without
consent

Frances Fyfield

without
consent

Viking

VIKING
Published by the Penguin Group
Penguin Putnam Inc., 375 Hudson Street,
New York, New York 10014, U.S.A.
Penguin Books Ltd, 27 Wrights Lane, London W8 5TZ, England
Penguin Books Australia Ltd, Ringwood, Victoria, Australia
Penguin Books Canada Ltd, 10 Alcorn Avenue,
Toronto, Ontario, Canada M4V 3B2
Penguin Books (N.Z.) Ltd, 182–190 Wairau Road,
Auckland 10, New Zealand

Penguin Books Ltd, Registered offices:
Harmondsworth, Middlesex, England

First American edition
Published in 1997 by Viking Penguin,
a member of Penguin Putnam Inc.
1 3 5 7 9 10 8 6 4 2

Grateful acknowledgment is made for permission to reprint excerpts
from *Archbold 1994,* edited by James Richardson, re-issue volume 2,
December 1993. By permission of Sweet & Maxwell Limited.

PUBLISHER'S NOTE
This is a work of fiction. Names, characters, places, and incidents
either are the product of the author's imagination or are used fictitiously,
and any resemblance to actual persons, living or dead, events, or
locales is entirely coincidental.

CIP data available
ISBN 0-670-87682-8

This book is printed on acid-free paper. ∞

Printed in the United States of America
Set in Granjon
Designed by Sabrina Bowers

For my brothers,
Ian and Simon Hegarty,
with love

I am very grateful for the help (and inspiration) given by Detective Sergeant Julie Proctor, Vulnerable Persons Unit, Islington Police Station; Dr Dene Robertson and Dr Vesna Djurovic.

without consent

'It is an offence for a man to rape a woman.

A man commits rape if (a) he has unlawful sexual intercourse with a woman who at the time of the intercourse does not consent to it; and (b) at that time he knows that she does not consent to the intercourse, or is reckless as to whether she consents.'

prologue

Home was where the heart was.

She smelt. Stank. The rank smell of perfume mixed with grass and sweat, city smells and those of harvest, soil beneath her fingernails. Shivering in the heat of the night with the jacket round her shoulders which she wanted to shake off although she needed it for warmth. Needed it, needed it, the lapels damp with saliva, and oh yes, there had been real tears in her eyes as she stumbled home. Look, we don't have to do it this way, she'd said. We could do it nice and ordinary in your car; take me away from all this and I'm all yours, she'd said, and he'd laughed. A lovely laugh, he had, low and sexy and full of promise. Jesus. There was nothing to fear. But she had been so frightened, like now, feeling the air had been punched out of her. She could imagine the fingerprint bruises on her ribs. You're perfect, he'd said; a few bruises won't harm you. Bruises to the sternum where he'd held her down. They'll fade soon, he'd said. I'll make them in the shape of a flower.

She heard footsteps coming down the stairs, imagined, accurately, a young man in carpet slippers coming down to put out the rubbish, closing the door quietly, knowing that what he did was important. Then she began to cry.

Silence. Only a kind of semi-silence in this man's room, high above the street. The slight vibration of anxious traffic but no voices.

It was not enough for him, the ordinary way of doing anything, or so he told himself. Or maybe it was the humiliating fact that it was shameful and undignified to be so obsessed by anything at any time. Sex is not life, simply a part. For some, he supposed, sex was a necessary release of tension, instead of this idle curiosity of his in which he could never admit that necessity ever played a part. Bearing in mind what women submitted themselves to all the time, he could not see that he did any harm.

Such women. The shapes and sizes of them filled him with wonder; each body as unique as its own fingerprint, each set of reactions different, each set of needs and stimuli unquantifiable if broadly similar. The thought of so many of them blundering through life without anything amounting to satisfaction filled him with pity. He saw himself as a man who loved women and wished that they could understand and value themselves more, and also, take themselves a little less seriously; appreciate a joke, perhaps. God knows, there had been enough jokes played on him to last a lifetime, and he was still smiling. In his view, a feminist was a person who considered it morally indefensible to cause pain to any woman; the object was to cause pleasure; there was no point otherwise. Of course, if the life were already so diminished, so beyond the prospect of pleasure, it might be as well to cause pleasure in the ending of it, but he was not sufficiently practised to consider himself in the role of

God. One of these days, he might perfect the most poetic form of death. A sublime accident.

You were born to make women happy, his own mother had told him. Also for the healing arts. Yours is a double vocation, my child. The ice clinked in the glass beside his desk. There were flowers in the vase, variegated carnations, rather sterile in their perfection, he thought. A box of chocolates. He sipped the drink reflectively. Alas, ice and lavender oil were not sufficient for every kind of burn. Nor were drink, pleasure and the exercise of power always sufficient antidote for life's crueller reversals. So many of his ageing women acquaintances could have told him that.

He pondered these and other matters in front of his computer. The blankness of the screen did not alarm him at all; it was hardly the same as facing an empty page with nothing better to do with himself. He could copy onto this space sections of alarming medical and legal text, although the latter, with all its Gothic splendour, always made him regret his choice of career. Medical science was not ennobling. In his experience, doctors were worse liars and rogues than their legal counterparts who tended to be at least more guarded in their promises.

Physician, heal thyself.

The vase holding the flowers was an artful sculpture of female genitalia. The broad base represented the uterus; the ridge at the base, by which he would lift it, the cervix, opening out realistically into a flower-like shape of the labia minora and labia majora. An artist's slightly fanciful impression of the vulva, in other words. A frivolous creation which the girl who cleaned consistently and typically failed to recognize for what it was. He often found it helpful to explain anatomy if one began from the outside in. In actual life, as he knew, the labia closed with the tidiness of a bud, concealed beneath a convenient mound and carried round as normal by women who scarcely knew how any of the reproductive and sexual machinery worked. This polished wood structure was hardly a useful educational tool for hopeful men either, but it was warm to handle and looked, without the flowers, like a decorative candle holder.

He could not explain why he was as he was or did as he did. The random development of his own tastes astounded him as much as the history of his life, but he felt saintly and worthy in comparison to some mindless procreator of the aggressively macho sort. *He* would never foist some unwanted, unsupportable, screaming child into the world; that indeed was a sin, raw and unadorned in its sheer wickedness. He nodded at the screen; the screen agreed.

He smoothed his already smooth pate, tapped it with the middle finger of his right hand. He had his own rationality, that was all; along with the conventional overtones which were enough to show him he was not really mad in his entirely sane fear of retribution. His was the fear of an innocent man who can never really be understood.

What was it they could ever say that he had done wrong? Nothing! And who would give evidence? No-one? Nothing was done, my dears, without consent.

He looked at his watch. It was not a distinguished implement, but a type made by the million. Dark outside now, but still warm. His lovely little girl would be home. Fearless about the dark. Safe in the hands of a man who would never awaken her.

Almost a soul mate. Not a friend.

Almost a lover.

chapter one

Listen, Bailey said.

Once upon a time, there was a girl, going out.

Dressing for the party, she had felt she was worth a million dollars. Somehow that phrase meant more than the sterling equivalent of the day – the last of her life as she had known it – and she might have been worth more. Coming down for a moment from the quarrel with her mother, the third this week, and putting a jacket over what her father called her itsy-bit skirt and the skimpy top, wearing it as if she would never part with it, rather than shed it as soon as she got there, she had a sudden surge of rebellious love for her repressive parents. They weren't so bad, some of the time. For a brief moment, she knew that she was safe as houses, because she had this room to come back to and this number to call, although the only reason she was worth so much to herself was the fact that after three weeks' diet, her waist was where she wanted and her ribs stuck out. Not a milligram of surplus flesh, although, if she ate as much as a bread roll, her stomach came out like a balloon. The answer was not to eat.

'Bye, Mum. Bye, Dad . . .'

'Let's see you,' he called. She stepped into the living-room, pretending great haste even though she was early. The jacket was buttoned. She had on a prim little choker round her neck, which would go from throat to handbag before she had reached the end of the road. The make-up would go on in the bus.

'Very nice,' he said, reassuringly, thinking nothing of the kind. Why did this child have to look so fierce and why on earth was she so addicted to black? Why did she go about with that girl who was so much older and prettier? One quick peck on the cheek, given and received in an over-powering atmosphere of multi-layered perfume, and she was off before Mother came out of the kitchen. Because Mother was harder to fool.

Later on, when they picked her up after the police had called, she stank of booze. The itsy-bit skirt was torn and stained. The child whimpered, but did not hug; could not bear to touch. Her thighs were scored with scratches; there was detritus under her nails. She was scantily dressed; it was presumed she had been stripped prior to her foetal curl in the gutter where she was found. A few bruises.

No knickers, no jacket. In the presence of her parents, she said she had lost them. That was all she uttered, apart from sobbing. Even after hours with a sympathetic woman in a nice little house with pictures on the wall.

'Well?'

Helen West, Prosecutor, sat on Bailey's sofa, still listening. They did this sometimes, a kind of dress rehearsal for tomorrow's challenges, both occasionally mourning the co-incidence of their professions. Senior police officer, experienced Crown Prosecutor. It was not a relationship she would recommend, but she was stuck with it, like the fly which had fallen into her drink. Bailey had a creased face and a fine way of telling a story. He animated his narrative with verbal cartoons and embellished the whole thing with gestures, but as soon as he said, 'Once upon a time', she knew the story was going to be doctored with his own opinions and recounted in a style he would never use in front of a judge.

'Drugs?' She questioned crisply.

'Negligible, from her demeanour. I'd guess not.'

'Booze?'

'Plenty.'

'Semen?'

'Saliva, yes. Here and there; not there. Semen, no. Several abandoned condoms around, but a lovers' trysting place. Bodily fluids also in the gutter. And no, she isn't a virgin. Not quite.'

'That's not enough,' Helen said.

Bailey watched the graceful figure of his betrothed cross the broad expanse of his living-room and thought of his ex-wife, for whom his traveller's tales from the police force had always taken second place to what they should do with the bathroom in preparation for the first child. He might as well have been out to stud. Oh, silence, he told himself, don't fall into clichés as if you were obliging someone on the psychiatrist's consulting couch. That woman had her needs, you had yours, which coincided at the time and might still if the child had not died. A child who would be the same age, give or take a year or two, as the girl in the story. He found himself repeating, what a pity, the trite words hiding a multitude of sins. His stomach growled. The last year of his life had seen the development of an ulcer.

'The way you tell it', Helen said, settling easily into the big fat settee he would never have possessed in his married life, 'gives me all the clues to the verdict. Silly little seventeen-year-old goes out to party, as described to parents, to whom she lies habitually, about dress code, about everything. Goes shimmering in there, dressed in nothing.' He was silent.

'The bloke for whom she's wearing all the glitz does not pitch. So she salves her disappointment by drinking a bit more and then a bit more and ends up in a scrum with a stranger. She doesn't have the faintest idea what a half-naked, flirtatious girl risks.'

'She wanted love.'

'She had love, the silly little bitch. She wanted attention.'

Helen took a sip of coffee. One bottle of wine in an evening was enough. He could continue, since it never seemed to affect him; she would not. There was a level of control in her he both admired and resented. She was a beautiful woman, after her own fashion. The kindest he had ever met, easily the most imaginative, the most elusive, the most measured. He wondered if she had agreed to marry him for the same hormonal reasons which had affected his wife. Helen was in her late thirties, about a decade his junior.

'Her parents are howling for blood. They insist she was raped,' he said. 'Someone must hang, they say, namely the boy with whom she left. Spotty little oik, who says he tried to kiss her, but she shoved him and ran off. He says she had other fish to fry. Someone she was meeting; someone older.'

'No case,' Helen said. 'Not even if she swore it was him. She could be a victim; she could be a cock-tease. Unless, of course, he caused the scratches. But I'd bet she did them herself.'

'Right. Her own skin beneath her fingernails.'

'And tomorrow, how come *you* have to explain to mum and dad why the evidence is insufficient?'

'I don't. Ryan does. He asked my advice on diplomacy.'

She made a mocking gesture, using two fingers to point a gun at her head, and pulled a sympathetic face.

The lovely Ryan was not always her favourite man. Bailey's bag carrier when first they had met, progressing since then, onward and upward. Capable of being outrageous and treated by Bailey as the son he never had. There was a fidelity between the two of them she accepted, because she had no choice. Personally, she doubted Ryan deserved it, but there it was: a mutual devotion without rhyme or reason, just like any other kind of love.

'Ah well, early night, then.'

Bailey moved to sit beside her, put his arm round her shoulder and felt her rest against him, willingly. They were easier together since their decision to marry; she joked it had probably caused the ulcer, but it had altered something, although he was not sure how. In a moment, he would clear the last of the glasses and papers from the table. In Helen's flat, litter remained at least until morning, perhaps the same weekday of the following week. One thing they had proved: compatibility need not involve a common domestic attitude.

'Tell me, love, do you always regard this subject with such a bold and jaundiced eye?'

'Do you mean sex cases? Rape? My current, almost exclusive stock-in-trade? Yes. But drunken teenagers don't raise my heartbeat. Oh, I'm sorry for a kid like that; something happened to her, but you can't make a case out of *naïveté* betrayed.'

Would they make love tonight or not? The idea rarely lost its appeal, except when she was tired to her bones. Perhaps she would let it happen, perhaps not. If she did, would that be rape? The idea was laughable. Rape was the exertion of force; Bailey had enough power over her already, although she did her best not to let him know.

He was sound asleep by the time she reached him.

The night light was a pale darkness, glowing through the window. Bailey lived so high above the ground, there was no need for the curtains he despised. From the front windows of her basement flat, Helen could see the feet of people walking past, sometimes peering down, but at the back, there was nothing but the garden. She missed her home, especially the solitude of her garden, and then, when she was in it, she missed the light of Bailey's vast attic. When they were married, they would live in exactly the same way.

His sleep made her perversely sleepless. He would wake if she touched him and his sleep was the unfeigned unconsciousness of the just, the result perhaps of a pragmatism she could not share. He believed in fate, and telling himself that you could only do the best possible with what you were given. No 'if onlys' for Bailey. You did what you did, apologized if necessary, and then you slept. Soundly. Did he really want this marriage, or was it his version of courtesy? In Bailey's eyes, a relationship as long as theirs would have to be honoured somehow. Loving Bailey was one of the best things to happen in her life, but she had a mortal dread of being owned and knew she could still throw it all away. Out of fear.

Failing to sleep opened the floodgates of all those things left undone or badly done. Cases swimming before her eyes. Visions of her previous married life, plus visions of all those odd and brutal couplings she read about on paper and which filled her waking hours with speculation, making her feel like a voyeur.

They should not have been talking about rape before going to bed.

Something had happened to that little girl. She wondered what it might have been.

'All right,' Aemon Connor said, in tones which combined both aggression and resignation. 'That's fine. That's absolutely fine. If you don't want to, that's fine by me. You frigid little cow. Was a time you couldn't have enough of it. Don't worry about it. I can always get someone else.'

Brigid whimpered in the darkness. He was refusing to hear it; he had listened long enough and conversation never cured anything. She complained it hurt; so, if it hurt, why couldn't she use her imagin ation? He could tell her what hurt, all right, and that was a mammoth state of arousal with nowhere to go. She was his woman, remember; his wife, even; what a joke, when she just wouldn't do it any more.

He lay on his side, him fuming and her still snuffling, opening his mouth to speak. He could not stop talking.

'I could get someone else tomorrow. And then where would you be?'

There was a long silence, until he felt her fingers moving timidly to touch the back of his head.

'Changed your mind, have you?' he muttered. 'Thought you would.' Forcing himself inside was difficult enough, even without listening to the sounds she made or noticing the passive resistance which seemed second nature. The process was brief and noisy. He held her down by the shoulder and in the aftermath of climax fell into a deep and suffocating sleep. Later, having eased herself from under the bulk of his huge, drowsy body, she felt for the marks of his hands and wished herself dead.

The bathroom to which she tiptoed was splendid. There was a power shower among the black marble tiles and a bidet with gold-coloured taps which she used religiously, especially at times like these, to wash away all traces of him.

She had no idea how to live outside this house. It was her home and her prison, and living in such a place represented the pinnacle of all achievement. She liked this bathroom best; she had made it her own, and she could hide behind the door after doing her duty as a good Catholic wife. She could also sit and lie here too long in contemplation of avoiding it. Praying to God and occupying the bidet at the same time seemed faintly obscene, but Brigid imagined God would forgive her that, at least, since he demanded so much of her otherwise, and was supposed to forgive a great deal more than her husband. Dedicating the act of sex as a penance for the holy souls also seemed indecent, but might ensure a blessing in advance. Maybe Aemon was right and she should have been a nun.

You used to love it, he'd said. He said that every time, taunting her. There was a muffled shouting from outside, her name called, 'Brigid, Brigid . . . where are you?' sounding as if he was lost. God help us, he was awake again after insufficient drink to anaesthetize. She touched the lips of her vagina, swollen like cocktail sausages, almost screamed, reached for the lubricant from the cupboard and answered him.

'I'm here, I'm here, in a minute.'

He hated to wake up and find himself alone. It was an insult to his manhood: it gave him nightmares.

Aemon and Brigid, happily married.

In a neat little terraced house, light showed from every window, as if the occupant owned shares in London Electricity, or could not stand the dark. Around three a.m., a solid form could be seen, balanced on a ladder, silhouetted against the window to the left of the door, painting the ceiling of the living-room. Anna was in a sweat. The radio played softly only because she was a considerate neighbour. What she really wanted was a house pulsing with vapid, heavy-beat noise, amplified to fill her head. Anything to block thinking and aid the manic activity which had continued since early afternoon.

Ceiling, two coats, a small area, quickly covered; the whole place a bit of a doll's house. Walls could be finished in an hour, possibly tomorrow. The washing-machine hummed in the kitchen; third load today. Curtains hung damply; she would paint round them. The carpet had already been shampooed. She was doing things out of order, but perfect decor, logically created, was not the object of this exercise. The achievement of cleanliness was.

The ladder wobbled; Anna clutched, swore, saved herself from falling, and watched the paint tray fall to the floor, face down. Scraping the white ooze from the ruined pile with desultory energy, she realized that bending over made her dizzy and she could not see straight. All that white, glimmering against the unsteady light of the naked bulb which swung from the ceiling; her eyes were no longer able to comprehend colour. Or the fact that there might be someone outside, looking in.

She might as well paint the carpet, too, and be finished with it; the thought made her smile. All this work had done the trick; she was so tired she could scarcely put one foot in front of the other, and at last the place smelt of nothing but emulsion.

Anna held one hand in front of her face, watched its tremor, and delivered the now-familiar lecture. You can cope, girl, you can cope; it's all the rest who can't. Talking to herself, out loud; that was another thing to be cured, but not yet. The hand trembled; the burn marks on her arms were fading; her legs had the substance of jelly. She could sleep now.

As Anna tried to ignore the spots in front of her eyes while sticking the paint roller in a bucket of water which suddenly seemed red instead of white, the phone by Superintendent Bailey's bed bleeped without apology. He did not need to look at his watch to know that it was shortly after three; he always knew the time.

'Bailey. What do you want?'

It had been a joke on regular squads that Bailey always sounded as if he had a woman with him. Probably had too; the man had been a bachelor a long, long time. Going out and staying in with a lawyer from the Crown Prosecution Service was seen as another lascivious eccentricity which went with his good suits. The wearing of the one on his back and the other on his arm, bordered on some undefined treachery. The men who claimed to know him longest were placing bets on this marriage. Ten to one, it would not take place at all, five to three it wouldn't last a year. They had different kinds of faith in Bailey. The existence of Helen West did not exactly do him any favours.

The voice on the other end of the line appeared to hide an element of amusement. Sometimes, in the comparative regularity of his newish role, Bailey forgot that working for Complaints and Discipline was still, potentially, a twenty-four-hour shift.

'Islington. Sorry to disturb you, sir, but we've got a problem. Allegation of rape.'

'Against whom?'

The officer sounded as if he was reciting from a reading primer for under fives, spelling the sounds as he spoke.

'Detective Sergeant Ryan, sir.'

Bailey paused for a moment's palpable shock.

'I can't investigate allegations against Ryan,' he said. 'I know him.'

The voice coughed. 'That's the problem, sir. We've tried everyone else on the complaints rota, but everyone knows Ryan.' He paused for effect. 'Everyone.'

Bailey knew what he should do if he were going straight by the book. Get up, look up all other available numbers, tell this sergeant who did not yet have a name to continue his exploration down the list, because yes, he knew Ryan. Far too well. Knew him as a man of flawed intelligence, deliberate blindness, sexual fecklessness, indiscretions of all kinds. A man lacking in imagination, dogged in loyalty, but finally, in the last two years, emerging from a chrysalis, abandoning frustrated youth in favour of some degree of wisdom. Bailey had tutored him, forgiven him, covered up for him, believed in him, right up until that recent point where the belief was justified and Ryan had suddenly taken off and learnt to think, wonder, take responsibility and ask real questions. He had grown, shed his juvenile prejudices like unwanted skin, and learnt the art of patience, the way Bailey had always hoped he would. Looking at Ryan as he was was like looking at the man Bailey himself had once been. What retrograde nonsense was this? Stupid, stupid bastard.

The pause was long enough for the sergeant to cough again. 'Sir?'

'On my way.'

Bailey was precise. In the same way that he knew the time, he knew where to find his clothes. Helen stirred, listening. Bailey knew she couldn't quite fathom his absurd loyalty to Ryan any more than he could himself, and felt a flash of annoyance that the phone call should make him peculiarly, defensively embarrassed, as if she could guess that this was more than his paid duty. He touched her shoulder and left without a word of goodbye. Singing in his head as he went for the car, not Ryan, not Ryan, please. Not just as he was making good. Not Ryan and rape.

With that good-looking boy there would never be the need.

Bailey made himself drive slowly, although the instinct was to race and the sheer emptiness of the streets was an invitation to speed. Emptiness was a relative concept in London. There were always people. In these God-forsaken early hours there were simply fewer, plying the night-time trades, some of them innocent, some not. The factory making dresses for tomorrow's market, the loading of goods, the post-midnight clearing out, the parties which never stopped and the increasing numbers of those sleeping rough. He regretted that his duties no longer really included this twilight zone of all-night pit stops: conspiracy, danger, chat, street light. The night isolated people, made them more truthful. You poor old man, he thought to himself ruefully, they'll make a gardener of you yet. Set you to trimming roses in distant suburban police stations, or polishing the commander's shoes. Instead of this loathsome business of pruning, examining the varied complaints against officers of his own kind.

Oh, surely this was a storm in a nightclub cocktail? He knew in his bones it was not. Ryan, you bloody fool. What now? You always had a weakness for women and they for you. Bailey found he was thinking of the girl with something akin to dislike, already formulating disbelief in what she would say. He shook his head. This would not do.

The back of the station yard was lit with orange light, as if to reduce the white paint of the cars to a sickly cream. Bailey went to the back door. Better than going to the front and possibly running the phalanx of waiting relatives, supposing there were any. The interior corridor was a similar warm and oppressive yellow. He was met with the distant courtesy his role demanded. Everyone knew Ryan, a convivial and popular character, while several more knew Bailey, who could not be thus described. No chance, Bailey thought, of an incident like this failing to enter the history books.

The duty inspector was embarrassed, a symptom rarely apparent on ruddy red features such as his, unless he was talking about his daughters with the boastful and nervous pride he reserved for their achievements. The existence of a family made wild men tame, gave them different perspectives; it had done that for Ryan, albeit slowly. However many years he had taken to fall into respectful love with his own wife, he had still done so, although only after he had led her a merry dance, and she him. Boys will be boys, and girls retaliate. The rape story was told, dispassionately, the voice avoiding judgement.

'Decent enough girl. No record, works in a shop. She knows Ryan on account of being a witness in one of his cases. Seems like she went to a disco with a girl who got into some kind of trouble on the way home, and she's giving evidence about what time they got there, what time the girl left, that kind of thing. Anyway, Ryan takes the statement and they get along fine, and he goes back to tidy it up, and they still get along fine. Then, according to her, he meets her for a third time, purely social. He starts to pester her. She lives with a bloke. She and Ryan – Shelley Pelmore she's called, sir – go out for a drink. On the way home, he suggests a walk in the park and he rapes her. Or, at least, he tries. Penetration, but no ejaculation.' The inspector coughed apologetically. Another source of ridicule for Ryan. Didn't even make it, poor bastard; couldn't keep it up.

'Obvious signs of resistance. Sir.'

The police service was an army with a self-appointed officer class, so Bailey understood. Respect had to be earned and, in the eyes of this man, he had not earned it yet.

'Now why on earth would he do that?' Bailey wondered out loud, making light of it. The inspector caught his drift, laughed briefly.

'See what you mean, sir. Usually he only has to ask nicely, although everyone says he's quietened down. But then why do politicians go with tarts, even when they've got groupies and their fragrant wives at home, sir? Dicing with death, someone's idea of fun.'

'Do you believe her?' Bailey tried to get the plea out of his voice. The cough was repeated.

'Can't say, sir, can I? I haven't met her, wouldn't know if I did. They were seen together in the pub. He says they met by accident, chatted, that was all, gave her a lift, went separate ways.'

'Who reported it?'

'The boyfriend. Found her on the doorstep. Brought her in. She's in the rape suite up at Holloway. We can't deal with her here for obvious reasons. Ryan's in the detention room.'

'Well, come with me, will you? I can't see him alone.'

Another long hesitation.

'Oh, one more thing, sir. When she came in, she was wearing Ryan's jacket . . .'

He would need a witness to ensure fair play – no hidden intimacies between himself and an old pal – and also because he needed someone to stiffen his own backbone when he saw Ryan. Bailey might as well have been looking at the victim of a car smash, one who was resigned to being told that apart from being blind for life, the legs would have to be removed as well. Ryan's handsome face was puffed; he had not avoided the disgrace of weeping, which had made his eyes red and his skin blotched as if it was bruised. There was a smell of drink, not overpowering but noticeable, and the different, overlying smell of perspiration and soap. He sat on the bench in his shirtsleeves above creased cotton trousers. On their entrance, he placed his hands behind his back, guiltily. Bailey had the distinct impression that he had been biting his nails. He swung round on the other officer, almost falling into him.

'Has he had a shower?'

'Sir, yes. At home, before we collected him.'

Ryan's face had opened into the beginnings of a smile before Bailey spoke. Then it closed into sullen lines and he turned his eyes to a long examination of his hands. Nails bitten to the quick, Bailey noticed. In as long as he had known the man, Ryan had never bitten his nails. Not even in the long reaches of the night, when nerves turned men into anxious boys.

'Has he been examined?'

'Not yet, sir . . .'

'For Christ's sake, that should have been first.'

Bailey swung on Ryan with the anger of a parent trying

to prevent himself from slapping a child out of sheer disappointment.

'What have you got to say?' Bailey barked at him.

Ryan shifted. His voice was surprisingly firm.

'Nothing, sir. Nothing at all.'

And he turned his head to the wall.

chapter two

'. . . if at a trial for a rape offence, the jury has to consider whether a man believed that a woman was consenting to sexual intercourse, the presence or absence of reasonable grounds for such a belief is a matter to which the jury is to have regard, in conjunction with other relevant matters, in considering whether he so believed . . .'

Rose Darvey measured the distance, sprinted up to the empty cardboard box and kicked it. It sailed upward and hit the casing of the neon light with a satisfying crack, bounced off the wall and landed. Inspired by the length of the corridor and its dull grey paint, she repeated the kick from the other side, watching as the box hit the casing for a second time. That should do.

'Yeah!' Rose shouted, waving her fist. Who said football training was no use to a girl? 'Punch their lights out,' she muttered. Dribbling the box before her, she made for the swing doors. She had to do something – anything, as long as it was overtly physical – before a day in court; frustration was the price of dedication to a career which involved so much enforced immobility. Perhaps she should have gone in for politics. That, at least, allowed a person to shout. In the life of Rose Darvey, Helen West had much to answer for.

Redwood, self-important yet timid Branch Crown Prosecutor, master of this flagship, came out of his office with the speed of a startled guinea-pig. Rose beamed at him with the usual unnerving effect. Rose Darvey and Helen West were clones of each other, he thought fearfully, the pair of them separated only by a decade and a half in which Helen had learnt alternative methods of insubordination. Helen could smile just as sweetly as Rose, but relied on guile, abuse of dignity and dumb insolence, while this one, who could have been her daughter, played her games with more palpable falsehood. She shimmered with energy, like a fighter hanging on the ropes, impervious to the strictures of a referee, waiting for the chance to punch a kidney.

'Lovely day,' said Rose.

'Isn't it,' he said faintly, noting the crack in the neon light which everyone hated, wanting to say something about it, but not daring.

'You're in early, sir,' Rose chirped with a terrible display of politeness, her smile reminiscent of a small animal baring its teeth. She could make 'sir' sound like an exquisite insult, no offence intended.

'Yes.' He felt himself beaming in response; fat old cat. Redwood was always in limbo; once he started a conversation, he did not know how to stop, but stood there, hovering. Rose knew that one sure way to make him move was to pick her nose, an action which, understandably, sent him running for cover. At the moment, she had other things in mind.

'Why are we turning down so many rape cases, sir?'

He rocked on his heels, felt for the wall to give him support. The suddenness of the question jolted him into an untypically truthful response.

'Because they don't work.'

'Pardon? Don't work? That ain't no legal phrase I ever heard of.'

'They don't work,' he repeated.

'Don't work for who? The fucking Treasury?'

Redwood fled. The corridor fell into silence.

From the distant end, Helen West hoved into view, coming closer beneath the subterranean lights, three of which Rose had managed to damage. She looked good today, Rose remarked to herself: loose jacket; nice skirt, fitting like a dream; good legs. No wonder that dour old scroat Bailey liked her. She wasn't bad for an old lady.

The cardboard box landed at Helen's feet. Lacking the benefit of football training, she picked it up without a second glance and put it over her head. Rose whistled and prayed for Redwood to come back out of his office. Two demented women would keep him demoralized for a week.

It was cool in here, air-conditioned freezing. Helen continued up the corridor, blind as a bat, and turned left into her room without breaking step. Some day, Rose thought, without wistfulness, all this will never be mine.

She was one third of the way through legal training, and so far she had found the exams a breeze. She could count on her fingers a fistful of achievements, namely, the beginnings of an impressive qualification, a borrowed family and a man she was going to marry in a matter of weeks. The career posed several questions and many more doubts; the marriage did not. Rose scurried down the corridor, looking out for signs of her own vandalism. Now they really would have to replace the fucking lights which drove everyone mad, but then, if the establishment refused to listen to intelligent requests, they had to be otherwise persuaded.

The office of the Crown Prosecution Service, north central, lay at the apex of several insignificant streets and was not itself a landmark. Facing Helen West's small room, over a narrow stretch of road, there was another set of offices, with remarkably better equipment and a plethora of underworked employees. Helen had suggested rigging up a pulley over the road so that they could send over photocopying, or receive, in recycled carrier bags secured with clothes pegs, the day's faxes. Over the road, the people were engaged in the long-distance management of a paint production company; their office was light, bright and far from grey. Over here, the office fixtures bore signs of wear, redolent of a surly atmosphere and an environment devoted to the creation of nothing but hierarchies. The pursuit of justice was an unprofitable sideline.

Each occupant of each office was supposed to operate on a 'clear desk policy', translated by Rose to mean, put your mess in a filing cabinet and close the door. Policy directives such as these reached the in-trays on a weekly basis (word-processed, single spaced), three-page essays on how to use the new expense claim forms, operate the front door, apply for stationery and photocopying or retrieve a file from the distant limbo of storage, where it could only be accepted for final oblivion if subdivided into bundles no thicker than three inches. Helen had asked if anyone could keep a clear desk when the bureaucracy spat forth such volumes of forms, statements and exhortations which had nothing to do with the practice of law. Redwood said rules were rules.

Helen kept her room in accordance with the keep-the-desk-tidy policy by storing most of the paperwork which she was not actively hiding on the floor. There lay white files, bound with tape, bulging with paper in varying thicknesses and states of order, festooned with yellow post-its, reminding her of the next thing to be done, and when. She stepped in between the serried rows each morning, read her own messages to herself and hauled forth the ones where some kind of action was imperative. An immaculate system, she thought. The files were slab-like stepping-stones on a grey carpet patterned with coffee stains.

Rose piled one file on top of another and sat astride them. Helen had removed the box, once used for copying paper and invaluable for other purposes, from her head, improving her appearance dramatically. Her hair was not even ruffled and remained tied back neatly in a black scrunchie. Very lawyerly, Rose thought. You could almost believe she was the real thing. Rose adored Helen with a fierce devotion which was not always devoid of criticism.

'Are we really going back to the Crown Court today, Aunty H? Are we really?' she asked in a passable mimicry of Redwood's whine.

'Only if you're good.'

'What does that mean?'

'You should know by now. Don't taunt Redwood so early in the morning. It's bad for his digestion.'

'Is it OK in the afternoon?'

'Yes, especially in the afternoons. Especially during policy meetings.'

Helen was passing down the first line of files, kicking them into symmetry before she pounced, hauled the burden to the clearish desk and struggled with the tape. Rose pointed at it.

'Is this one going to work? I mean, to coin a legal phrase not yet found in the Latin, will it work?'

'Doubt it.'

'Why? That poor cow was raped, good and proper.'

'Nothing proper about it. Date rape. He says she consented; she says she didn't. It all depends on which of them makes the more impressive witness. She wasn't very good at giving evidence in chief yesterday, was she?'

Rose shrugged. 'I believed her, but then I s'pose I'm

nearer her age. There's a couple of girls on the jury listening hard, but then there's a couple of mothers who've probably got sons just like him. Testosterone tits.' Rose clasped her hands between her knees, an automatic reaction which was nothing to do with the subject matter of the trial. It was all in the air they breathed: the pollen of rape.

'What beats me', she continued, 'is why even girls don't believe other girls. It's not as though every female over the age of sixteen knows much about sex. Oh, I mean, she may have done the business, but that's not the same thing as knowing anything about men. You want them to like you. You can't believe they'd actually hurt you. You think they can stop and you think they can read your signals. Girls are romantic. That's why it's so horrible. It can't be half as bad being raped when you're older. You've got less belief to shatter.'

'Oh, I don't know about that,' Helen said drily, checking the papers, looking at her watch. She had clearly stopped listening and Rose was annoyed.

'The problem with you, Aunty, is too much respectability. I think maybe you've got it in for youth, you. The number of rape cases you personally have turned down over the last three months . . . well, speaks for itself. You're positively encouraging testosterone to tread all over timidity. I mean, why did you bother to run this one?'

'Bruises.'

'You turned down the husband and wife one, too. What a pig he was.'

'There wasn't any choice about that. Those kind are virtually impossible to prove unless the couple have separated. One person's word against another.'

'And you turned down the one with the man in the basement flat,' Rose went on, hotly.

'Oh, come on, Rose. You know that gave me sleepless nights. She picked him out on parade, but he was nothing like her description of him and there was no forensic and he had a sort of an alibi . . .'

'And he's done it again. And he'll do it again . . .'

'Probably. Keep your door locked when Mike's not around, won't you?'

The concern in her voice broke Rose's antagonistic mood. She smiled, the grin lighting up her bright eyes, creating dimples in her cheeks and even softening the spikes of her hair.

'Naa,' she said. 'If I get any intruders, they won't be after my body; they'll be after his, or the wedding presents. Time to go, is it?'

'Yup.'

Rose stood in front of the small mirror to the left of Helen's desk. A policy statement on dress code for court was expected daily. She ran her fingers through her hair.

'Mike wants me to stop being punk and go curly. Only for the wedding. What d'ye think, Aunty Helen?'

Together they considered the most serious problem of the day.

'No,' Helen said finally. 'Unless you buy a wig.'

'Blond? To go with my flowers, d'you think?'

'For sure.'

Rose's infuriation with the random nature of justice was always an item festering on a hidden agenda. Although she could recite it, Rose did not understand the Code for crown prosecutors, which so clearly underlined the difference between truth and pragmatism. The Code said that prosecutors should only initiate those cases where they considered there was a reasonable prospect of securing a conviction. That meant, in Rose's eyes, that they had to consider the likely result before considering the facts. It seemed outrageous to her that these middle-class wankers should base their decisions on second-guessing what the jury, or the defence, would do; taking prejudice, skill and incredulity into account before they were even expressed.

She stood up and began systematically feeding paper through the window, passing through the policy dictates contained in the in-tray with all the delight of an old lady feeding birds.

The taxi fare to court would require a form in triplicate if it was ever to be reclaimed. Helen was unlikely to bother, happy enough to have the prickly Rose alongside again for the day. As they plunged into the gloom of the court foyer and dumped their baggage for the usual check, Rose pulled at Helen's arm.

'Look, I meant to ask you earlier. One great big favour . . .'

'What, buy you the wig for the wedding?'

'No. I want you to talk to someone.'

'About what?'

'Rape.'

At this time of year, the yellow fields of the north were full of rape. Brilliant yellow flowers, so vibrant they were positively vulgar in an English landscape; luminous by night, brighter than wallflowers, but the scent of the blossoms heavy and foul. As a farmer's son, Detective Sergeant Todd approved of his homeland, approved of rape in that agricultural context. Rapeseed oil, fit for a thousand uses, his father said. He was homesick for the sight of those flat and ugly fields so full of valuable produce. It would be nice to harvest something in the spectacular dryness of this August, and see what you had done.

'What's he trying to do?' Todd asked Bailey.

'Kill himself,' Bailey grunted.

'Clever, when you think of it, although I suppose when you do, it isn't, really. Not for a copper. You go straight home. You have a shower and put your undies in the washing-machine. I bet Ryan does that every night he's home late.'

'Ryan's wife might have put the stuff in the machine. She may well swear she did. Just like she said he'd been in all evening, when you lot went to pick him up. Poor woman.'

DS Todd reserved his small supply of sympathy.

'Well, she wouldn't pass her GCSE in telling lies, that's for sure. It was obvious she was saying the first thing that came into her head. Pointing the finger at him even more. As if she'd assumed his guilt.'

'Don't leap to conclusions,' Bailey said mildly.

'Difficult to avoid. I don't see, at this stage, how even the CPS could find a way of turning this down. Even without any forensic. Even if they don't go for rape, make it attempted rape or indecent assault; same difference. She's covered in marks, wearing his jacket, and all he'll say is, no comment.'

Todd was keen as mustard. Imported from another police force, he was one of the few who did not know Ryan, even by reputation. He was not a man for gossip, Bailey concluded, but one whose sharp nose touched the grindstone with dedication every week he was not on yet another training course. Bailey smiled at him to cover the dislike he would not show. He recognized all too well the necessity of having about his person throughout this ghastly mess a nit-picking stickler to whom Ryan was a stranger.

'Was he drunk, I wonder?' Bailey asked.

'Oh, merry. Not so drunk that he didn't remember to

take his wallet and warrant card out of his pocket before dunking his shirt into hot soapy water.'

'Hardly evidence.'

Nothing was more debilitating than Bailey's strange sense of grief. Todd and he sat together in the canteen, relieved at its relative emptiness. From the direction of the counter, over the Formica-topped tables and plastic plants, raucous laughter sounded as two large West Indian ladies poured glutinous soup into the heated container which would render it inedible by lunch-time. Soup was always on the menu, even in August. A few coffee drinkers huddled together, as far distant from Bailey and Todd as they could make it, as if whatever contagion they carried could drift and move above the smell of fried food.

'C'mon on then,' Bailey said reluctantly, uncurling his long legs. 'Got to go and see about a girl.' The chair he pushed back made a loud fart-like noise on the floor. The place fell as silent as a church.

The station by day was an entirely different building to the station by night. This time, they traversed the front counter as an easier route to the suites at the back, passing *en route* the counter queue. It comprised mainly young men shuffling and scratching, signing on for bail; drivers producing documents; ladies with tales of stolen handbags, the air thick with subdued anxiety. While Todd excused himself to find the gents, Bailey took his chance, nodding to the custody sergeant, who pressed the buzzer through into the cells, watching without a word while Bailey practically ran to Ryan's cell and opened the flap.

'You all right?'

There wasn't much else to say. Ryan was sitting still, staring at nothing. He turned a blank face on Bailey, then looked away. Something was said which Bailey almost missed.

'Pardon?'

There was a glimmer of a smile, the voice only slightly louder.

'I said, I never liked that jacket, sir. Never.'

There was little enough Bailey could do for Ryan without showing signs. Keep him clean and tidy for one. Get him out of the cell soonest and try and use some form of telepathy to stop him crying. His gaolers, those solid uniformed men, were bound to see that as an admission of guilt.

There was something terrible about a man weeping. Mrs Mary Ryan had read many a magazine article about the virtues of the new kind of man who wept at the drop of a hat, in case the hat was hurt, and was otherwise honest about his emotions, but it was not a culture with which she was familiar, or one she expected any man of hers to embrace. True, she would have preferred more honesty from her husband, or at least a greater ability to articulate when something was on his mind, instead of which he would put on a mood and hang around like the walking wounded, sulking and barking and waiting for her to guess the cause. Crying, however, was another matter. Tears were her prerogative, and even she did not shed them often. Daughter of a police officer, married to a police officer, with one of her sons dreaming of nothing else but becoming one of the same, she was watching the possible demise of every tradition which kept her family afloat, and there was her husband, her conquering hero, with a face puffy from tears.

Mrs Ryan hugged Mr Ryan and, in its way, the embrace was heartfelt. She was not a hard woman, merely a practical one, and they had been together a long time. Married far too young, of course; twenty-one apiece and with all the sense of a pair of kids, so that each of them had kicked over the traces a few years later, taken their marriage to the brink once or twice, then, after more than a decade, got a grip. On her way here, driving with automatic care and rehearsing a dozen versions of what to tell the kids, she had made herself remember all she respected about Ryan. He was generous to a fault, he was funny, he did not judge, he was ultimately reliable, and yes, she loved the way he looked; always had. She scorned the assumption that sensible women did not bother so much about a man's looks, when really, the way they looked, if they looked like Ryan even on a bad day, always helped them get away with murder. That handsome mug would go down well with a jury, she told herself, and shook her head in disbelief that she should think such a thing. It would never come to that.

He was not a pretty boy today, though. Seedy was the word which sprang to mind.

'You'll be out this afternoon,' she said briskly.

'Who says?'

'Custody sergeant. Your bloody precious Bailey left a message with him to tell me.' Mrs Ryan, who had always secretly credited Bailey with the development of her husband from imbecile to grown man, now felt and spoke of him as an object of hate, purely for his current power over their lives.

'Bailed for further enquiries. Something like that. What did you tell them?'

'Nothing.' She nodded, approving, but wanting more.

'What's the Brief like?'

'OK. I only did what he said.'

'For once.'

Mrs Ryan produced the Thermos of coffee and Mars bar which the sergeant had allowed her to bring in. They seemed such a pathetic offering in the circumstances, she almost put them away, but the chocolate seemed to bring colour to his skin.

'A Mars a day helps you work, rest and play,' he remarked, his voice a touch stronger.

'Did you get any breakfast?' she asked, resorting to the lowest level of wifely consideration, conscious of what she was doing and even more acutely aware of the atmosphere of the place. Echoing footsteps, a muted banging on the wall from somewhere, the conflicting smells of disinfectant and urine.

'Didn't want breakfast.'

She could see why.

'Oh, I bought you a newspaper.'

'Thanks.'

All speech was desultory. She felt as if every word was being overheard and could scarcely raise her voice above a whisper. There was also that sensation peculiar to hospital visits: the fear of saying anything which was not banal and the acute guilty desire to escape. Get out. He seemed to sense it, and for that, she felt a rush of love for him.

'You'd better go, love. No point both of us being stuck in here, is there?' He attempted a laugh. Although she wanted to go, being invited to go still felt like rejection. Perhaps he simply wanted his space back, so he could cry in peace.

'S'pose not.' She rose to her feet gratefully and rang the bell, then sat down to await the response, dying for those footsteps to come down the corridor towards them. She was aware of him watching her.

'What are you thinking?' she demanded; a last attempt to make this encounter fruitful.

Ryan stretched his legs so that they touched the wall opposite. Single cells were not designed for the swinging of cats.

'I'm thinking that I shall never, ever again, bang a bloke up in a cell without thinking long and hard about it first.'

You might not have the chance, she thought. You might never have the chance. You are going to be formally suspended from duty this afternoon, whatever else happens, and our world will come to an end. How could you do this to me?

'I never think of Old Bailey, without thinking of your Bailey,' Rose said as they stuffed the bundles of paper and files into the back of the taxi, this time without attempts to keep them in order. 'They have the same craggy appearance.' The afternoon sunshine made them blink. Out of the cooler corridors of the court, they felt like moles ascending into daylight. Rose's face shone. She was chattering for the sake of making noise, hiding the fact that she was angry and disappointed.

'Didn't take them long, did it?'

'No, not long. Probably the weather.'

On a day like this, even the most conscientious juror would want to be gone. Back to a flat, a house, a bus ride, away from sordid tales of bodily fluids, out of the gloom and the security checks, into the warm sunlight.

'Half an hour.' Rose tugged at the ends of her hair, found one longer lock, stuck it in her mouth and chewed. 'Half an hour to brand that girl a cheap little liar.'

Helen protested, mildly.

'No. He only had to show that his belief in her consent was reasonable at the time, even if he accepted in retrospect that it was wrong. The clever part was that he was careful to avoid calling her a liar.'

'Won't make any difference to the way she feels.'

'She'll probably recover,' Helen said. She looked cool in the heat. Her right foot steadied a box of paper at her feet.

'What a cold-hearted bitch you are, Aunty West, honestly.'

Helen did not reply. There was clearly a better occasion to mention that the deepest and most terrifying of humiliations, rape included, did not always send a life into an inevitable downward spiral. Rose herself was a fine example of recovery. Rose, who was still so young, but had never been allowed innocence. A father from hell, a history of abuse and promiscuity, from which she had risen, like the phoenix from the ashes, frightened of nothing. Proud of her, Helen also envied that huge capacity for life which had made the transformation possible, and, while trying to ignore Rose's comments on the frozen state of her own soul, wondered if the remarks were true and whether it really was a cop-out to make yourself indifferent to the things you could not change.

'You were saying something earlier on about a favour,' she said. The taxi bowled out into Ludgate Hill. The vast spectre of St Paul's rose before them in majesty, the steps littered with brightly coloured people. They looked normal; they had decent lives, wore their best and most garish clothes, each with his own history. Helen wanted to go inside, feel the cool, mingle with gawping visitors and pretend superiority. Rose was fingering her hair into sharper spikes, a sure sign of determination. Hers was a life which made religion, even religious buildings, anathema. Her father had always carried a Bible, even on his way to abuse little girls. Rose now believed in a different set of gods.

'Yeah. I want you to talk to this friend. Well, I don't know. You might bite her head off and tell her to go and get a life or something.'

'Oh, for Christ's sake stop talking in riddles. What do you want me to do?'

Rose took a deep breath of exasperation, then enunciated her words as carefully as any real lawyer on a pedestal.

'Michael's cousin. She's doing my flowers. I like her a lot, as it happens. Eight years younger than you; nine years older than me. Work that out for yourself. Only, she's been attacked, by a man. She told Mike's mum, but she won't say much and Mike's mum says it's been like watching someone shrivel up, but she won't do anything about it. You met her at my engagement party, remember? You two got on like a house on fire.'

'And you want me to talk to her? Forget it. There's social services, Rape Crisis, Victim Support, all that . . .'

'And none of it would do. Don't ask me why, it won't. You're the right age, you know what it's like to be attacked, you can pull words out of people. Will you do it?'

'No. I haven't got the skill.' Nor the time and certainly not the inclination. She was trying to recall the woman she had met, remembered a large girl, a midwife by profession. The taxi turned sharply, diving through a dark narrow street, throwing them together. Helen could feel the heat of Rose's skin. Papers littered the floor, ignored. All that paper, representing nothing but loss for everyone concerned.

'Typical,' said Rose, righting herself. 'Bloody typical. I can just hear what's in your head. Me? Never! I just prosecute; I can't do anything else; I don't want to understand. I don't want to find out what it's like, and I don't have time to help anyone, 'cos I'm so busy doing my duty. Like some doctor; I just inject, I just prescribe, I can't prevent. Look, it's because all these counsellors are such bloody experts that she won't go. She doesn't want psychobabble. She wants a nice, dry, sympathetic lawyer. One with my personal seal of approval, which you are about to lose.'

'Why won't she talk to you?'

Rose turned her head away.

'Oh, don't be so silly. I'm too young.'

Rose, you have never been young. Youthful and energetic, yes, but never young, Helen thought, slightly amused and certainly perplexed. Odd that she could withstand the bullying of a judge, the intimidation of Redwood, the vicious dislike of defendants and still have absolutely no armoury to defend an unreasonable request from Rose. She had a sudden flash of what it must be like to be Bailey, locked in his friendship with Ryan, made as malleable by it as a piece of putty.

'When?'

She meant, when was the woman attacked? but the single word was taken as acceptance of the demand. Rose was good at that. She had an angular face with a wide generous mouth made for smiling. Redwood was right to remark that Helen looked like an older, calmer version of Rose; she seemed unaware of how much the girl modelled herself on her. If she had her hair transformed into soft curls, Helen was thinking, fondly, this little devil might be able to fool even more of the people more of the time.

'Triffic. I'll give you her address. I mean, I did tell her this evening would be fine, but I expect you could re-arrange.'

There was no such thing as totally free will, Helen decided. Nor any such thing as predictability when the will was so weak.

Much of the time, she did not like being in charge, especially of human beings. Rose could have been right. It was a dangerous state to have reached if she really did prefer to meet them on paper.

chapter three

'The House of Lords has upheld the Court of Appeal in deciding that there is no implied consent to sexual intercourse within marriage, and that it is therefore possible for a man to rape his wife. The argument that "unlawful" meant outside the bond of marriage was mere surplusage . . . it was clearly unlawful to have sexual intercourse with any woman without her consent and the use of the word in the subsection added nothing.'

Brigid Connor was taking tea among the friends of the parish, ostensibly to organize preparations for the visit of the Bishop, who would confirm several children in their as yet half-baked faith and inspect the church with a view to allocating funds. This seemed to necessitate a wholesale spring-clean of the church itself, although Brigid privately thought it would be better to leave it as it was, since there was little point painting over the cracks which they wanted the man to see. The episcopal visit was distant enough to take second place to gossip of various kinds; Brigid would be able to add little. She detested parish activity and had no great affection for the other ladies who approached it with the enthusiasm she was capable of assuming, but never feeling, and she disliked the uneasy knowledge that they were all in the same boat.

They formed a sanctimonious posse of the better-off kind of matrons, who did not work, either because they did not know how or because they had no need. They were an unglamorous version of the ladies who lunch, all of them considering it poor taste to be flashy, to show off the baubles or the boobies, while each, to a woman, pretended they were poorer and busier than they were. It was the cars that gave them away rather than the clothes. Each time Brigid met one or the other, she hoped for a kind of breakthrough into friendship. Or, failing that, some kind of clue as to how it was they seemed to manage their lives so much better than she did; something she could copy, so that she could laugh as they did. But she stood on the fringes, looking in, watching intensely, making them uncomfortable, all the time afraid they might discover how much she envied their self-command.

Did they live in a state of mortal sin? Did they fear hell and any repeat of pregnancy as she did? They were a small element of this particular parish; minimal in comparison to those parishioners at the other end of the scale. This coterie existed to give, the bulk to receive, like a vast nest of baby birds with open mouths, Brigid thought, without condemnation. She had often wished she was one of the needy poor, then she might have greater licence to trouble the priest. One of the other women, only a couple of years Brigid's senior, married young and looking forward to grandmother status by the time she reached a well-preserved forty, was showing the others photos of her daughter's wedding. Brigid had attended the service, without an invitation to the reception. She saw herself, skulking in the corner of one of the photos outside church, with her hat askew, and, looking at her shadowy depiction, felt shame in it.

'Didn't she look a dream? All that lace . . .'

'Her granny's veil, that was, you know. Must be a hundred years old. Beautiful, isn't it?'

There were photos pre-ceremony, photos after, careful to

include costly cars and all the best frocks, or so it seemed to Brigid. The one thing which struck her most was the picture of the bride arriving with the veil over her face, ready to float down the aisle in ghostly anonymity, although everyone knew who she was. The veil said it all, Brigid was thinking. You arrived for your wedding shrouded in complete ignorance, thinking you knew about life, the universe and everything, while knowing nothing. Least of all the fact that you were a sacrificial lamb, for whom being in love was not going to help one whit. At least that was the way it had been for her. Might not be the same for a modern girl; but eighteen, this bride, for God's sake. How much could any girl know at eighteen?

The photos were bringing forth a flood of reminiscence, some of it surprisingly frank by their standards.

'I remember my wedding night,' one remarked. 'Lord, what a fiasco. I never thought I'd recover.'

'Was it such a great thing, Mary? Did you have to step over it?'

They all snorted with laughter.

'Course, it's not like that now,' Mary continued. 'Not that it ever really was. I was a virgin, God help me, but as for my sisters . . . Nobody actually produced a shotgun, but Daddy might as well.'

'That was me,' Brigid murmured, suddenly spontaneously bold. She only had to know, within rough parameters, the ages of these women's children to know that the had-to-get-married scenario applied to more than herself. No-one was shocked.

'Me too,' said another, after a pause. She was another plump one, who knitted between bites of her cake; the last thing she needed. 'Not that I have regrets, mind: I mightn't have got him any other way,' she said with her mouth full and they all laughed again. 'And surely', the plump one went on, 'there's few enough years when the sex stuff matters that much. Thank God the old man seems to have forgotten all about it.'

'If only,' Brigid said, further emboldened by the laughter. She spoke too fervently, her voice too loud. Now they were all staring at her, waiting for elaboration. She giggled, feeling herself blush.

'I mean, I wish mine would forget about . . . it. He never does though.'

The pause this time was distinctly awkward. The hostess stood up to refresh the tea.

'Well aren't you the lucky one?' she said, not unkindly. Everyone knew that Brigid, even in the maturity of her late thirties, was one brick short of a load. 'After all those years. It must be a wonderful thing to have a man who still wants you.'

Brigid knew how she must have sounded: boastful instead of bruised. And her Aemon such a handsome man, too. Barrel-shaped, with the kind of ruddy complexion which suggested rustic honesty. A big man with vivid blue eyes and a fine crop of hair, like his brothers. And his daughters, playing with their cousins for the summer. She had failed them all.

She went home via the church, where confetti drifted across the steps and the traffic roared by. God help her; it was only a small thing to bear, wasn't it? Sex, marriage, her own existence.

At the junction of the main road and the avenue which led to her home, she faltered and made an excuse to detour to the shops. It wasted another twenty minutes. The front door to the apartment block was a door of glass, which threw her own reflection back at her with warped accuracy, like a silly mirror at the funfairs of her childhood. She bent in the middle; her forehead was huge, the carrier bag enormous and the necklace round her neck too bright. Nearer the door, as she climbed up the steps, she became a small neat woman with an overlarge bosom and overtinted red-blond hair which was nothing but an artificial imitation of what it had been. She looked capable enough, but with shoulders too narrow for a body to cry upon and a dress with a pattern as busy as the confetti she had seen.

From the windows of the apartment Aemon had built, she could see downhill to the bowl of London. In the near distance were the gasometers of St Pancras. Touches of green between rooftops; railway lines sneaking out from the vast sheds of the station, suggesting freedom. All she had to do was go, but there had been a touch of cold in the morning air, an early-warning sign of a summer on the wane. Brigid did not want to be up here; nor did she want to be down there in those streets, either. Even in those shaded areas of green which showed the coolness of a square or a park.

Too soon for a drink, or was it? Drink, bath, warmth within and without. Ablutions and alcohol to rid herself of the dreadful guilt about taking pills and going to the doctor. Confessing things she should only confess to a priest, without hope of redemption now. No, no drinkies, not yet. She had will-power sometimes; it was the will itself she lacked.

If Helen West was resenting the superior will-power of Rose Darvey, Anna Stirland resented it more. Rose had a talent for subversion which was nicely complemented by her appetite for conflict. Anna could see that someone might rue the day when Rose had been persuaded to train for the law, even though the day when the child would, qualify was still a long way off. She could imagine Rose filling the courtroom with her own version of heavy breathing and an office with the same. The effect on her fiancé's family was exhilarating: they were weak with love for her.

Because of Rose, Anna had agreed to meet Helen West. OK, she had liked Helen on one meeting, but she would have preferred another context for the second. Anything to get Rose and Rose's future mother-in-law off her back: she should have kept her mouth shut. Anna was rehearsing the lines to make this less embarrassing, such as, I'm sorry, this is all a big mistake, fuck off. The sheer lack of imagination in her own nervous anger infuriated her all the more, but at the same time, there she was, tidying in expectation of a guest who would notice. Dusting surfaces already clean, looking at the whole doll's house with a critical eye, as if she were selling it. Some chance – she'd sell it if she could – she hoped that the sound of the doorbell was announcing someone responding to the advertisement. People might think the hasty decision to sell was the reason why she had suddenly taken to spending hours after midnight painting the walls. That was the way it went, she chanted to herself in the same singsong rhythm she used to the agent. Once you make it nice, you don't want to leave, do you?

If the woman on the doorstep had said hallo, extended some nice warm paw for shaking and announced herself with platitudes or small talk like the estate agent, Anna might have gone into her prerehearsed speech, but the visitor stood sideways on to the door, looking away down the street, one hand extended in Anna's direction, offering a bottle of wine, which, once accepted, left Anna no option but to ask Helen in. A clever ploy, she decided later; they had not even looked at one another's faces before they were both trapped.

She noticed again the scar on Helen's forehead. It curled from one eyebrow into the hairline and could easily have been covered by arrangement of her long hair, but she did not seem to mind it. Anna remembered Rose's verdict on this woman, heard Rose's lecturing voice, telling her: she may look buttoned up, you know, Anna, and she may talk a bit precious, but there isn't much she hasn't done. She didn't get that scar in a road accident and she has been known to bite people.

'What a nice kitchen,' Helen said, genuine enthusiasm taking away the polite banality of the compliment. Anna looked around; it was a more than nice kitchen, full of old pine, carefully chosen pictures, dried herbs and flowers lending it a musky smell. A door stood open, leading on to a small backyard laid out with narrow flower-beds in full bloom. Pink and white geraniums prevailed in tubs; roses climbed the wall. The glass panes in the door gleamed.

'I know what I want in my kitchen,' Helen continued, 'just as I sometimes think I know what I want in my life, but I never quite seem to achieve it. Something goes wrong between concept and execution. I expect it always will. I'd have thought about hanging dried herbs there.' She pointed to the wooden clothes pulley above her head, holding pans and flowers. 'And then I would have continued to think about it. Not done it.'

Anna fussed, uncorked the wine clumsily, poured un-steadily, the sound of it comforting. The glass she handed Helen was unusual, heavy and old; the wine cold and pale. Nothing in the kitchen was new; all of it revealed an owner who specialized in thrift as well as taste.

'I make an effort with my house,' Anna said, choosing words carefully, 'and I love flowers, because I can't do much with my person. I think I do it to compensate to the world. Or myself. I'm not sure.'

'I don't think I quite follow.'

'You should,' Anna stated with a touch of impatience. 'But then you probably live in a different world. Beautiful people do. I'm a rather ugly woman, in case you haven't noticed. It follows that I feel obliged to create something like beauty around me, so that I can justify my own existence.'

She was plain. Not plain enough to warrant the description of ugliness, but still a slab of a woman, apart from the eyes. The kind of woman who had never quite looked like a girl; too full a figure from the age of eleven. The type who would play wallflower and act chaperone for lovelier, livelier sisters or cousins. A face which had assumed responsibility as soon as other children shed it, but not, Helen thought, as plain as all that. Anna spoke of herself ironically, as if she were birthmarked or disabled to the degree that she was an assault on the human eye, instead of being on the wrong side of ordinary.

'I think you should get a new mirror,' Helen said honestly.

Anna rose and placed the wine in the fridge. She had the light-footed step of the heavy woman who had somewhere learnt to dance, a grace and economy of movement which also cast doubts on her own bitter self-deprecation. She did not seem a person who accepted defeat lightly, nor one who had looked at her world without issuing a challenge. If anything, she would be obsessive about making the best of what she had, Helen guessed; not today, perhaps, but on other days. She felt uncomfortably obtrusive, warning bells telling her to leave because Anna was right to resent the presence of anyone who could not mend her fractured self-esteem, least of all someone who did not want to try. Am I a man's woman or a woman's woman? Helen asked herself, remembering teenage years in which she had eschewed the company of either sex, but especially the female, for the sole unspoken reason that they were the ones most likely to expose her deficiencies. She had been a beautiful, reserved child, features which, taken together, had isolated her so much she had envied the big, fat, fearless and competitive girl who led the class and was the doyen of all their opinions. Anna could have been one of the same kind, who took her bulk and her dimples and turned them into virtues, moved on to another popular persona. Becoming one of the boys; something Helen had never been.

'You would suit lace,' Anna said, her face suddenly breaking into a grin which did indeed show dimples, hollowed into the cheeks, bunching the flesh of her face into a picture of good nature. 'You could get away with lace and ribbons. Rose tells me you're getting married.' She could deflect conversation away from herself with suspicious ease, Helen observed; she did it as to the manner born. They could quite easily have sat as they were and discussed the wedding garments.

'I hate lace, ribbons, buckles and bows,' Helen said. 'And Rose tells me you were attacked and can't talk about it. Can't, won't. Rose talks a lot, about other people.'

'So does my aunt. I didn't swear her to secrecy. Obviously not,' Anna said, quick to defend Rose. 'I've been dripping on people, that's all. I shouldn't have. Rose is too young and too happy, it isn't fair.'

She leant back in her chair, which creaked under considerable rather than formidable weight. Shapely weight, as if all her proportions were exaggerated. Not fat, simply too much. Not a lady for wearing Lycra, that was all.

Helen liked her. She had liked her on first sight. For all her reserve, she could fall into instant and profound liking and, all of a sudden, it was imperative to help. She put to one side the thought of Bailey's terse phone call with the news about Ryan; also the daily cases which made it seem that rape was an epidemic, sexual assault an everyday occurrence which she judged by a set of well-established, horribly objective criteria. The questions here were different.

Anna Stirland shrugged and let out a sigh.

'I'm a nurse,' she said. 'A midwife. A competent caring person with professional skills. I've been wiping bums since childhood.' She hesitated. 'In other words, I'm one of nature's sensible people and I'm ashamed of how I've dealt with this so far. And yes, I can talk to you; I have to. Perhaps you could regard it as a piece of dictation. Take it down like a lawyer. That way it might make sense.'

'I shan't fall into a fit of the vapours,' Helen said.

'Because you've heard it all before?' Anna asked mildly. 'You haven't, you know. I bet you haven't.'

At six-thirty in the evening, Detective Sergeant Ryan was formally suspended from duty, denied access to his office and instructed to go home and await the result of enquiries. His own detective chief inspector did this with Todd as witness, Bailey lurking on the sidelines. Ryan looked as if they were sending him out into the world naked, Todd thought with some satisfaction. The DCI thought the same, albeit with greater sympathy. Ryan had been so indefatigably popular, a man's man with a taste for women; the sort they admired. It was Bailey who arranged the car to take Ryan away; no-one else had formed Bailey's conclusion that if left unattended, Ryan's departure from the station would demonstrate the shortest route between the back door and the nearest public house. Ryan looked at him, wryly, each of them second-guessing the other.

Bailey watched the car disappear, driven by a woman constable. He wondered what, if anything, the two of them would say to one another and reminded himself to ask her later, slightly ashamed of the subterfuge. The pursuit of truth was all, was it not? All legitimate means were allowed. Or perhaps the pursuit of some niggling ambition that Ryan would let slip in private to the driver, some definitive clue to his own innocence. Rape is a crime which calls for vengeance, Todd had said, portentously, revealing a churchgoing tendency.

Barring Bailey's progress in the car park stood a blonde girl, hands on hips, looking at him belligerently. He recognized her as a detective, one of Ryan's sexual offences team. It occurred to him that, so far, the irony of Ryan's current work taken in conjunction with the offence they would likely charge him with, had escaped him. Yesterday, Bailey had been giving Ryan advice on the diplomacy of dealing with incredulous parents; today, he was *en route* to see another set, the ones who belonged to Ryan's own victim. It was all offensively circular.

'Sally Smythe, sir. What are we supposed to do with Ryan's cases?' It was an accusation, spat out with minimal pretence at politeness.

'I don't know. Carry on. He won't be back for some time.'

The blonde looked at him as if he was solely responsible for the doubling of her workload, the demise of her life and the appearance of her first grey hairs. Bailey began to walk towards his car, away from Todd; there was an implicit invitation for her to fall into step beside him.

'Which was his biggest case?'

'They're all big. Indecent assault, buggery, you name it. And he had an ongoing thing . . . Oh, shit.' She was gabbling, on the verge of tears. 'How could he do it, sir? How could he?'

'To you? To me? To the victim?' Bailey asked lightly, touching her arm with the slightest gesture, enough to suggest commiseration, but not camaraderie.

'He was good,' she said, fiercely. 'Really good. Getting better. I know none of us liked the appointment at first, but he had this case, eighteen months ago. Broke his heart. After that, he seemed, well, he seemed able to identify with the victims. If we can't, he said, who can?'

'Tomorrow at ten,' Bailey said, watching Todd catching up, 'I'd like to look at all his casework. There might be a clue to his alleged behaviour. It is only alleged, you know.'

She nodded dumbly, peeled away and left him to watch her plodding footsteps with regret. If Ryan's career was blighted, then so, by infection, was hers.

The evening sun raised a pink haze as they drove north, Bailey at the wheel with no need to consult a map. Vague directions would do equally well; he had known these streets since childhood. They were in the no-man's-land where Islington merges with King's Cross in a series of used-car dealerships, traffic lights and treeless thoroughfares which hide from view the pleasanter, leafier roads of a mixed hinterland. They sat behind a belching bus, watching it shiver with fumes in the heat, Bailey longing for the privilege of a fast vehicle with a siren to move everything from their path. Traffic cried for vengeance, as well as rape.

He scorched past the bus and into the side-streets, put on a turn of speed through a series of back-doubles. He flung the car round corners on a small industrial estate, took it up a cobbled alley-way, round the back of a parking lot and back on to the main route again, tyres screaming. When they arrived at number fourteen Roman Court, Todd was pale and Bailey felt calmer, not ashamed for shaking his passenger's composure.

They would not be talking to the victim. She was resting in her own flat, her mother said, and that was not, in any event, the purpose of the visit. Bailey had seen her statement already; it was background he wanted. Something to make the girl more than a silhouette and a name on paper. Something, perhaps, to stop himself disliking her.

The parents were not of the kind accustomed to being deferential to the police. Middle years, old enough to have watched *Dixon of Dock Green* on TV and then read three decades of newspapers detailing the destruction of that avuncular image. Mr Pelmore had twice been stopped for speeding and Mrs Pelmore had once been the victim of an overzealous store detective, so both of them were experts on the law. They saw themselves as minority honest citizens; fully employed, subject to harassment. Shelley, their daughter, was one of three children. Looking around, Bailey imagined he could guess an enthusiasm to leave home, even, as in Shelley's case, to live with a boyfriend less than two miles away.

'She's a good girl,' the mother said, as if anyone had yet suggested otherwise. 'A sweet girl. Quiet.'

A parent would always claim a girl was good. Bailey had waited years for one to boast that his or her child was gloriously, colourfully bad. The father was silent. Both sat in their living-room, defiantly occupying their regular oatmeal fabric covered chairs with uncomfortable wooden arms. Two dining chairs had been produced for the officers to sit facing them, perhaps to emphasize the fact that the interview was on sufferance. Tea was not offered. The room itself personified contemporary gloom: dark-blue carpet, patterned blue curtains, light-blue wallpaper with heavy borders near the ceiling, fittings of orangey-coloured wood. The shelves housed no books, but contained instead carefully arranged china figures of ladies in crinolines, shepherds and shepherdesses, dogs, cats and horses, all prancing together in sterile contemplation of a large loud clock on the opposite wall. Everything was depressingly tidy. Bailey remembered that his own flat had been given a similar description by Helen some time since, but his flat was different. It was eclectic. There was another passing thought, as he let the words flow over and around him, while he arranged his own face in an expression of rapt and kindly concentration. Would he and Helen sit thus, in chairs like this, when they reached the stage of Darby and Joan? The thought made him shudder. He never wanted to be fastidious. Not about emotion; not about anything.

'Yes,' said father at last. 'A very good girl. Always worked, Shell. Never cost us.' Bailey could not help himself; he leant forward with his arms resting on his thin knees. His legs were too long for the narrow room; Todd thought he had a face like a hatchet.

'What exactly do you mean by "good"? Do you mean good in school, good at helping blind people at zebra crossings, kind to animals, or not many boyfriends?' He spoke with all the congeniality of a cobra, but quietly, scratching his head as an afterthought to suggest genuine confusion. Both mum and dad bridled; mother spoke first.

'I mean a good girl, that's what I mean! Not one of those

dole spongers! And she lives with this decent bloke. Been going out with him since she was sixteen. Works hard, he does, too. Electrician; works shifts. They got a flat on a mortgage. Getting married.' She spat the last with a note of triumph.

'She liked animals,' father added as a delayed reaction. 'Least, she did when she was a kid.'

Mother darted from her chair and produced a photo album, as if by magic. She placed it on Bailey's lap with a smart thump and retreated to her own seat to sit with folded arms. Todd sensed a conversational hiatus, filled it blithely, looking at the bovine face of dad.

'What kind of animals?'

'Pardon?'

'She didn't really like animals,' mother interrupted, anxious to avoid anything which might suggest a lack of hygiene in any sense. 'Only gerbils and things.'

Bailey was suffering from a desperate desire to laugh, another to scream. He was turning the pages of the album, seeing Shelley as an overdressed baby, held aloft by her mother like a trophy; Shelley at school, earnest in socks; Shelley with her mates and cousins on her thirteenth birthday, a pretty child, refusing to smile for the camera. He felt only relief that these parents had never met the age of the camcorder, the better to depict in movement what was, to his jaundiced view, that fleeting sly expression of their child. Did not like animals. Having reached the point where the photos tailed off, Shelley aged fifteen, he snapped the album shut and placed it back in Mrs P's lap. She had the impression of a large pale ghost coming towards her and retreating, quailed slightly and blinked. By the time she looked again, he was back as he had been, legs crossed this time.

'When was she getting married?' Todd asked, looking like an earnest bank manager, almost cocking his hand behind an ear for the reply.

'What do you mean, *was*? She still is, isn't she? Next month, sometime. She isn't dead, is she?'

Oh, she lied, she lied. All mothers know the date of a daughter's wedding. Did they? Bailey was getting married himself, sometime next month. When the weather was fine, whenever; month decided, date not fixed; a register office do. Left deliberately vague, God help them both. Summer, Helen had said. We'll think about the arrangements two weeks before. It occurred to him, in this frozen room, just why they might both be so diffident. This daughter's mother seemed to regard a wedding as a prize for winning a race.

'He's a lovely lad, her fiancé,' Mrs Pelmore said fondly. 'Lovely. It was him reported it. Then, after the police came, he phoned me. He's good to her. Steady.'

'Did you know about her other involvement with the police?' Todd asked.

'She's never been in trouble with the police,' dad cut in.

'I know,' Todd said easily. 'But there was an occasion, not long ago, when she went out clubbing with a friend, and the friend had an accident on the way home. Shelley helped us with information. We think that's how she met Mr Ryan.'

Mrs Pelmore looked blank.

'How often do you see Shelley?' Bailey asked.

There was a long fidgeting pause. Mother opened her mouth to speak and closed it again. Father hauled himself upright, the bones of his elbows crunching on the uncomfortable chair. Mother put out a warning hand which he ignored.

'She never comes near us,' he said, flatly. 'Not if she can help it. He comes, though, her boy. He comes to see us. That's how we know how she is.'

'I know', said Anna Stirland, 'about rape. Oh, I don't mean in a legal sense, I mean I know about violation. I work with women, you see. It's a kind of violation, having a baby you don't want, by a man you don't love. I don't meet many men, though in my kind of environment there are a lot of them around. Men seem to like me well enough, but they don't, well, look at me. I'm one of the lads, a good sport; they'll put that on my gravestone. To tell the truth, I don't do much looking either; no point in a great lump like me flirting, is there? Only when I look at these baby kids, I know how I'd like my life to go: in the direction of a household with a nice man and a couple of children. Especially children. Well, I'm over thirty and the prospect gets ever more remote. I just don't like men well enough to try. Then I met John. That isn't his real name. I'm not going to tell you his real name.'

'Why not?'

'You'll see. And if this is dictation, you aren't supposed to interrupt.'

'Sorry.'

'He worked in the same place as me. We got on well. I used to watch his hands and think, God, you are the most beautiful creature nature ever invented. He had all the humanity I like in a man; vulnerability, too. Not the sort of drivel you'd put in a statement, is it? I suppose it might have been obvious that I went into spasms whenever I saw him, but the others didn't seem to notice, so I thought he hadn't either. We copers have self-control, you know. Yes, you probably do know. What would have been more obvi-

ous was the fact that I sparkled when he was around, became the life and soul of the party, full of wit and energy.
Falling in love must be like that. I've always hated the
phrase. I thought the best thing would be to be friends first,
let love, or whatever you choose to call it, grow like a plant.
But desire isn't like that, is it? It's a bloody affliction. It has
nothing to do with approval, mutual feeling and appreciation, nothing at all. It's a ghastly virus, immune to medicine.'

She gulped her wine. Helen sat in front of her notepad,
trying to make herself as anonymous as a shorthand-taker
at a board meeting.

'And we were friends, I thought. He has a special smile
he reserved for me; he seemed to seek me out, even when
every other female in the place simpered and would have
thrown their knickers at him, given half the chance. So I
let hope spring eternal. Perhaps one day he'd say, let's have
a drink? How about dinner sometime? The one thing I
wasn't going to do was make the suggestion: I was too
scared of rejection. I sort of prayed it would come from
him. It's always better to live in hope than risk the negative,
don't you think? Well, it is if you look like me. Such sensi-
tivity, I have.'

Her fingernails were neatly trimmed, Helen noticed.
There were flecks of paint on the back of both wrists. Anna
stuffed her hands into the long sleeves of the kaftan she
wore, as if hiding them.

'But no, he didn't take whatever bait I was offering, not
in months, and then he was posted somewhere else. A man
with a career path, you see. I was devastated at the thought
of not seeing him again. So there I was, acting out of character, saying, why don't you come round to supper before
you go? He said he couldn't, but he'd drop round for a

drink sometime. I had to be content with that. Had to? I *was* content. Doesn't take much to please me. I worshipped him.'

Helen caught a waft of scent from the garden. It would be pleasant to eat at this table, with the doors open like this and the blaze of flowers outside.

'I waited, of course one waits, but not all the time. He turned up, like they do, when least expected. It was that hot spell, a couple of weeks since; freakishly hot. Midnight or so, too late for a casual call. I looked a mess; it made me flustered. I was in the living-room.' She jerked her head in the direction of the first room off the hall which Helen had only noticed briefly. 'I was doing my ironing. Well I tried to smooth myself down, fetched us a drink, but it isn't easy to look both alluring and casual when all you have on is a long T-shirt. I was too flustered to get the ice; he did that.' She gulped.

'I put down the drinks: gin and tonic, first things first; I was joking and had my back to him. I wanted to unplug the iron, put the board away, because I didn't want the damn thing littering up the room. I wanted . . . I wanted him to see what a nice room it was. Admire me for it. Pathetic, isn't it?'

'No,' Helen said. 'It isn't.'

'And then he was on me. No preliminaries, no nothing. I thought at first he was hugging me from behind, fooling around, and I didn't want that. I didn't want a quick poke, for God's sake; even I can get one of those if I want nothing more. I wanted sweet words, admiration, some sort of tentative beginning, some curiosity about *me* . . . Oh, I don't know what I wanted, I didn't even want him to see my bare knees.' Her voice fell into silence. Helen wondered if it was permissable to smoke a cigarette and decided not.

'Oh, do smoke if you want. I think I'll have one too. It's amazing the number of nurses who smoke, you know. Doctors, too.'

'Was he a doctor?'

'Did I say that?' Anna said sharply. 'No, I didn't say that. Of course he wasn't a doctor, how could he be? A sort of technician, really.' She took the cigarette with a shaking hand.

'I fell onto the iron. He pushed me down against it; it fell over. I don't know if he meant to do that, but he must have known it hurt, because I screamed. My arm was burnt.' She pulled back her sleeve. There was a triangular imprint of a fading burn mark, still livid.

'The board fell over. I fell with it, I think; on my stomach, against the iron, then I rolled over against it again. I was lying on top of it, screaming; he seemed to be pressing me down. I think it was then I realized he meant to do me harm. I started struggling, but I was kind of paralysed, too; I could only focus on how much the burning hurt. Next thing I knew, he'd hauled the T-shirt over my face. I was on my back, couldn't see anything. I began to cry, I think. I thought he was going to rape me, kill me, I don't know what. I couldn't move. He held my arms down, but there was really no need. Even when he moved and I heard what I thought was the rustling of paper, I didn't move. Then I felt this thing going in between my legs. I think I'd already made a half-conscious decision to stay still. Something stuck up me. Rammed. I might have passed out for a minute.'

The ash on the end of her cigarette smouldered and dropped onto the clean table. Helen brushed it away; it burnt slightly against her palm.

'I don't know why, I thought of a sixty-millilitre syringe.' Anna's voice had gone down to a murmur, as if she was speaking to herself.

'You can use them for irrigating a womb . . . and other plumbing operations; they're sort of phallic shaped, cold . . .' Her voice hardened. 'I was simply aware of being fucked and being icy, icy cold. My stomach in contractions; me, fighting with the T-shirt, getting my face free. The fucking stopped. I certainly can't call it anything else but fucking. Certainly not making love. I somehow sat up, got the shirt over my head, and there he was, sitting in the chair laughing. Me, naked, flopping all over the place; him, sitting with his legs crossed, immaculately dressed as usual. He favoured the smart casual. Nice white cotton tops, smart linen-look trousers, handsome belt.'

'Dressed?' Helen murmured, incredulous.

Anna extended both her arms, shaking them free of the purple kaftan sleeves. The colour of it suited her. The burns were almost symmetrical.

'So was I, dressed, I suppose. I was wearing three large burns. And I was so cold. And then what did he do? Swallowed his gin, came over to me, kissed me on the forehead and said, there, poppet, that was what you wanted, wasn't it? Then he left. He was . . . pleased with himself. As if he'd done me a favour. There's more wine in the fridge,' she added. 'Could you get it?' The fridge was empty apart from the bottle. It looked new and reeked of cleanser.

'Isn't it funny that I can put wine in that thing, but not food?' Anna said chattily. 'It's all his fault.'

Helen kept her expression calm, privately thinking, The woman has flipped. This is not making sense.

'I hadn't even got to my feet by the time the door slammed,' Anna continued. 'And I heard his footsteps going down the road before I moved. Then I looked down between my legs and I thought I was bleeding. A sort of red-coloured trickle was coming out onto the carpet. I stood up and it dripped on the floor. By this time, I was imagining some major haemorrhage. What had he done? Was it a knife? Hadn't I noticed any pain, only cold, because the burns hurt so much and that was all I had room to feel? Bleed to death, go on, I told myself, but I knew it wasn't blood.'

Anna started to laugh. 'It was a popsicle. One of those cheap ice lollies kids like so much, like a long icicle, wrapped in polythene; horrible things, but I kept them in the freezer for neighbours' kids. Should I laugh? He laughed. Get the girl all lathered up, then cool her down . . . it is funny, isn't it?'

'No. It isn't funny.'

'Promise me it isn't funny . . . When I sat on the side of my bed, I was weeping strawberry juice. Tell me, lady lawyer, was that simply a joke, or was that rape?'

Helen cleared her throat, reached for wine and cigarettes simultaneously.

'According to the letter of the law, no, that wasn't rape.'

Anna began laughing, a grim and mirthless chuckle.

'No,' she said, 'I don't suppose it was. That's me, isn't it? Not even worth that.'

chapter four

'Where, on the trial of any offence under this Act, it is necessary to prove sexual intercourse (whether natural or unnatural), it shall not be necessary to prove the completion of the intercourse by the emission of seed, but the intercourse shall be deemed to be complete upon proof of penetration only. According to the old authorities, even the slightest penetration will be sufficient . . . It is submitted that this remains the law under the present statutory arrangement.'

Shelley remembered that when she had finally reached home on the fateful night of her meeting with Ryan, she had smelt. Hot-night sweat of rage and fear with overtones of heavy perfume. There was mucus on the jacket, tears in brown mascara rivers on her face, filth embedded in her torn clothes. When Derek had found her, he had not touched her. This had been, he explained, the actions of a careful man who had seen films about the need to preserve evidence in cases such as these.

First, he had put down the rubbish bag he had been carrying and then sprinted for the phone. Highly sensible, a police officer had conceded, but Shelley did not think she would ever forget the fact that he had not hugged her.

Their lives were full of patterns and plans. Derek was like her mum and dad: constantly in a state of vigilance against the awful threat of the unpredictable.

*   *   *

Derek Harrison watched Shelley Pelmore get up and open the curtains he had just pulled closed. She did not open them completely, since she did not wish to contradict him, but enough so that she could see the opposite side of the road and the darkening sky from her window seat of oatmeal coloured fabric from Ikea, identical to that possessed by her mother; such good value. They now had a matching pair of such chairs, replacing the cushions she had possessed. Derek's reason for the replacement was that sitting on cushions meant you had to go such a long way down to the floor and such a long way back up again, and even though she might reckon herself double-jointed, he was not. The same argument prevailed when it had come to acquiring a new bed to replace the double mattress. Derek was the master of do-it-yourself, but he liked to have her around when he did it, requiring an assistant and admirer for his skills. Mostly, it was his money that went on improvements.

I don't resent it, Shell, how can I? he would say as she demurred every time another length of wood appeared. It's our future I'm building.

A future in bricks and mortar, shelving and three-piece suites stretched before her. Matching crockery and washing-machines to save them from falling into animal behaviour. Ready-made, machine-washable curtains in pastel shades to make sure they could distinguish themselves from the creatures in the jungle outside. Shelley was twenty-two and worked in a shop in the West End. She got a discount on clothes of which Derek approved; he didn't like her shopping anywhere expensive, so that when she did, she scrunched the garment into a small parcel and hid it away. Brick by brick, Derek built their future; she could feel the walls of it surrounding her. Sometimes, the prison had the comfort of a padded cell; at others she wanted it bulldozed to the ground. Derek was so kind. Everyone approved of him. She had everything she wanted.

'I think I'll go to work tomorrow,' she said.

He looked up in surprise. On the floor between his feet, sitting neatly on a double thickness of newspaper to save the carpet, were the innards of their vacuum cleaner which Derek was mending.

'Oh, no, I wouldn't. It's too soon, lovey, after all you've been through. It's only a couple of days since . . . You need your rest.'

'Two days. I don't need rest. I need something to do. I feel much better, honest, and if I don't go to work, the old bat will think it's time she got someone else . . .'

Shelley could hear the whine in her voice; a rising note of panic singing along tunelessly behind it.

'There are laws against unfair dismissal,' he said primly.

'I know there are, but they don't count for nothing if you get the sack. You can spend weeks fighting it or you can put up and shut up, the manager knows that. Anyway, a couple of days on the sick is all I can get away with before anyone asks questions. And we've got a sale this week.'

Shelley liked work, usually; work was a laugh. The corollary of not going to work was having to stay at home, in this flat, cleaning it, fussing round it, making custard for apple pie. Derek worked on the vacuum cleaner. Silence reigned, apart from the sound of a screwdriver, tapping the filter free of dust.

'I don't want to tell them, at work, I mean, Derek. I just don't.'

'No, of course you don't. Why should you?'

He dusted his hands, stepped across to her and patted

her head indulgently. Then he sat down again and continued tapping the filter. The small sound grated on her nerves. She knew his industry did not imply any criticism of her for fouling up the machine in the first place, but that was what it felt like.

Between them both, the television glowed and people were murmuring at one another. A police officer appeared through a door on the screen and Shelley squirmed at the sight of him. The trembling spread throughout her limbs; she pulled her knees into the chair and clasped her hands around her calves.

'What's going to happen, Derek? What are they going to do to him?'

He looked at the screen, puzzled.

'Sorry, love, I wasn't watching.'

She wanted to shout.

'I don't mean the man on the telly. I mean that copper. Ryan.'

Derek's hands ceased moving and he gave her his full attention. She had had the benefit of his 100 per cent solicitude for forty-eight hours; he never seemed tired of giving, darling Derek.

'Charge him, put him on trial, lock him up and throw away the key, I hope, after what he did. But we don't know, love. Most likely they'll cover it up, just because he's a copper. They stick together, you know.'

'I don't want to give evidence,' she said, her voice tremulous. 'Do you know what he did for a living? He was doing sex cases. That's why I had to go so far, all that way, to that other police station; I couldn't go where anyone knew him. Why didn't they take *him* somewhere else? 'Cos I couldn't be on his territory. I don't want to give evidence. What's the point?'

'You can't let him get away with it, Shell. And you mustn't worry. I'll be with you all the way. Now and for ever.'

Such a good man, the best she would ever find. The girls told her so, warned her not to lose him. Shake him off a little from time to time, sure, but never risk losing such a man in a million, who worked hard and didn't mind if she went out alone, didn't even mind if she came home late; loved her enough to give her freedom. Look, Shell, he would say, I don't like clubs and discos, and I got all these late shifts, so you go on and have fun, girl. I like you having a good time. The unspoken context was his own plan to have her knee-deep in babies and living a million miles from town within a couple of years, but perhaps that was an unfair interpretation. He wanted any wild oats sown so he could reap the crop; he would turn one blind eye, admire with the other, as long as he kept her.

She looked at the world outside, listened to the traffic, felt her heart contract with fear.

'I'd better iron some gear for the morning,' she said, uncurling from the chair. 'I'll do it for you,' he said. 'You just sit still now. Want a hot drink, love?'

'Tell me again,' Helen asked Bailey. 'Just so I get it straight in my mind.'

The meal was finished, to mutual satisfaction. Steak for him, fish for her, because fish was something she reserved for the occasions when she did not have to cook it. She was superstitious about fish and always imagined it would leap out of the bag on the way back from the shops, find a drain and try and swim back home. There were lights in the roof of Casale's, suspended from branches, giving the effect of Christmas decorations in a barn. The floor was uneven, the chairs rocky and the proprietor rude to a fault. It was a small price to pay for the food.

'Not that much to tell. I'm told Shelley Pelmore seems nervous, truthful and she's very pretty. I'm never quite sure whether it favours a prosecution case to have an attractive victim, or a plain one. Depends on the argument. If the issue's consent, it's better to have them pretty, because juries will believe she had every right to refuse . . .'

'Well, well . . . I take it you aren't actually saying that a plain woman hasn't any right to say "No"?'

'Helen . . . I'm simply saying that a jury is more likely to assume that a pretty lass can pick and choose. She'll have more men after her. She's likely to have more confidence, reject what she doesn't want, demand more. A pretty girl has more power, that's all. On balance, unless she's provocatively sexy, when her looks go against her, she's more likely to be believed.'

It was not a conclusion Helen wanted to accept, but she remained silent.

'Anyway, this pretty woman, girl, is out in a pub, West End, after work, a regular hang-out for the girls. She's met Ryan before, I told you about that. He knows where she lives, because he's been there to take a statement . . .'

'About the other rape case? The non-starter case he was telling you about, where the girl won't say . . .'

'Yes. Ryan happens to be in the West End, meets her this time by accident. They get chatting in the pub. She liked him in the first place, she said; he made her laugh. He says he'll give her a lift home, but they stop in another pub, near her flat, for another drink, ostensibly to talk about her friend. As far as Ryan will say anything at all, he says she wanted to stay in this pub near St Pancras, decided she'd wait for another friend and didn't want to go home yet, so he left her there. That was it. The sum total of his evening's acquaintance with Ms Pelmore: one lift, two drinks, left her to meet someone else. Shelley says they get back in the car to complete the journey to her flat, but halfway there, Ryan stops on the edge of the park and makes . . . suggestions. She laughs at him; he seems to lose his temper, comes round to her side of the door and says, OK, get out and walk. She gets out, not particularly worried, but shocked as hell, because she doesn't expect a copper to come on like that. He drags her into the bushes, telling her she's asked for it; she resists and then stops because she already hurts, and bingo. He mucks her about, tears her knickers, puts on a condom, shoves it in, but can't come, gives her a slap, then leaves her. He drives off; she staggers home.'

'Where the ever-loving boyfriend finds her on the step. Wearing Ryan's mucked-up jacket. How does he explain the jacket?'

'He doesn't. He won't. Not even how there came to be another condom in the pocket. Such a responsible man.'

'Traces of her in the car?'

'Bits of straw from a straw bag she had on the back seat. Not conclusive, because she was in the car anyway. Bits of hairy fabric under her nails, from his jacket. Soil. She had scratches . . . bruises.'

'Her friend had scratches. The other one you told me about.'

'Not the same. The only skin under that little girl's fingernails was her own. Shelley had soil from the park. There might have been skin under Ryan's fingernails, but there wasn't, for the simple reason he'd bitten them to the quick before anyone took samples. Now, would you say the man had a case to answer?'

'Yes. I'm glad it won't be coming to me.'

'What a crying, bloody awful shame, and I still don't want to believe it.'

Bailey looked as if he might begin to beat the table, an outburst curtailed by the arrival of coffee and four chocolates which he ate, absent-mindedly.

'Shall we talk about something else? Weddings? Births, marriages and deaths?' he said. She had once thought his habit of changing the subject with such speed was evasive; now she knew it was merely habitual, a symptom of a crowded mind, full of separate, easily accessed compartments.

'Marriages first. I thought later this month. Two weeks tomorrow. We always said we'd do it by special licence, midweek. No time for thinking. Put the date in your diary, for God's sake. We can have a party later. To dispel second thoughts.'

'That's just a couple of days before Rose. Fine. Daren't tell her, though.' She hesitated. 'I thought you might want to postpone it until this business with Ryan's over.'

'Nope. If life's negative, I want to do something positive.'

Helen nodded. So they had agreed. Their wedding would be spontaneous, eccentric and private. Suddenly, he grinned, leant across the table and kissed her.

'This is your ever-so-decisive husband, Miss West. Don't change your mind about changing your name, will you? I like it as it is. We can be like all those characters out of Jane Austen. Husband and wife addressing one another as Mrs Smith and Mr Smith. Never Helen and Geoffrey; far too familiar. You'll be Miss West, even first thing in the morning, and I'll be Mr Bailey.'

'Don't expect me to call you sir.' She was laughing now, covering the slight feeling of awkwardness and embarrassment which afflicted her whenever she thought of this forthcoming event, a thought recurring every single day but only long enough to put back in a box marked secret.

'Take ourselves by storm. I'll fix it. Think of it like a medical appointment. This way you haven't got enough time to plan an escape.'

He grinned again, the smile which was imprinted on her imagination. Bailey's smile lit up his lined face and made it look like a map. Age was only intermittently kind to him: he could look cadaverous, but his eyes were brilliant, aware of her ambivalence about marriage; accepting it. He was not bullying her, just following out their mutual conviction that this was the best thing to do. God knows where we'll drift if we don't.

You will be a very distinguished old man, Helen thought, and how well, how very well you know me. I do not think I really deserve you at all.

Ryan loved the City of London with a passion. He could have opted to be a City of London constable instead of an officer serving with the Metropolitan, had it not been for the little matter of family tradition, and the more important detail of his size. Six foot had been the minimum for the City; some of the men looked like giants in their helmets. He was only five ten in stockinged feet. In boyhood, he had attempted to stretch his own size by holding on to the wardrobe door with his outstretched arms, his feet hooked under his bed, maintaining the pose until it hurt. In retrospect, he reckoned this exercise had stunted his growth rather than increased it. I should've been stopped, he told himself; I should have been stopped from doing a lot of things. Dozens of defendants had told him the same.

The City was quiet on the brink of dawn, with a pink sky flowering above it. Six o'clock in the morning and the place was beginning to exhale the dark, inhale the prospect of the day. Too soon for all the ants to begin scurrying. St Paul's station disgorged cleaners and dealers into tall and taller buildings. The steps of the cathedral were empty of tourists. Ryan felt as if he was a free man, in charge of his car, without hindrance from traffic, therefore in charge of his own destiny. Life might have been different if his career had been spent in the heart of the financial centre, where crime was white collar and committed on paper and the pubs shut at seven, turning it into an elegant and substantial no-man's-land, inhabited by security guards and less temptation.

He cruised past the Central Criminal Court, crossed the lights and entered into the square by St Bartholomew's. The contrast delighted him; beautiful buildings: the church, the ancient hospital, and the throng of the meat market which had been in full swing since five. If all else failed, he might become a porter, lugging carcasses into vans, but porters operated a closed shop, even if his size didn't count. Shame; he enjoyed working the early shift. Ryan stopped to buy coffee, sipped the froth, replaced the cap, and put the carton on the passenger seat, carefully. The pink of the sky was fading. He turned the car east.

'What did you do with your jacket?' his wife had asked, persistently. 'How did you lose your jacket?' Then she tried to make a joke of it. 'I don't know, one of your best jackets remaining in custody; you could have given it to the charity shop. I don't understand you, really I don't.'

Ryan could see that she was being courageous and that he, by sticking to his story of simply forgetting the jacket, was making things worse. He had always been so punctilious, if generous, about clothes. If he had said he had given the thing away, he might have stood a better chance of being believed, and if his wife doubted his story, she was making a spirited attempt to hide it, although incredulity leaked through the façade, like honey through a comb.

No jacket this fine morning. Jeans, old trainers, sweat-shirt and a two-day growth of stubble. He might have been back in the old days of early-morning stake-outs with Bailey, dressed like the yob they were trying to catch, hoping to find him at home with his pyjamas round his ankles. Ryan tried to remember how many times he had conducted a raid on the wrong house, always careless about reading the warrant when he was all fired up and ready to go; he shivered to remember how Bailey's subsequent ingratiation with outraged citizens had saved his bacon. That and countless other times.

Could details of the defendant's past behaviour be given in evidence? Ryan wondered. Would he be vilified for all his flirtations? The female's sexual history could not be given in evidence, that he knew, but could they put the historical screws on him?

For the moment Bailey's help lay only in all that early training in self-discipline. Much of which had been ignored.

I loved you, you sod.

Ryan reached the public house where he had encountered Shelley Pelmore on the night in question. It stood, locked and barred, with a pile of rubbish sacks outside; only the pubs in Smithfield were open at this hour, another reason for the attraction of the City. He waited outside with the engine idling, an underpowered car, to his mind, but reliable enough for his short-distance-driving wife. His own car, like his jacket, was still in police custody. Ryan remembered with a stifled groan how new that car was, how much of a novelty to him. If the car had been an old banger, more like the Peugeot, would he have given the girl a lift? Probably not. He had wanted her admiration and respect; he was still a show-off, and she would have despised a runabout like this.

He drove on, taking the route he had used from the first pub to the second, remembering something else. That car, his car, had been so new that it had still had paper covering the rubber floor mats in the front. The girl had remarked on it, torn the paper on her side with the heel of her shoe when she got in. For no reason he could fathom, he had found this annoying, and since the annoyance highlighted a fussiness of which he was faintly ashamed (a car was only a car, for fuck's sake), he had crumpled up the paper and thrown it away. That had been on the way home, when he was sick of her silliness. She'd remembered the paper, of course.

Stupid, worthless little cunt. Silly bitch.

The backstreets shaded him from the early sun, which hit the windows of The Wheatsheaf, an incongruous name for a pub hard by a station, in territory best described as an urban wilderness of roads, but still the best of the local soulless drinking barns. By now, Ryan was halfway home again, going against the traffic which was perceptibly heavier. Pedestrians were still abed. He left the vehicle and crossed the road, uncertainly. Which way were they supposed to have gone, he and the girl?

He had pretended not to understand the question during his interview, where all his energies had been spent in saying nothing and avoiding Bailey's eyes and his all-too-familiar voice. Instead he had listened to his lawyer asking for clarification of this and that, making sure they both knew the exact extent of the allegation and its geography. An interview under caution, even where the suspect remains stubbornly silent, must describe the case against him completely. Bailey knew that. Ryan had known that too, even as he had clung to the dim hope that Bailey's comprehensive questions, articulating every detail of the accusation, were designed to help him build a defence. Really he knew otherwise: Bailey was only being as thorough and beyond reproach as Bailey normally was. There had been an ice-cold atmosphere in that interview room.

There was a slight morning mist over the park where, according to the questions, he had stopped the car and dragged her out, put on his condom, tried to do the business after a few choice threats and blows, left her there and driven off. Only a prat, and a very angry prat, would have done that, but he had been angry. What was he supposed to have done with his condom? Ryan brushed away a fly which buzzed round his head, sounding almost friendly. A careful prat, more careful than the average rapist who never used rubbers, would have taken it away, put it somewhere, like on the floor of his car, possibly, then chucked it. He would have put it on the paper on the floor, passenger side, which she had torn with her heel. That would have been why they asked him about the paper, wondering out loud why he had chosen that evening, of all others, to dispense with it on the way home. Because it was torn. If he had decided to break his silence and say what a clever bitch to remember the paper at all, he would have been doubly damned. It was always the details which counted. Hairs and fibres and paper.

Any amount of penetration is sufficient.

There was a crowd of chattering starlings above the trees in the park. He knew this lovely shabby park well. It was somehow preserved while the buildings around it, marooned but still splendid, bore witness to better days. The trees, in full leaf, screened the small area of grass, making it cool; the planting of blooms was meticulous. Pinks and blues in serried rows, neatly interspersed with greenery. Ryan loved gardening, an anomalous but not uncommon addiction for a police man and the one thing which reconciled him to living in the suburbs. That and his kids.

There was an old lag sitting on a bench. By daylight, this was an old lags' park and Ryan wondered how many of them, old, young, indifferent, knew about the mortuary at the far end with the separate entrance for wagons, next to the coroners court. You could hear the refrigeration hum, close to. Ryan fished his cigarettes out of his pocket, proffered two and watched a wizened and dirty hand take them from his own fingers and hide them in one of many pockets.

'They can accuse me of anything,' Ryan told him earnestly. 'Anything at all. Only they mustn't ever suggest I'd roll all over the flowers . . . Think of that! Would I ever?'

The man nodded. The day had begun. Ryan heard the squeak of a baby carriage and saw a woman coming towards him, making noises at the infant in the pram. He wondered if the child was hers, or if she was simply employed to guard it, and whether he could ever think fondly of any baby which was not his own. The sun through the trees caught the brown of the girl's hair, dishevelled round a pretty, utterly preoccupied face. I may never look at another woman again, Ryan thought, except in a magazine.

He felt the time without looking at a watch. Parking restrictions in half an hour. Shelley Pelmore lived three streets east. Ryan tried to envisage the easiest route between that address and this park and then tried to envisage the route a girl might take late at night. One route if she were trying to get home without being seen, another if she was simply trying to be quick. He jogged the first choice in ten minutes, the alternative, back to his car, in eight.

That was enough for this morning. Give it another half-hour and his wife would be awake, ready to resume her persona of stoic, all-forgiving, casual calm, and only ask him one more time about his jacket. She would never once dare to ask, did you fancy that girl? Did you? Afraid of forcing him to admit the truth. Oh yes, I did, I did, I did. I wanted her.

Helen West had taught Rose the importance of the written word. Rose did not realize quite what a flair she had for it. She could write as she spoke, with the same clarion quality, never pausing for a better way to say it, as if she had understood all along that a person who will not listen is also one who will not read, so there was nothing to be achieved by compromise or prettying it up. Rose had had an excellent education in the fundamental rules of self-expression. Granny next door had done that. Dead now, like her mother. Rose had the kind of family history which might have curtailed her capacity for love, instead of increasing it.

Now look here, Mike, you bum, I'm sorry we had that row yesterday, although I'm not sorry, really. I'm only saying I am because I can't tolerate sulking. I hate those plants, always have; they look so bleeding dismal and I don't care who the fuck grew them, neither of us has time to water the buggers so they're dead, OK? You said our attitude to living things made us incompatible. You do talk a load of shit. Go on then, leave if you want, before it's too late. Getting out of a wedding is far less trouble than a divorce. You don't have to do this bridegroom stuff if you don't want, even if it was your idea. You don't have to do anything you don't want, right?

As long as some things are clear. You've given me more breaks than I ever knew existed and I just want to say thanks for that, and if anyone ever bad-mouths you when I'm around, I'll break their jaw . . .

It took five minutes to write. Rose cut the crap about how she loved him to death and felt she would die without him. If he didn't know now, he never would. She left the note on the kitchen sink, thought about splattering water on it to look like tears. Naa, that was creepy and she knew what ailed him: all that stuff about family planning and pills; they never agreed. And then pre-wedding nerves and everyone getting at him. Hated to be on show, did Mike, unless it was in some sporting event, and he could not re-gard his nuptial celebrations as that, he took them far too seriously. He'd hang for her and she for him, but he re-garded their wedding as a solemn sacrament, while she viewed it as the best party ever.

A man on the crowded underground stood too close; closer than he needed. Rose twisted round, so that the over-large buckle of her handbag hit him in the soft of the groin, making him flinch. She smiled at the ring on her hand and then smiled at him with her white teeth clenched in a growl.

A woman loved.

She thought of the man she had told about all of this, in the clinic.

It reminded her of another thing Michael didn't always like: her, talking too much.

chapter five

'It must be proved that the accused had sexual intercourse with the complainant. The prosecution must prove either that the girl physically resisted or, if she did not, that her understanding and knowledge were such that she was not in a position to decide whether to consent or resist. If, however, a woman yields through fear of death or through duress, it is rape.'

He did so prefer the legal text.

No-one has ever been afraid of me, he told the screen. There was never any need. I would never make a woman pregnant and that is so often their greatest fear. Besides, they will let me do anything. They all need love.

It is noble in me to give it.

There was a difference, of course, between a woman and a girl, but no difference in their peculiar kind of endurance. Insane stoicism. Didn't they know how to avoid? To take the pleasures of passion without the risks of childbirth and disease? What issue of consent could there ever be if women from recent history submitted to this?

'In the application of leeches, so often necessary in cases of inflammatory congestion of the cervix uteri,' he read, *'the patient should be placed in the same position as for labour and a conical glass passed up to the uterus; care being taken that no part of the vagina is left around the rim . . . as the bites of the leeches are not painful when the uterus only is wounded, but excessively so if the vagina is . . . Eight or ten being the usual*

number, the speculum applied closely to the uterus, carrying the
leeches along with it, and allowed to remain until the leeches
fill . . . generally, twenty minutes.'

He had never seen a leech, except in illustration. They had a
greater association with jungles than surgeries in these unen-
lightened days, but, come to think of it, both places had plenty
in common, and a medical man was really only a kind of leech.

'Occasionally it is necessary to detach one . . . readily done by
dipping a camel-hair pencil in a solution of common salt and
applying it to the head . . . It is a good plan to apply the speculum so that the mouth shall be external to its margin, as in some
cases, troublesome symptoms arise from a leech crawling into
the cervix uteri and there adhering . . .'

He gave a brief snort of laughter, which echoed loudly in the
quiet of the library. There was often something comical in the
most pedantic of texts. He turned the laugh into a cough and
rubbed his head, in order to look as if the cough troubled him.
Then he examined his neatly trimmed nails and wiped his hands
down the synthetic fibre of his trousers. Silence prevailed. In the
late afternoon, the heat had become stultifying, even in here. He
thought of the hungry little leeches and he thought of ice in a
long glass, a mild form of anaesthetic to the skin, a deceptive
ameliorator of heat. Ice and leeches; they might have done for
him as well as anything else. No-one should despise primitive
medicine in favour of the supposedly more sophisticated.

A leech could be useful. Provided it remained detached about
its business. Common salt will detach a leech. Air will dispatch,
and detach, the woman or the girl.

I want to be loved, he admitted.

I want, even more, to be in control of passion.

They called it the Rape House. It stood two streets distant
from the police station, conveniently placed for Sainsbury's

and the market. Inside were five small rooms of miniature, late-Victorian terraced building, similar in size to the home nurtured by Anna Stirland, less than a mile distant. The area was roughly boundaried, tapering away into the complicated wilderness of King's Cross on one side, some of the streets gentrified, some defiantly refusing. The Rape House – for use of vulnerable persons only – lacked the polish of its neighbours and the key tended to stick in the lock, making DS Ryan repeat one of his familiar ribald comments, *ad nauseam*. 'Can't get it in,' he would mutter. 'Story of my life.' Ryan's remarks did not always stop on the right side of downright offensive. Personally, Sally Smythe did not think it mattered as long as his actions showed respect and he didn't wisecrack in front of the punters. Sex remained the stuff of rude humour, whatever anyone did for a living, she thought. Police officers were allowed bad taste, same as doctors.

The local authority had given the house to the police, for indefinite use, as an alternative to the rape suite inside the police station, which had been comfortable enough, but only reached via the front desk and a mile of corridor, which was enough to make any nervous victim back out quickly. No paperwork was done in the Rape House; no computer terminal was visible. The décor reminded Bailey of a dentist's waiting-room: three prints on the wall showing landscapes, each aligned with the other in remarkable precision; a chintzy sofa; glass coffee-table and venetian blinds to block out the light. There was a slight smell of disuse in the kitchen, drifting into the surgery, and another room designated for use as a nursery; enough residual stuffiness to indicate that no-one lived in the house. Nightmares might find themselves embedded in the clean walls, but no-one slept here.

Bailey felt slightly out of date and ashamed of it. He and Ryan's colleague were padding around one another like cats, with her muttering, I'll make you a cup of tea, shall I, treating him with condescension because this was her territory not his, adding in a touch of sarcasm with the sugar. For Lord's sake, the man could read; he'd read the files; why did he want to chat again, and why here? Lucky for him there was no ongoing investigation, no late-night allegation, no current attack which would demand that she sat here with the complainant for one day, two, three, as long as it took to piece together a statement which said it all with minimal need for revision. The Rape House was redundant for a few blessed hours and, even in the heat, felt chilly.

'What was it you wanted to know, sir?'

'How many of these cases get as far as the Crown Prosecution Service?' he asked mildly. The easy questions came first.

'About half. There's no point them seeing the complete non-starters, is there? A DCI has to mark them off, though. No point sending them the false allegations either.'

'Many of those?'

She fiddled with her hands in her lap, feeling faintly treacherous.

'Yes.'

'Any particular reason why, do you think?'

Sally Smythe warmed to a theme. Perhaps this austere man, whom Ryan had mentioned so often, really wanted to know.

'There's always been a lot, but it's hardly political correctness to say so. Sexual attack and women's rights get a high profile. Probably more complaints now because it's common knowledge we take them seriously, so the rotten complaints increase in proportion. Girls know they risk nothing in coming to us. They get kid-glove treatment, no recriminations, no lectures. Don't get me wrong, I'm not over-cynical, nor was Ryan, but a lot of the time we're a free counselling service. Victims they may be, but not always victims of rape.'

Bailey frowned. Sally did not scent disapproval; she didn't scent anything; his lack of reaction disorientated her.

'Was Ryan tolerant about that?'

'Very. Although he did less of the interviewing than we did. Obviously, some of them don't want a man in the room. There's always two of us. When he was here, there was always a woman officer as well.'

He stirred his tea and smiled at her. The effect on his gaunt face was almost shocking, making her respond with a grin before she knew it had happened.

'Give me a typical outline for a false claim. If there is such a thing as typical.'

She thought quickly and shrugged.

'A woman or a girl says she's been raped, attacked, say, three days earlier. She's thought about it, wants to complain, but she'll give three different versions of how it happened. The description of the attacker will vary too, but she won't know his name, even if she says she's seen him around. We don't try and trip her up; she does it herself, trying to tell us things which can't be proved or disproved, not clever enough to get it right. Sometimes it's sheer fantasy, sometimes a real event from some time past, or a real event distorted, sometimes it's straight off the telly. Troubled ladies. Then there's the semi-false, like, oh, I dunno, someone having it off with a family friend, relative, something; wanting to tell themselves it was rape when what

worries them is the fact they consented, or were outma-
noeuvred. Then there's those getting revenge on boyfriends. Or hiding an illicit encounter.'

'Do you always know the liars?'

She hesitated, outraged. Liars was a harsh description
for the desperate.

'Yes, I think so. After several dozen, yes. I didn't to start
with, nor did Ryan. You learn from the ones who tell the
truth. There's a difference; it hits you in the eyes.'

She was becoming a touch impatient, slightly self-
conscious, felt as if she was giving evidence which could be
used against her. She was not fond of the sound of her own
voice. Bailey had uncurled himself, begun pacing. You
would never hold down my kind of job, sir, she wanted to
yell at him: the person asking questions is supposed to ask
in a manner which will put the person answering at ease,
and then keep them there; it says so in the training manual.
Her mind ran on to other things to fill the silence. Pathos
and bathos, such as how to get back from the lab the patch-
work quilt on which a brave and honest victim had been
raped and buggered by two burglars. The quilt had been
made out of cut-offs from her children's clothes, pieces of it
torn in the process of analysis for stains, but she still wanted
it back, if only to prove that the one set of memories it in-
voked were far more important than the other.

That's what I deal with too, she wanted to tell Bailey:
bravery. And that's what Ryan was good at. Finding the
truth.

'What I really want to know', Bailey said carelessly, as if
all previous conversation was irrelevant, 'is why Ryan kept
this file?' He was flourishing a slim folder, using it to fan
himself before he handed it across.

'Which file?' she asked stupidly, blushing as if Bailey had unearthed something incriminatory. There was no such thing, after all, as a totally clean record. If he were to delve around in anyone's career, even if their daily progress was far less documented than that of any police officer, this spy could always find some embarrassing piece of shit. Even furry little rabbits leave turds. It must have been Ryan who said that.

Bailey sat and the room grew smaller. Putting on his glasses failed to make him human. He rose again and pulled open the fussy venetian blinds, letting in light through the small windowpanes. The blinds had always stuck before, even when new – Ryan had comments for them, too – but these long fingers of his older mentor commanded obedience out of inanimate things and, suddenly, there was light. Sally was afraid of Bailey, the way, as a child, she had been afraid of the old woman in the story who lived in the forest in a cottage made of cake.

The computer print in the file blurred in front of her eyes. She sat bolt upright, reading the faint lettering, resentful, ready to come up with any old answer. The print was made for daylight. She was half aware that Bailey had left the room; there was a distant flush of the lavatory cistern and the sound of the kettle boiling again. Then he was back. Sounds echoed in an unoccupied house. More tea, as if to prove he could make it better. She hated tea, the drink of comfort and a swollen bladder.

The windows needed cleaning, she noticed; he made her aware of such details. They were smudged rather than filthy, but enough to deserve attention.

'I know what it looks like,' she said. 'He's got the names

and addresses and descriptions of several no-hopers. Girls who've been in here. Cases which'll go no further. And their witnesses, few that there are. He's got that disco girl and Shelley Pelmore, the one he's supposed to have raped. And I suppose you're thinking it may be his version of a little black book, aren't you?'

'They have one thing in common,' Bailey said evenly. 'All those names. All those girls, women, I mean; he's quite specific about that, they're all unmarried. Perhaps one or two of them would appreciate a visit from a good-looking sympathetic policeman. Liars maybe, vulnerable maybe, but so far, incapable of completing their accusations and maybe needing a nice broad shoulder, or something of the kind.'

She would have flared at him like a rocket hitting the ceiling in that confined space; she could, after all, see exactly the way it looked. To the naked eye this small compendium of names and addresses was horrifying. We do not rely on photos of victims, she wanted to say, but surely he knew, even in his old-fashioned way, how that would make them feel. We make pictorial histories; we write notes as if computers did not exist. Here was Ryan's inventory of the victims who had never got beyond the DCI's no-action dictate. Not all of them; only some: five, or was it six? Bailey seemed drunk on tea. It was an added insult that he had the kind of long lean frame which need never resort to saccharin in order to keep it in that awkward state of angular thinness. Skeleton on legs, Ms Smythe thought, despising him with a clarity of thought which took in the file, too. Her face was red and chubby. It was her turn to get up and pace the room.

'It wasn't a file for Ryan's personal use. It was *ours*. Ours; the product of 'ours and 'ours; oh, he did like a pun. If you'd read further, you'd see.'

'What would I see?' he asked gently.

She sat, but moved again.

'Oh, I can't expect you to understand his code. Or to see why there was any sense in him recording these particular women, I mean, or the kinds of places they lived in, what jobs they did. Even Shelley Pelmore's friend; you see they all had jobs.'

'Jobs, I presume, they wouldn't want to lose? By doing silly things like shouting rape for the second time, for instance? Unlikely, also to report a smiling police officer at the door with a bottle of vino?'

Sally forced herself to stay calm.

'Look, you were the one who talked about gut reactions, I didn't, and he didn't much. Oh, for Christ's sake, the gut digests, doesn't it? Look. What we've got on this patch is a serial sexual pervert. He's been around for a while. He doesn't have an established way of doing anything, sir, but he rapes without trace, and he may have killed without trace. All the ladies in this file are those who would not, or could not, complete a statement, however long we gave them. They could not, would not, name an assailant. They were blurred in their accounts, they described fantastical things . . . There was never any forensic evidence . . .'

'They were dead ringers for the false allegations you describe. No names, no precision, change of story. Vulnerable ladies. Fantasists maybe; unhappy, maybe. Ideal for a man with his prick out at every traffic light.'

It was at that point she twisted her left hand into the cord of the awkward venetian blinds of the doll's house which was the Rape House; regretting politics, regretting everything apart from the fact that if Ryan was going to be done to death on evidence such as this, she had better put the record straight.

'Look, you sanctimonious, dirty-minded bastard. They weren't even the prettiest. Can't you read?'

'Sometimes,' Bailey said, humbly. She continued at the same speed, well beyond listening, her voice stronger and stronger.

'This was Ryan's collection. It has a system, you see. A small collection, you will note, not quite the stuff of a little black book. A few witnesses, maybe working alongside, giving evidence of victims' habits, maybe a link. What we think these girls had in common was one single perpetrator of whom they were ashamed. Some nameless shitface. And Ryan's got the pathologist he's spoken to on the file as well. No-one would dare seduce her.'

'I know the pathologist,' Bailey said. 'She's very attractive. And I don't understand,' he added, sounding obtuse, a man without visible gut and all too apparent guile. 'Don't understand.'

She took a deep breath, spoke carefully.

'The ones in this file are the real no-hopers; nowhere to go, no names, no forensic, nothing to toy with.' She was so close she could have spat in his eye, which was exactly what she wanted to do. 'But they were the ones we believed. We believed them. You hear me? They had no case and we believed them.'

The cord from the venetian blinds came away in her hand and she sat down abruptly.

'The problem is, sir, no-one believes *us*.'

'Perhaps I should go and see them. Check the black-book theory.'

She laughed.

'You do that, sir. Not a long list, is it? Especially since two of them are dead.'

* * *

There was a moment, later on, when he sat in a pub, nursing a half pint and mulling over what Sally Smythe had told him, that Bailey missed Ryan so intensely it was painful. And pathetic, he told himself, to find no pleasure in a drink unless that silly fool was sitting next to him. Ryan had a rare cunning for finding an excuse to get into a pub. He could fabricate an informer who must be seen, or a rumour that the drinks were free, but Bailey had never thought that such petty deceptions made Ryan a liar. He was fond of conspiracy theories, though; capable of inventing drama when life was too dull to be endured, and plenty capable of getting Sally Smythe to go along with some fantastic theory if he believed in it himself, even if his commitment to the idea had some ulterior motive.

What theory and how fantastic? Bailey spelt it out to himself, as explained by Ms Smythe, a woman under Ryan's influence, of course. Oh, what a joy it would be to have the luxury of listening to someone and believing what they said without a second thought.

Ryan's theory hinged on his belief that there was, out there, a rapist with a difference. Quite a different animal to the rabid man who leapt out of bushes to satisfy a sudden surge of lust on any female, of whatever age, who happened to be passing. Different, also, to the ex-lover, raping out of revenge, or the sly next-door neighbour or date rapist who mixed rape with seduction and pretence. These were merely distant cousins to Ryan's rapist. One way and another they wanted sex. This one wanted gratification of a peculiar kind.

Bailey looked around the bar. No candidates here. Ordinary men with ordinary desires and shirtsleeves.

At best, at his most normal, this creature was a performing trickster, a manipulator, who learnt as he went along. A man who wanted to tease and control, who made up the rules *en route*, sometimes clumsy with it, because the delight, of course, was crude. The achievement was to leave a victim so ashamed that, even if they began the formalities of a complaint, they would never complete the process.

It was an awful pint in a pub for those on the dole, with the Catholic church about next door. Downhill were the train termini and a view of London, swathed in a mist of heat.

A foul kind of magician, then, this mythical attacker, with blunt factual Ryan on his tail. Possibly a man with allies. Or a figment of Ryan's overfevered imagination, created to add purpose to the sometimes mundane and ever-seedy business of the Rape House. A fiction to allow him to preserve the names of the fantasists; keep a dossier of vulnerable women who might, after all, like indoor love with a married man, no strings attached.

The door of the pub burst open. A young woman with a dog, regretting the row of her entrance, went outside and did it again, only quieter, as if the second entrance would make her invisible. Something to sell, or buy, perhaps; nothing to celebrate.

Bailey could not see subtle plotting as part of Ryan's stock-in-trade, not for the sake of sex alone, unless he saw himself as some romantic counsellor, helper of the afflicted. That was more like it for a heavily romantic man who still believed that people could be helped despite their own resistance. He lied sometimes; an honest liar. Try that for a character reference, as if any character reference was going to help a policeman charged with rape, or save him from the extra brutality reserved in prison for his kind.

The thought made Bailey sick. His stomach growled.

If Ryan were put on trial, on the decision of some separate faceless bunch of lawyers whose decisions Bailey felt he could quite safely predict, the defendant could be acquitted. Easier, for such a good-looking man with so much to lose, charged with such an offence; the jury might not have it: they were soft on police officers. Ryan could come out of there, the exonerated darling of the tabloid press, but Bailey despised that kind of result. He was either innocent or guilty, not to be consigned to that half-life of disbelief in between.

Look at the black book, then, find an excuse.

The bottom line was wanting him free.

'Well? What did she say?'

'Who?'

'Anna, of course. Who did you think I meant?'

'Rose, if I was going to tell you, do you think I'd do it here?'

'Oh, see what you mean.'

The Central Line of the underground was tolerable for once, although not a suitable venue to discuss anything personal, even for someone as uninhibited as Rose. They sat together; Rose fished in her purse for a list.

'All we've got to buy, Aunty H, is a complete transformation of me for less than a hundred pounds. Inclusive of shoes, bikini and a full frontal lobotomy. Got to put the old me through the mangle of the Dickens & Jones sale and collect a fully-fledged wifeling at the other end. Got that?'

'I thought you said you wanted a dress.'

'Oh, that too. I don't think I've had a dress since I was twelve.'

Rose would be married in an outfit yet to be found. She had drawn the line at a frock of virginal white, not on account of any hint of hypocrisy it might imply about her lifetime's experience, but because she thought white was tame. The closest she had got was a sort of ivory shirt, tried on beneath Helen's critical eye and giving rise to smothered laughter in a changing-room. Rose had resembled a waif in someone else's silken dishcloth, her skin bleached by the sheen of the material; a sort of sickly bimbo without style. Suits she could handle, dresses not, but she still craved a dress. She longed to flounce away from her own reception with a wobble of fluffy skirt.

'Hope Michael's in when I get home tonight,' Rose announced cheerfully. 'As of yesterday, he was leaving for Timbuctoo.'

Never mind the perfidy and wickedness she dealt with on a daily basis; if wonderful, solid, kindly Michael were to scoot, do a bunk, lose his bottle about Rose, then Helen really would lose her faith in human nature. It was frayed already, but not that much.

' 'S all right. He's twitchy, that's all. I mean, he's the one with all the family complications I ain't got. He's the one who's got to cope with his Aunty Mary, Uncle Stephen and 'orrible little cousin, Jim. To say nothing of all his mates at work, ribbing him, warning him marriage is the end of life as he knows it, and telling him he shouldn't be marrying someone like me. He's bound to listen sometimes. I can see the pressure, really. Thank God for his mother. Are all men such babes, Aunty H?'

She seemed unfazed, much to Helen's relief. Opposite her seat, a man lowered his newspaper to look at them. His eyes rested first on the tube map above their heads; then he appeared to examine the roof of the carriage; then stared briefly at Helen, longer at Rose, frankly curious. Rose noticed.

'Hallo,' she said, boldly. 'Nice weather, innit?'

He smiled, nodded acknowledgement and retreated behind the newspaper again. Helen noticed immaculate shoes, casual trousers of some synthetic fabric and a pair of brown hands, before the train rumbled into Oxford Circus. As she passed towards the door, she noticed the top of his head, the skull shiny brown, like polished wood. The indentations in that sculptured skin showed up in the station's artificial light, the dome oddly tactile, so that she almost wanted to reach out and touch it, like the knob on a banister. She compounded Rose's cheekiness with a grin of her own, surprised to feel a *frisson* of attraction for an impertinent stranger so completely bereft of hair.

'Are you always like that with men on the tube?' Helen asked as they crushed together on the escalator, where it seemed the whole world had suddenly joined in a headlong rush to escape the subterranean oppression. She always expected someone to begin howling with rage on the up escalator out of the underground, because of the sheer slowness of it and the pushiness of passengers, but resentment was more conservatively expressed. Behind her a shopping bag, carried like a weapon by a determined woman, brushed her legs. She turned, somehow expecting to see the bald head further down. It was a foolish expectation, even in an ideal place for strange hallucinations. Rose was answering her as they put their tickets into the gates and started up the stairs, avoiding the inevitable someone who could not manage the machinery and held up the queue.

'He wasn't a stranger,' Rose shouted back.

'Who was he then?'

'He's a doctor. Saw him yesterday. Stared up my fanny; must have recognized my voice. I talked too much.'

She did not elaborate; Helen did not ask. Shopping fever had descended on Rose's brow and her face wrinkled with concentration. There was the mild state of madness induced by Oxford Street in all its tawdry splendour; the one place where Helen failed to detest crowds.

There was method in the madness, too. Unlike Bailey, who shied away from shops like a frightened filly, crept into them and out again as if he was on a secret mission, Helen and Rose stood at the threshold, breathed in the scents of the perfume counters and knew they were home. The method was no method; there had to be a purpose to justify the expedition, but the purpose could be abandoned. It took Rose half an hour to fall out of love with the idea of a dress (Look at this, Aunty H . . . I wouldn't wear it to go to bed in . . .) and fall into adoration with the idea of a trouser suit she had seen (perfect shape, foul colour). They were on the trail; out of this place, on to somewhere else, looking without real expectation for a facsimile of a suit with the same buttons, but not that tasteful and overbred shade of sludge. In the meantime, Helen had purchased three pairs of stockings and a hair-slide and Rose had bought a pan. If that was all they got, it really would not matter. Heavy on the blood sugar, though, as Rose put it, necessitating frequent sit-downs and caffeine fixes. It was understood, after initial quarrels, that Helen would purchase these overpriced beverages and also the cake, which was part of the proceedings, the paying arrangement being an acceptance of Helen's motherly role and their unequal financial status.

'*They* know how to shop,' Rose said, enviously, counting the bags of two delicate tea-drinking Japanese ladies in Liberty's café. 'They've got fifteen carriers each.' She sipped and put down the cup with a clatter.

'All right, Aunty H, now tell me what Anna told you.'

Typical Rose, waiting for the right blood-sugar level, never really forgetting anything; but that was another thing about large shops. All the ladies, as well as the minority of men, sipping liquids and giving one another their whole-hearted attention, talked nicely in whispers, like a lot of low-voiced conspirators. Revolutions could be planned here; coffee-shops in the anterooms of spending halls were exactly the right kind of place for secrets and the baring of the soul. Indiscretions would be taken away, wrapped in tissue paper, back to the realms of suburbia where they would no longer exist.

'I don't think I can tell you. She didn't swear me to secrecy or anything, but she didn't want you to know.'

Rose nodded, curious but unperturbed.

'I s'pose I've got to respect that. Did you tell Bailey?'

'No, but I might. In fact I'm sure I shall, but then, he doesn't know her. There's a difference.'

Rose nodded again, mature about such things, well versed in the need for respecting confidence. She was a fabulous gossip, loved it; she also knew what not to repeat and what not to demand.

'Did you like her?'

'Yes. Yes, very much.'

Such value in the faint praise offered like that. Rose finished a mouthful, sat back and rubbed her stomach.

'I shouldn't have had that, Aunty. On account of the traditional pre-wedding diet,' she said without much conviction, using the pastry fork to subdue and then eat the last of the crumbs, only satisfied after the last was swallowed. 'Two more questions, Aunty, then I'll leave it alone, promise. First, was she raped, and second, could you help?' She mimicked the Redwood voice.

Helen was choosing words with the care which so often infuriated Rose. All she wanted was a quick response, the flush of shopping fever temporarily suspended.

'If she's telling the truth . . .' and Rose noted that the 'if' was not emphasized, merely used to introduce that lawyerly note of caution she so loathed, '. . . then she was assaulted in a way designed to make a complete and utter fool of her. Using means so silly that the telling of it would make a fool of her all over again, because it sounds like a joke. Her assailant was someone she admired, with a cruel sense of humour. She's adamant about not going to a professional. Perhaps it helped that I didn't laugh.'

Rose chose not to say that this all sounded like a load of cobblers.

'And she's equally adamant she won't say who it was.'

'Protecting him?' Rose asked, incredulously, always dismissive despite herself when Helen got formal. Shop till you drop with this woman, she'd told Michael, but never say you know her.

'No. Protecting herself from further ridicule. She might be coming round for a drink and a meal next week. That might help more. And she loves her work. That will help too. Did what I could, Rose. Not much.'

'Sure you did.' That was enough. Some kind of result, Rose supposed; enough to mean it was time for her to abandon interest. It surprised her to hear that Anna loved her work, that wasn't what she had heard, but if Helen liked Anna and Anna liked Helen, something had been achieved. Helen always underestimated her own power. She doesn't even know how lucky I feel to know her, even when she gets things wrong, Rose thought, scraping back her chair, treading respectfully over the distinctive bags which fanned out from the next table, moving gingerly with the steps and smile of a cat. She had no time for people buying porcelain.

'Why are you so afraid of getting married, Aunty H?' she asked as they passed through handbags. Neither had much use for leather; shocking prices.

'Dunno. I suppose because I did it once, hated it and found out I'd married a thief. He didn't even know the meaning of truth. An utterly lovable thief.'

'Must've been his body.'

'We've got an hour,' Helen said in a voice grim with resolution.

'Monsoon? Principles?'

There it was, fifty-five minutes later in neither of these premises, but hanging in the window of an establishment neither had considered. Not a dress, not a trouser suit: a jacket made in heaven.

chapter six

'If, at a trial where any person is for the time being charged with a rape offence to which he pleads not guilty, then, except with the leave of the judge, no evidence and no question in cross-examination shall be adduced or asked at the trial, by or on behalf of any defendant, about any sexual experience of a complainant with a person other than that defendant.'

Shelley Pelmore understood shops better than the back of her hand. She had haunted shops ever since she was allowed out on her own. West End shops were the stuff of dreams when she was a kid, especially the ones where music boomed and nobody cared who you were and you had to shout to ask the price of anything. Not that she had even whispered in those distant days, or dared to ask particulars of what she could never afford. On one single occasion, she had been stopped by the store detective, leaving with a vest tucked up the sleeve of her jacket. A vest, of all things! Nothing gorgeous, just an ugly piece of thermal underwear, chosen on a November afternoon, simply to find out if thieving was as easy as someone had said it was. Her informant had lied about the ease, but it had been a bitter wintry day, and Shelley's wise reaction on arrest by a woman who resembled her mother was to burst into tears, say she was sorry, but oh, she was so cold and it was colder still at home. A pretty child; thin, pinched, distressed, she had been forgiven with a brisk pat on the arm, accompanied by a kindly warning. Even now, she could still feel the shock of that hand on her sleeve.

She had felt genuine distress, a mixture of shame and horror over her own incompetence, but by the time she was halfway home, she could see she had been wise in learning her lesson with a vest. Anything more covetable would not have been forgiven as easily. Shelley never did it again. It diminished her love of big shops for a few days, but the light and warmth, the colours and the merchandise, were too strong a lure. It was preordained that she would work in a shop of large proportions and escalators, another childish passion, and only a question of time, she told herself, before she would own a shop of her own. Progress was slow, pay was lousy; she was not much further forward but it had ceased to matter.

The problem was that shops had lost their allure; she was waiting for it to come back. It was quite a while now since anything gave her a buzz, unless it was skin.

'Can I help you, madam? Just browsing?'

Suit yourself, you old cow.

Shelley had moved from hapless trainee in a department store to experienced sales assistant, almost to floor manager, until she'd had that fight with another girl which put her out of the running, although, mercifully, not out of a job. She had learnt from her mother, knowledge retained like a talisman, that to be out of a job was the greatest disgrace on the planet, so she stayed for a while, although she knew she was not going to progress any further. Instead she took a sideways move into a far classier, up-market South Molton Street designer boutique, which felt like a kind of promotion. Escalators wearied her by then.

A friend of hers, who was leaving to have an unwanted baby, had recommended Shelley on a temporary basis. By the time she wanted the job back, Shelley was well dug in amongst the expensive clothes, indispensable to the manageress and not to be ousted by a mere plea of loyalty. End of friendship; so what? Shelley had other friends, other distractions; she flitted among the silk chemises and linen jackets, dressed in the shop's stock which suited her model figure, shining with suppressed sexuality; a brooding presence which gave the display an added cachet. She despised the fat customers all the more, because she knew their secret ambition was to look as sultry and tempestuous as she did inside these clothes.

She had told Ryan some of this. Something about the frustration of selling to fat cows with no looks and much more exciting lives. And about being best friends with the manageress; the kind of friendship which led her into clubs and pubs as a willing ally, trailing along with a couple more girls, all exceedingly slender, with the unspoken misunderstood purpose of giving the older wiser woman some kind of support as she cruised the bars, looking for something special with a bank balance to match. Shelley never did know when she was being used. As friendships went, the one with the manageress could be blown away in a puff of smoke, but Shelley had never known that, either.

'What you been up to? Two days off and thinner than ever, well, I don't know. What's the matter, Petal?'

'Period pain,' Shelley drawled. 'Won't happen again.' Knowing she was being watched. Let down this brittle creature more than once and the coveted job and the fun which went alongside might be at risk, and worst of all, the man of her dreams and nightmares would not know where to find her.

* * *

Derek was right: Shelley was tired to her bones and might well have been better resting at home. She was too nervous and edgy to be at her best. When the phone rang at the back of the shop she jumped, and when she steamed the creases out of a blouse her fingers were nerveless and clumsy.

Perhaps, if she told the manageress what she had endured so recently, there might be sympathy; or disbelief. Besides, she was unsure of her ability to tell the story in the way she had told it when they took the statement; any repetition would confuse. She panicked when she thought of having to repeat it, live through it all again. The only person she wanted to talk to was him. She painted her face, teased her hair and waited.

Late afternoon; the two brown hands appeared in front of her on the display cabinet which housed the underwear: pure silk, made only for those with sufficient time or domestic help to keep them beautiful. The display was a fine froth of cream and lace: colour of the month, *café au lait*. His hands on the glass were enormous and alien by contrast.

'I'll have two of those, miss. Please.'

'The briefs, sir? Which size?' Her voice trembled; her fingers fluttered among the lace.

'Your size.'

'Any. You choose.'

'Your colour.'

She wrapped them with an attempt at the air of indifferent insolence she had perfected with the fat ladies, her heart beating like a gong and a sheen of sweat breaking out on her face, pausing in her fussing with the tissue paper to swipe her hair back from her forehead.

'How would sir like to pay?'

He handed over the card without a word; she put it briefly to her lips before passing it through the machine, stood watching the slip emerge for signature as if that piece of paper held the secret of the universe. 'I must see you,' she mouthed at him as he bent to sign. The bag rustled as she handed it to him, noticing with a kind of anguish how the varnish on her nails was chipped and untended. They had taken scrapings from under her nails, a sample of saliva from her tongue and swabs from her vagina; she wanted him to know all that. She wanted him to know how well she had done and how bravely she had endured. She ached to touch the burnished crown of his head, finger the smooth and repellent ridges of his skull, but she desisted.

'What a lovely day,' he said loudly. 'Far too good for working.'

'Yes,' she said. 'No choice about it.'

'Ah well. Perhaps you'll be able to take a walk in a nice shady park later on. If not today, tomorrow? Something to look forward to . . . So wonderful to have these places.'

'Perhaps,' she said.

Watching his retreating back, she felt the sweaty mix of revulsion and excitement which made her stammer. The breath of the manageress was on her neck. Long manicured fingers, without chipped nails, straightened the back of Shelley's collar, patted it back into shape, feeling beneath it the dampness of her skin, sidling round to check the price of the sale.

'Three times in a month that mean old baldy's been in here. The mistress must need some pleasing, or is he a conquest of yours, sweetie?'

Shelley suddenly had a vision of the rape suite in that faraway police station as a place of safety.

* * *

Maybe the life of a well-off Irish Catholic lady would be better if she had worked. A little job in a shop, perhaps. Brigid Connor watched the afternoon light turn dark and felt down her spine the threat of a storm. Late summer brought these alarms; she was less afraid of the thunder than the lightning. Oh dear Lord, if a storm were to burst over her head, she would run and hide in a cupboard, and if the devil himself had come to the door, she would fling her arms round his neck. Such nice eyes that doctor had, so kind. It was he who had stumbled upon the truth, only by letting her talk without saying anything. All she had wanted was for him to find something wrong with her, something which would make sex impossible, but there was nothing to be found. Maybe it was he who had sent the cutting from the newspaper. Maybe it was one of the girls. Brigid eyed the drinks trolley. It was Aemon's favourite affectation, as if they ever threw cocktail parties. She knew she would succumb, despicable though it was to be sipping anything other than tea at four in the afternoon, with a storm coming on as well. If her husband found her laid out and comatose, she would blame the lightning which brought with it that everlasting fear of the wrath of God. Punishment; the apartment destroyed by a bolt from heaven which would consign them to hell and then do the worst thing of all, bounce them back, the same as they were before.

Taking a tincture was a new habit she had learnt from the parish sisters, who were not, she had come to realize, quite as obtuse and fatly comfortable as they seemed. Perhaps one of them had sent the newspaper cutting.

There was a ritual which had come to precede the tincture habit, like many of her rituals, which she vaguely recognized as a sign of something not quite right, although with the clarity of vision afforded by the first drink she could say there was nothing unusual about her own neuroses. It was beginning to occur to her that her careful rationing of drink might not be such a brilliant idea. Aemon had a thing about women and drink; hated it. Should he find her under the influence, it would either make her untouchable or, if it did not, she could sleep through the whole process. For the moment, she could not bring herself as far as putting that theory into action. Pride of a kind forbade it and, besides, she did not have a lifetime's experience of practice. Life might have been different if she had learnt, long before, to enjoy the taste of alcohol.

It did such dreadful things to the skin, so she'd heard. Made a female flushed and wrinkled before her time, her mother said. Made a man inherit the belly more suitable to a pregnant woman, so she had noticed of Aemon. Ah, drink is a terrible thing, sister. She thought all this as she ran the bath, thinking at the same time that only a woman with nothing to do bathes twice a day, but so the ritual demanded. It was a variation of the idea that a bath was therapeutic, relaxing, good for the soul and the body, cleansing enough to eradicate past and future sin. Sins such as taking the pill, denying Aemon his ambition for a son, offending God on both counts, and then telling the doctor all about it. Brigid simply liked this bathroom as a fantastic resort; it was big, beautiful, blousy and soft at the edges.

So was I, once, she thought, sadly, looking at her depleted figure in the comforting, obfuscating steam of the bathroom mirror. Tits, of course, famous for her tits, straining at a T-shirt and well able to pass the pencil test first tried at school. A girl had good tits if she could move around easily with a pencil held beneath each. She sank into bubbles, arose in front of the mirror, the top half of her festooned with foam, which she wiped off, using her hands, to save the towel.

'You're a highly attractive, healthy woman, yet, Mrs Connor; hardly a wrinkle. You could mother children if you wanted. You can do whatever you want, but from what you tell me about your lifestyle, maybe that could be improved . . . if you're worried about your own appeal, don't. That's not the problem, is it?'

So said that fine-eyed doctor, and she supposed that her appeal, as he put it, defined her existence. Being handsome, or not, was what dictated life and got one married out of a poor life into a rich one with a bathroom like this. She held the newspaper cutting over the steam and wondered again who had sent it. Whoever it was might have been kind, or, equally, malicious.

The print blurred in steam as Mrs Brigid Connor read, yet again, about the woman who claimed her husband had raped her, buggered her, generally messed her about. Asian names, therefore not applicable to herself, even if the result of the case had been hopeful, which it wasn't. All very well, they said, this business of marital rape, but it was difficult to prove. Almost impossible. Brigid had set little store by this piece of paper, watched herself squash it in one fist and pull the lav chain with the other hand. She was a kind of hostage in here, dreaming of ways out. Using the law was unthinkable: she'd never dare and Aemon would always win. In the heat of the water, she cleaned her fingernails with a toothpick and removed some imaginary dirt from between her toes. There might have been a faint hope that Aemon preferred his wife less aggressively clean in the same way that he would like her to be dressed in something other than an apron – her standard uniform when she was cooking. She was a woman kept, in a certain style, maybe, but still kept, in a towelling robe which took the damp off her skin and smelt, vaguely, of rose petals, with the under-lying musk of moisturizer. Perhaps all these ablutions made her smell of a tarts' parlour; she didn't care.

Brigid was hovering round the drinks in a flurry of de-light, towelling robe knotted tight, perfumes in order, with at least an hour to spare and the first big gin down before there was any chance of himself being home.

Speaking for herself, she couldn't understand why any-one bothered with the tonic. Lemon and ice out of a silver bucket, that was fine. She was standing with the second tumbler cooling her palm when the doorbell rang. Modest in the towelling robe which clutched her throat and reached her ankles, she moved to answer it. There was a porter downstairs who was supposed to deter Jehovah's Witnesses and double glazing people. Brigid never hesi-tated about answering the door, in fact she often prayed for it to ring. As far as she was concerned, the only danger in her life already lived here, and he was not expected for a blessed interval yet.

There was the man with the nice eyes, the one who had understood all she had tried to avoid saying between the lines of expressing non-existent symptoms. It seemed like a long time ago, but it could only have been a matter of days. He smiled, of course, that is what any visitor does, and stood on the threshold, waiting for the invitation to come further. 'Oh,' was all she could say. 'Oh, it's you; do come in.' Flustered and a little unsure whether she was pleased, embarrassed, puzzled, Brigid's thoughts would have been clearer, except for an overriding guilt of the most obvious kind. She was still holding a tumbler of neat gin in one hand. Amply covered, but not properly dressed, at four-thirty in the afternoon did not give a good impression either; the most she could say for herself was that she did not look like a slut and she was, at least, thoroughly washed.

'All alone?' he said politely, not needing a response. The place somehow smelt of someone who was all alone in it far too often; there was not a dint in a cushion to show where anyone had sat. 'I was passing,' he added. 'Thought you wouldn't mind if I called. It seemed to me, you see, that you were rather unhappy. It stuck in my mind that that was the case. Forgive me if I intrude.' He had moved to the picture windows. 'What a lovely view.'

The threatened storm had not emerged and the summer skies were clearing, leaving a sky of non-uniform grey and patchy cloud. Brigid knew every detail of the view; she had stared at it for hours. Knew that they stood at the tallest point of Clerkenwell and from here, the best apartment in the place, she could see the huge buildings which only looked poetic from a distance. From car level, driving round those streets, they seemed treeless and depressing; from here the amount of greenery was surprising. There was even a glint of canal water, and the sweet umbrella of St Pancras Gardens.

'You aren't intruding,' she said.

'I thought you needed . . . therapy, Mrs Connor,' he said softly, still facing the window.

'Therapy?' she echoed, watching his hands, held behind his back, the fingers on one hand tapping the knuckles on the other. All of a sudden she felt slightly woozy, the effect of a large shot of booze on an empty stomach and the first still doubtful sensation of fear. Such nice eyes.

He did not answer and his silence was unnerving.

'Would you like a drink?' she asked, noticing the quaver in her voice.

'No. Put it down and come and sit beside me.' He motioned to the shiny leather sofa; a long, deep, squashy piece of furniture which sighed noisily as they both sat, a further cause of embarrassment.

'Therapy, Mrs Connor. For a lovely mistreated lady.'

There was no expression of appetite on his face, only neutrality; the bland look of a scientist examining a specimen which has aroused interest rather than passion. He had seized the lapels of the rose-scented robe, pulled it down over her shoulders and pinioned her arms before she had an idea of what was happening. The knot of the tie belt was neatly unlooped; he pushed aside the volume of thick soft flannel. She stared down at herself, mesmerized, helpless, then closed her eyes in protest at her own exposure. Her mouth was dry. Carefully, he released one full breast and took the nipple into his mouth. There were the soft gurgling sounds of a baby at the breast; she had a dim memory of that, the most erotic experience of her life. First the right teat, then the left, like a child feeding, wet and warm until the mouth withdrew, leaving the nipples hard and pointed. She felt the brush of his slightly shiny shirt against her skin, his mouth trailing a moist line down her abdomen, his delicate fingers pushing apart her thighs without much resistance, although her fists clenched and she gritted her teeth. In a state of paralysis and profound shock, it was all she could do.

'Hush,' he murmured. 'Only therapy, Mrs Connor. You poor darling.'

The endearment, spoken so softly before he buried his mouth and she felt his tongue, was as shocking as his actions. Brigid had not heard a term of endearment, however vague and anonymous, in many months, only hoarse words of encouragement; hissed instructions, such as, move yourself, no, not that way; grunts of approval or discomfort. The uttering of the word 'darling' simply increased the paralysis. I should be screaming, she told herself, and braced herself for the effort of the shriek which failed to emerge. All she could hear was the sound of her own breathing and all she could register were his hands beneath her buttocks, raising her with supreme gentleness to his mouth. She kept her now wide-open eyes fastened on the ceiling light above her head, an elaborate thing of glass and chrome, as new as the sofa. A wild confusion of thoughts made her dizzy again, among them the knowledge that the scream would not be heard, that in a moment she would wake from a nightmare and find herself still warm from the bath, that her nipples were not erect and that this man was not a virtual stranger, but her husband. Or that he was that other boy, from all those years ago; the one she first loved. The ceiling light moved back into focus; she was counting the bulbs, six of them, and their shininess reminded her that she was in the present and that what he was doing to her was monstrous and if she was still alive she must shout or move, summon some power to resist, spit out that bile which rose in her throat.

She struggled to free her arms; moved one leg, ready to kick; raised her head, the better to scream; arched her back and felt him pressing on the inside of her thigh, so that the leg she had bent was pinioned, the calf hanging loosely over the side of the sofa, his fingers pinching muscle. And then, to her own horror, she ceased even these pathetic attempts to stop him. Tingling warmth spread as far as her hips, sparkling sensation concentrated in her groin, making the mouth of the orifice feel enormous. She tried to close her legs, squeeze sensation into submission, suppress it, ignore it, wrench back control for her own treacherous body, but it was too late and the mind would not co-operate. Brigid

Connor shuddered into sexual climax, moaning, biting her lip and drawing blood.

'Ice in your drink?' he asked. His face, with the nice eyes and the skull the colour of the polished walnut banisters which led up from the foyer downstairs, loomed above her and she closed her eyes, unable to look at him. The sofa exhaled as his weight left it. There was the sound of soft steps and a tinkle of glass, then he was back. 'Cool you down,' he muttered, or at least, there were words she only remembered later. She had been flushed hot, still fluttering. Then she felt the cubes of ice he rubbed between her legs, the ice melted from the bucket she had so carefully prepared, so that the ritual of the drink was less disgraceful and more like the ceremony of tea; it was then, and only then, that she screamed.

Later, the door closed behind him softly. There was fresh ice in the container. There were gifts on the table she had never noticed: flowers and chocolates. The crackly leather of the sofa was cleaned with detergent and Mrs Brigid Connor was back where the whole episode had begun: in the bath, weeping softly and numb with shock which the gin he had poured did not lessen. She tried to gather her far-flung, never-too-sharp wits to eradicate from her mind what he had looked like, what he had worn. A smart shirt of some shiny man-made fabric; trousers, beyond recall; nothing he had removed. No jewellery, no hair, no traces.

Brigid Connor had wept for imagined sins all her life, but she had never ever known such terrible, excoriating shame.

Rose Darvey had made intermittent efforts with the internal décor of the house she shared with Michael, and the various attempts at creating harmony showed the influence of Helen West. Helen's basement flat had been transformed into a sunny place full of yellows and blues; Rose liked it so much, the colours had become stuck behind her eyeballs. She was not a dedicated housekeeper any more than Helen, but she was still a compulsive nest-builder, wherever she had lived, and Rose had lived in many places since running away from home. She had made each of them clean and respectable; she was a devil with a paint brush which she used to put her mark on a place, but that done, enthusiasm waned. Frills, ornaments and dolls had disappeared from her life since Michael had arrived. She had adopted a minimalist attitude to furniture out of necessity; kitchen equipment was rudimentary because she refused to accept cast-offs. The walls were pale yellow, the blind blue-and-yellow striped and the mugs and plates echoed the theme. Rose thought that having a wedding present list for her friends and Michael's relatives was both absolutely gross and patently greedy. All she told everyone was buy something blue or yellow, and, if anyone could afford it, an electric drill for him.

They were lucky with this house. Rose had the low salary of an apprentice and a little nest egg from her granny; Michael's police wages were respectable; they weren't so badly off and it would get better, which meant that home improvements were not much of a priority. There was nothing which could not wait. The real priorities in Rose's life were loving him, working hard, getting on and having as much fun as possible. The paintwork would wait and the plants could die.

'Are we all right then?' she asked him as soon as she came in from work and saw his broad back at the kitchen sink, washing up the dishes from her breakfast. It was the nature of his shift work that they did not see one another every day, not when he worked nights. Sometimes three days passed. He did not reply. She put her arms round his waist; he flicked detergent foam onto her nose; she squealed and punched him lightly in the ribs. Then they were in one another's arms, hers scarcely reaching round his torso, the pair squeezing the breath out of one another, with enough oxygen left for a deep and endless kiss which seemed to involve every muscle and raise Rose's toes off the ground. When they withdrew, by an inch, she reached up and pulled his hair, looked at him with bold, questioning, playful eyes.

'Not leaving then?'

He held her head steady with two damp hands, kissed her again on the forehead, the nose, the lips.

'Thought I might postpone it. You know, think again, maybe in forty years, unless it upsets the grandkids.'

She looked at him seriously. 'How many do you think there'll be by then, Daddy?'

'Dozen or so. Give us a kiss.'

The reconciliations after disagreements were always thus. She had grown up in a house full of growling silence and threat; she could not bear bad feeling to persist. It got into the brickwork, she told him; then your house falls down. They fell to chattering. There was an accumulation of news on the days when he had come home after she left for work. A policeman's partner had to learn independence. Rose knew it already.

'Speaking of children,' he was saying, resuming the washing-up. 'Did you go to that clinic?'

'Yup.'

'How much did that cost?'

'Not much. I told you. I wouldn't have gone there unless Anna had persuaded me it was the best and she could get me a discount. It's very posh, but she was right. It's more comfortable than the doctor's – and there's no queue.'

They kidded on about children, wanted them madly, but not yet. So far, Rose had taken her pill, didn't like it any more than he. The idea of anyone spending much of their youthful life taking strong drugs of any sort struck him as fundamentally flawed; Rose teased him that it was his talent as a sportsman that made him think of all drugs as poisonous steroids. She giggled.

'Come upstairs, lover, I've got something to show you. You won't believe this.'

There was a bathroom and one and a half bedrooms at the top of steep stairs, their own room faced the road. Once the junk was cleared out of there they would move to the back, for the sake of greater privacy. There was a railway line shrouded by trees at the rear, a road with houses facing them in the front and no urgency about making the switch. The curtains in the front room were also blue and yellow. The offending dead plant, the ostensible cause of a row which had really been about something else, no longer dwelt on the window-ledge.

'This is what they gave me,' Rose said. 'A cap, like we said I ought to get. Anna told me how to put it in and said I'd got to practice with it for a week . . . and then go back, but I don't think I'll bother. There's a doctor there, asks all these questions . . . And you do feel a prat, trying the thing. I was glad it was Anna.'

'You mean she shows you, or you show her? Funny thing, isn't it?' He was trying to hide his distaste at the sight of a round rubber sphere nestling in a blue plastic box. It was the most unsexy object he had ever seen, reminding him of his baby cousin's teething ring.

'How on earth do you get it in?'

'Well, I'm not about to do the whole demonstration,' said Rose indignantly. 'And it isn't easy, I'm telling you.' She picked up the tube of jelly which came out of the same bag as the box. 'You put this stuff down the middle and round the edge.' She did so as he watched with some fascination. 'Then you squeeze it in the middle and, well, you know, insert it up your what's-it. Oh, shit.'

Rose had begun to giggle again. The cap was slippery, difficult to handle; a comic object with a wired rim, skipping out of her hand as she stood by the window, flying through the warm air with sudden momentum, resuming the spherical shape she had been trying to contain, landing, bouncing and finally rolling to a halt on the pavement below. They looked at each other and dropped to their knees like a pair of combatants evading a sniper, hiding their heads below the level of the window, desperate not to be seen. Michael raised his chin up to the ledge and peered over; Rose followed his example.

The cap lay slightly to the left of their front door, glistening slightly and looking like an accusing eye. Both heads: hers dark, his fair, ducked down again. Rose turned to slump against the radiator, clutched him and howled. 'Shh,' he said. 'Shh.' Great gulps of laughter consumed them. 'You go and fetch it . . .'

'No, I can't, I can't . . .'

Entwined again, comfortable on the floor with the old blue carpet and the dead plants and the curtains fluttering in the breeze. It was a quiet street, rarely deserted; there would be eyes in the opposite windows. The kiss was resumed where they had left off in the kitchen, turned into something soft and sweet and urgent; the only sound was the rustling of clothes until there were no clothes, and Rose saying, I love you, I love you, I love you . . . Him, saying the same.

The evening sun was lower in the sky by the time Michael next looked out of the window. He stood, this time, with the coverlet from the bed round his waist, looking down into the street once, then again. He nudged her.

'Hey, Rose . . . it's gone . . . it has, someone's nicked it.'

The doorbell chimed. Rose scrambled to her knees.

'Do you think it's someone wanting to give it back?' he hissed.

'No,' she said, scrabbling for her clothes and looking at her watch. 'It's your mum and dad.'

'Down the drainpipe at the back?' he suggested lightly. Rose, dressed on top at least, had stuck the modest portion of herself out of the window and shouted down to the two greying heads below.

'Coming!' she yelled.

'Oh no,' he gasped. 'Oh no, I can't stand it.' And Rose had the grace to blush.

chapter seven

'Sexual intercourse is a continuing act, which ends upon withdrawal. If, therefore, a man becomes aware that the woman is not consenting after intercourse has commenced and he does not desist, he will be guilty of rape from the moment that he realises that she is not consenting . . .'

'I did not consent to becoming what I am,' he wrote on his pad. 'I am tormented and thus entitled to torment . . .'

Wait a minute. He did not torment. He redeemed, gave pleasure, liberated; that was what he did. But there was this infection, coming through from the outside world, pushing him into this demeaning state of having to consider and reconsider the consequences all over again, becoming obsessive about the text, then reassuring himself. All he ever had to do, according to these texts, was to avoid penetration with any portion of his own body. (The tongue did not count; it was, in any event, almost entirely immune to infection; nor did a finger or an implement such as a syringe with a purely medical purpose. Such a penetration was not a rape.)

He sighed with relief. Books seemed so much more reliable than a computer screen in the sunlight of the day. Books were such solid items of furniture, demanding more effort to turn pages heavy with knowledge. Effort always equalled reward.

Next he read an article on baldness, advocating that the female of the species should note the bald man's legendary virility and, therefore, pursue him with the same lack of scruple she would use in the hunt after any other male. He shook his head, irritated again to find himself considering consequences. There was not a single hair left to fall from his body for collection by a forensic scientist, and that was not his fault either, nothing he had ever intended, simply another joke.

He rarely perspired; he was comfortable in clothing which was mostly synthetic, closely woven and highly unlikely to shed fibres fit for microscopic examination. So, as long as he kept his bodily fluids inside his body, he was safely beyond detection, unless, of course, someone not only protested, but complained. But women, in particular, were far too ashamed of pleasure to do that.

Love me, for what I am. For what I give you.

Stop that! Turn the pages.

'. . . Dilation of the cervix at virtually any stage of gestation will generally bring on uterine contractions which, in turn, lead to expulsion of the contents of the uterus. In vitro *decapitation, or foetal pulverization, were preferable to Caesarean section . . . Use a syringe with soapy water . . . Stir up the contents with a long sound . . . like pudding.'*

They should be grateful for me, for all I know and all I have to give.

Teaching them about pleasure without pain or consequence.

Filling them with comfort; filling them with air. Ending it.

'There is many a cleft stick with rape cases,' Redwood intoned. Someone sniggered and he ignored it. 'Redwood on Rape' sounded like a type of vegetarian delicacy. The *double entendres* would be indigestible and all the worse for being as unintentional as his dreadful puns.

Standing in a lecture room, he resembled what he might

have been in another life, possibly should have been, Helen thought with a rush of sympathy. An absent-minded professor, more at home with the written word and a legal text than he would ever be putting it into practice. Abysmal manager, worse public speaker, and, although he managed to suppress his knowledge of his own shortcomings most of the time, there was the occasional desperate realization of them which made him tearful. On the forum, doing his stint on an obligatory afternoon's training, Redwood tried to wield an illusory power. He still had some of the excitement of an academic to whom news, which has already travelled a continent, feels as if it has come to him first.

'What the law says', he announced busily, brandishing the notes which were already circulated to everyone in the room, including those members of staff who had not been able to formulate an alibi or leave the building beforehand, 'is that men can be raped.'

'It says "rapped" in my copy,' someone muttered.

'Typing error,' he snapped. 'Use your common sense.' He cleared his throat. 'There was never, of course, a time when men could not be raped. I mean they could be buggered, but it wasn't called rape, it was called buggery, for those under a certain age, whether consenting or not; once sixteen, now eighteen, but not with someone over twenty-one if they didn't mind, and anyway, you could sometimes charge gross indecency as well, but only in a public place. And now it comes under the rape umbrella. Very important to phrase the charge right.' He beamed; they all sat, bemused. Old news did not improve with his retelling.

'It's *all* rape, you see. So if a woman's been buggered, she's been raped; likewise a man. Vaginal or anal, it's all rape, is that clear? One section of one Act only. But you can always have indecent assault and buggery, if you like. In some circumstances. All depends what you can prove.'

This time the muttering was definitely Rose, but by the time Redwood swivelled his head and stared at her, the crown of her spiky dark hair was all he could see, her face bent in assiduous concentration on the notes in front of her; the model pupil, with nothing to give her away, apart from one long and slender leg extended over the other with a shoeless foot twitching madly, even whilst everything else about her remained completely still. Out of the corner of his eye, Redwood saw the door of the room open to let inside a palpably reluctant latecomer, giving Helen West the opportunity to slip out in his wake.

'A man can be raped,' Redwood continued less certainly. 'In fact, he has to be raped for it all to come under the same blanket of the same charge . . . What's the matter with everyone?'

By now, Rose was the only one in the front row who was completely immobile. She looked the very soul of concentration, the foot still, with a shoe on it.

'The same rules apply about consent, too. Oh yes. And evidence, of course.'

At the end of the lecture half of them were grey with sleep. Someone thanked Redwood for so enhancing their knowledge of the law, adding, beneath his breath, that it had done very little for the communal libido. They trooped out, smirking.

Once he was back in his room, Redwood wiped his brow and set about preparing tea. He had a secretary fit for this purpose, but he considered it bad for morale to have her make him hot drinks when she should be using her skills to type up memos and translate all those bureaucratic orders from above. Anyway, he positively enjoyed making tea to his own specification, drinking it out of the china cup he had brought from home. The interlude brought an illusion of civilization, all the better if he was not interrupted, so that when Helen entered after the briefest of knocks, she found him frowning. It crossed his mind to mention the fact that he had seen her leaving the lecture.

'Can I discuss something?'

It was a suspiciously humble request. He looked immediately for something with which to attack her in pre-emptive defence.

'In a minute, Helen. Look, is there anything you can do about the acquittal rate in your sexual assault cases? I've been looking at the figures; not good, not good at all . . .'

'You mean that losing every other one is hardly a fine track record? Well, I know what we could do about it. Send potential defendants on training courses, and tell them that what they have to do first is acquire a few previous convictions so that their fingerprints and DNA are on record. Then make sure that when they go in for an attack, full moon or whatever, they leave copious traces of bodily fluids and fibres from brand-new flannel shirts made of pure cotton. And then we could train the victims never to associate with men under forty they haven't known since birth, and should they be so foolish as to suffer attack, at least ensure they acquire enough bruises to make it clear they didn't enjoy it. Would that do?'

'Be serious.'

'I am being serious. There's a high acquittal rate because any case which isn't entirely clear-cut – the woman raped at knifepoint situation in a public car park – is always a risk, even if there's some corroboration for what she says. Look,

I want to talk to you about one in particular. Just to clear my mind, OK?'

'Rather than discuss it with Mr Bailey?' Redwood said cunningly. Helen's relationship with Bailey had always been a matter for speculation; Redwood did not approve.

'I don't discuss every case with Bailey, and oh, by the way, we're getting married, sometime, soon.' This was said in a rush. 'So I may need a day off, but if you could listen a minute . . .' She may as well let that news slip, she supposed, although it wasn't the purpose of the interview. For all his failings, Redwood could be a good sounding-board and that was all she needed. She was meeting Anna Stirland that evening and Helen wanted to be sure of her ground, although she was really sure already. Showing her insecurity, by asking about what she knew. Redwood nodded, stunned as usual by any tidings he had insufficient time to absorb.

'Supposing we have a woman, good character, sound of mind and limb, who invites a man she fancies round to her own house for a drink and a chat. He's perfectly well aware that she's very attracted to him, although in a shy kind of way. It's romance she wants, sex as well, but not yet. He pounces on her, causing her to injure herself, inserts an ice stick up her vagina and leaves. A joker, you see. She's so completely humiliated, she makes no immediate complaint to anyone until the nightmare of it makes her crack-up, by which time she's comprehensively destroyed all physical evidence, such as stains, and her injuries can't be dated. If she named him, currently she won't, would we look at it?'

Redwood was unfazed, shaking his head before her recital ended, only amazed by the speed of her delivery.

'Look at it? Yes, provided it came through the police in

the usual way. Then we'd turn it down. Even if we had a name. He'd walk out of a charge of indecent assault before the judge heard the end of the opening speech, you know he would. Defence? He wasn't ever there and she's a fantasist, or, he was there but nothing of the kind happened. The delay in reporting it makes it a complete non-starter. Why on earth are you asking?'

She hesitated.

'Confirmation, I suppose. Don't you ever do that? Seek a second opinion when you already know what it is? Call it frustration. What can the law offer a woman like that? Decent, responsible, maybe a touch obsessive. Oh, I don't know, I just hate the fact she hasn't got any form of legal redress . . .'

He lowered his face towards the fragrance of his tea.

'She doesn't deserve it if she won't ask for it. And I suppose what her recovering spirit needs is a spot of revenge? The best therapy? We all know about victims recovering far faster if their assailant's found guilty.' Redwood liked to see himself as a closet psychiatrist. 'Supposed to limit the extent of the damage. Well, if counselling won't do for her, there's only one way I can think of for her to get her man. How can she expect redress if she won't even accuse? One way. A frivolous thought, of course.'

The tea interrupted, a sip of it restoring his good humour.

'Tell me your frivolous thought. You don't have many.'

He sat forward over his desk, the china teacup nursed in his hands, his face lit with a grim smile.

'She'd have to lure him back. Make him do it again. Only this time, collect.'

'Collect what?'

'Evidence. Injury, fluids, blood.'

Silence fell in the room, apart from the sound of a man sipping his tea, enjoying his little joke.

'Well, I can hardly tell her that,' Helen said, flatly.

The noisy sipping of liquid was her signal to leave.

'Helen, if you're being asked for unofficial advice, rely on silence. The law's changed on the right of silence too. But not that much.'

Anna Stirland chose to walk to Helen's house that evening. It settled her mind – even a long walk, full of carbon monoxide fumes for the first half. She lived on the fringe of two districts, adjacent to where the summer dust lay in a ground-level cloud, disturbed by traffic, the identity of the place fractured by the massive dissections of road and rail. Even with the high proportion of inebriates and the rough trade in drugs and flesh prevalent in the environs of the stations, the area held her affection. It was a mixture of styles; a jigsaw puzzle with missing pieces; a dumping ground which solidly defied rejuvenation. There were terraces and squares, apartments carved from old institutional buildings, 1960's breeze-block monsters, flanked by traffic, opposite what she thought of as the church park, a green awning with a challenging if dirty statue near the gate. Anna walked down a fume-filled gulley, gazing with interest at the fly-by-night business enterprises which flourished in the brick-built caves of what had once been the arches of a railway viaduct. The furtive inhabitants suited caves; they dealt in cash and basic commodities. From here, a person could get a car rebuilt, a lorry disguised, a bathroom or new shop refitted overnight, a bus stolen to order; buy candles, bulk deliveries of halal meat, mirrors, take-away food, but never pay with credit card. Outside the station, there was a rank of panting taxis, eating up the travellers who emerged in clumps, anxious for the next destination. Avoiding the crowds, of whom the travellers were the minority and the drunks a sizeable proportion, Anna cheated and took the bus for the next mile uphill to the Angel.

Free of the immediacy of her own environment, she had time to relax and confess to herself that she had looked forward to this unsolicited invitation. Despite the circumstances of the second meeting with Helen, the bullying involved in the introduction at a time in her life when she doubted her judgement about anything and everything, she had already told herself that it was rare to like a person so spontaneously if it was not mutual. Therefore, if she liked Helen, Helen liked her. That kind of conclusion was not sound in a situation where lust was involved, Anna thought ruefully, but otherwise, yes, it was fair enough. She had usually known, although not always immediately, whom to trust. It was important to her to believe that Helen West was extending some form of friendship, as opposed to pity, or unfulfilled duty; even curiosity would have been better than condescension.

On the high pavement of the Angel, she began to walk again. The traffic was no less frenetic but less commercial, and here, the restaurant smells prevailed. There was one every twenty yards, not always with the same identity as its counterpart of the same time last year, wafting forth scents of spices, hot oil, curried chicken, tortillas, tomato sauce, bread, humanity, full bellies and good times. Anna thought of old friends and evenings out, wondered why it was that old friends could not help in her current condition, not that she had asked. Perhaps she wanted to keep her reputation with her old friends, not let them see her diminished; it was as if she owed the old friends a consistency she did not owe to the new. She paused to look at a menu in a window, cheered by the lights and the thought of food, horrified by the prices and slightly contemptuous of those who only came out because they could not cook.

It was then that she saw, up ahead among the straggling pedestrians, a shiny bald skull. It made her stop so abruptly that a girl running along behind cannoned into her with cross apologies. It was not him; nothing like him at all. It was simply a man, turning to smile at the girl he was ushering into a car; another younger man, dressed in garish clothes and possessed of a pricey motor, perhaps to compensate for the fact that his handsome head was as bald as an upturned bowl. He looked ten years the junior of her man. The car pulled out from the pavement with an arrogant burst of speed. Anna began to walk again.

How many lies had she told to Helen West? None of any significance; omissions rather than positive untruths, and she was not sure she wanted to remedy any of them. An irrelevant omission in failing to admit, out of a kind of shame which she resented herself, that while she had been a midwife for much of her life, and proud of it, she had succumbed to the lure of a better-paid job. It was a downright distracting lie to state that her bald-headed lover no longer worked in the same place, or had any command over her. How strange it was, the virtual impossibility of recounting the truth and nothing but the truth, the way she could relive in her mind what that man had done to her, telling herself a slightly different version every time, each remembrance adding or subtracting sufficient details to distort the narrative. That was what trauma did to the mind, she supposed: made her doubt her sanity and threw integrity into turmoil. She doubted she could ever take an oath to tell the truth.

She passed a wine shop and a cinema queue, dawdling,

and backtracked to look at the pictures advertising the film. Scenes of love, tension and violence made her shudder and she hurried on again. I want my old self back, she told herself; that is all I want. I want to walk around again with a perfectly normal set of reactions and a sense of humour. I want to be clean, decent and truthful. And what do I want from an evening with my new friend? I want her, someone, to know what it is like to have one's footsteps dogged by this all-pervading shame and anger. But I still can't tell the whole truth, which is that what he did to me might well have been a brutal form of therapy to cure me of my silly passion. Nor can I say that, yes, I have seen him passing many times, even when I least expect it, although not nearly as often as I think I have, and that every time I have that real or imagined fleeting glimpse, like now, I feel a panic-stricken sickness. A lump of gristle arrives in my throat and I think I am choking.

She had reached the crossroads where the restaurants gave way to trees. She stood for a moment, trying to remember the route she had memorized from the map she'd consulted before setting out. That was another symptom: lack of concentration. Dammit, she did not want to be suffering from a syndrome, or to be nothing but a mass of symptoms. She amended any expectation of what she might have wanted this evening to achieve. A shy foray into friendship, and if not that, a few hours' distraction would do.

'I can't cook, you know,' Helen said.

She lied, as well; that was all Anna needed.

The flat was a slightly untidy haven of multicoloured peace. Anna was aware of the moral superiority which

came from the knowledge that she was a far better housekeeper than her hostess, and on far less money. She touched
things, she admired, explored and settled like a wary animal. Most of all, she liked the garden: unplanned, overfull,
big enough for a cat to get lost. She would have loved to get
her hands on that garden.

Much, much later, after several glasses of wine and food
in the form of an endless parade of snacks, Anna told
Helen, lightly, speaking briefly, nothing heavy, that what
she really wanted was revenge, and Helen repeated, equally
lightly, Redwood's cynical formula. Lure him back, make
him do it again, collect evidence. She was only speaking in
the context of the options available for redress rather than
revenge; namely, none. They laughed about it; neither of
them aware at the time of how the idea might take hold,
like one of Anna's plants in parched ground.

When Bailey arrived, Anna left. He had made her feel
welcome; her discomfort lay in the fact that she had never
meant to stay so long and was not much at ease around men
at the moment, even though it was nice to refuse his offer of
a lift home and then be ushered into a cab. As if she was as
normal as she seemed. A capable woman able to unlock her
own door with that once-familiar pleasure in being home.
Ashamed to feel so diminished by some incident which had
not even threatened her health. And all the rest of her, still
burdened with love and lies.

Bailey stood awkwardly in the kitchen, the way he sometimes did, as if he had never been inside the flat before, instead of a million times at the last count. There were
moments when Helen wanted him to be in no doubt that
this was her territory, others when she wanted him to meld

in with the furniture, as comfortable as if he owned what was hers. His lack of resentment often amazed her; so did his humility and his complete acceptance of her ambiguous rules. She did not deserve him.

'Sorry,' he said. 'Didn't know you had company. Only I didn't want to be on my own.'

This was an admission, coming from him. There was far less of his almost obsessive reserve than there had been, but he was never going to be a man who admitted easily to need.

'Good. There's wine in the bottle and the night's young. Is it Ryan?'

He nodded. Helen put her arms around him. His body felt like knotted wood, slightly softened by age, yet hardened by the tension which seemed to sigh through his voice.

'Never mind a drink,' Helen said, 'you need a massage. Hot bath, maybe. Tender loving care, all that.' She kept her voice free from anxiety but his pallor was alarming. Bailey was ever thus: resisting the river of emotion until the damn was ready to burst. She never remembered the ulcer.

'I need inspiration,' he said. 'And a different job. And,' he added, accepting a glass and something resembling a sausage roll, both swallowed with indifference. 'And . . . what was I saying?'

'Exactly that.'

He sat at the kitchen table, marginally relaxed. She was almost up to speed on the Ryan débâcle she thought, but plenty could have happened in forty-eight hours. Such as some little snippet from the laboratory, some detail which made the whole thing worse.

'I've got to pass it over to that sanctimonious star, Todd,' Bailey said. 'I've got to. No choice about it. The girl's finalized statement is entirely convincing, needless to say. I've never bunked off a case before, and yes, I'm so angry with Ryan, I could spit.'

'Why did he do it?' Helen wondered out loud, feeling awkward about the fact that she had never felt at ease with Ryan, although confident she had hidden it. It was, in part, she suspected, a kind of jealousy. Ryan might know more about Bailey than she ever would; might even have a greater command over his affections.

Bailey rounded on her with red eyes.

'What do you mean, why did he do it? He might not have done it. Don't make assumptions.'

'Why not? You're sure, too, or you wouldn't be half as infuriated as you are now, or isn't it the thought of him being guilty which gets you down? You assume; you've got the evidence. Why can't I assume?'

He took a deep breath and attempted a smile. His stomach rumbled; the sausage-roll affair was a mere titillation, but the rumbling was his own fault for neglecting the simple business of eating. He had long since given up expecting, or even hoping, that Helen's fridge would automatically hold the makings of a man-sized meal. Sometimes yes, usually no; he was used to it.

'I'm sorry. I can't quite explain. I mean, I have to deal with my own assumptions and the evidence, which looks bad enough, but I find myself enraged if anyone else points the finger at him. Even when the stupid clot makes it worse, and even then I don't want anyone else suggesting that Ryan's guilty; I don't want to believe it, even though I do, actually, believe it. Am I making sense? No, I expect not. I loathe Todd.'

Helen stood behind his chair, kneading his shoulders. He reached for her hand and held it against the side of his face, resting his cheek against it. Bailey revelled in any sign of affection; he had been born and raised with a shortage which had turned him into a quietly demonstrative man.

'By an odd turn of coincidence,' Helen said, 'Anna, that girl you just met, my new friend; she might have been interviewed by Ryan. About a month ago. If she'd made a complaint, that is. She lives on his patch. But she didn't and she won't. She thinks her complaint is too bizarre for anyone to take seriously.'

'Why?'

She would have liked to have told him, but she doubted it would have made him feel better.

'You've heard enough about sexual aberrations for one day.' she said. 'It'll keep.'

At about half-past eight in the evening, Aemon Connor delivered his wife into the hands of the police, more by accident than by design. It was not a measure he had ever considered appropriate for any member of his family, although when his daughters were small, he had found the prospect of having them imprisoned singularly tempting. Now, he could have wished them at home, rather than summering with the relatives he believed would have a more beneficial influence on making them hardy than Brigid ever would. To allow any stranger into his apartment, unless it was to admire the handiwork and commission a building on the same lines perhaps, was anathema, but there was little else a man could do when his wife would not get out of the bath.

Would not, could not; he was unsure of the difference, only that by the time he actually saw her in there, having put his foot to the flimsy lock which provided privacy rather than security, she was cold. Attempts to communicate through the door had resulted in her humming, softly at first, breaking out halfway through the first line of a hymn tune he thought he recognized, into a bubbly laugh which was devoid of any quality of joy. Well, as he told the doctor, he'd known since the beginning that Brigid, despite a sweet and gentle nature and a fine singing voice, too, lacked a certain something in the brain department, but this was another matter altogether. What he would never mention to the doctor was the fact that he considered his gentle wife such a conversational dead end that he fucked her out of despair. It was all a man could do in order to stay sane and as loyal as his faith demanded. Nor did he mention to the doctor that his wife had not left her cooling bath – cold, in truth, but on a day like this not chilly enough for any signs of hypothermia yet – by voluntary means. When she refused to respond to an order, he had seized her by the arms first, then the waist, and bumped and dragged her out of there, swearing mightily and calling on God for a witness. He had put that damn bathrobe on her, the one she hid inside so often to make herself look like a nun, shoved slippers on her feet by grabbing her ankles and forcing her tootsies inside. Aemon also failed to mention that her passivity during all these manoeuvres, which was not to be mistaken for co-operation, had given him an embarrassing stirring of desire; the one thing she could always do when no-one else could, making her more infuriating than ever. Her skin was whiter than the morning milk, spongey to the touch. When he dumped her on the sofa, she had screamed, scrambled up to one end of it, curled her slippered feet beneath her and put her thumb in her mouth. Since this was the greatest sign of animation yet, he took it as a favourable sign.

He helped himself to a large drink to steady his nerves, then another. She seemed happy enough, until she fixed her huge eyes on him and giggled. She took the thumb out of her mouth, formed a fist out of her hand with the index finger pointing at him like the barrel of gun, whispering, bang, bang, bang. Soon after that, he called the doctor.

The medic was a dark little man, half Aemon's size, pretending he had better things to do than interrupt his dinner. Aemon did not like Asians, for being so much better employees than his fellow countrymen. He liked this example even less when he turned into an interfering idiot with ideas of his own. He was beginning to mutter about his wife needing sedatives or whatever treatment was recommended for hysterical women, when she interrupted, opened her mouth and said, very clearly, 'Please take me away, I've been raped.'

Brigid rarely completed a sentence, so it was not surprising that Aemon's jaw dropped. When she went silent again and the doctor turned to him for explanation, he was the picture of surprised guilt. Brigid's fragile wrists emerged by accident from that cloying gown, as if she was trying to shake it off. 'I hate it,' she hummed, 'hate it, hate it,' again sounding both clear and absent-minded. She had slender arms, where the bruises were beginning to form from his efforts to get her out of the bath, livid patches beneath her skin; the only features the doctor seemed to notice. Apart from the flowers and the unopened chocolates which he took to be the guilty gifts of a guilty man.

He asked her politely if she was able to get dressed and come with him. She obeyed with a brilliant smile. Aemon stood by in silent confusion, for once, lost for words.

To Sally Smythe, summer was a silly season and she could only feel relief that it was drawing to an end. The gaiety of skimpy summer clothes was not enough to compensate for the fact that the warmth brought out of the brickwork vulnerable persons in all their disguises, and as they took to the streets and parks, so did the other type of vulnerable person who was likely to attack them. Oh, the lure of the great outdoors. The last person who had sat in the Rape House had been extremely dirty: a back-packing tourist girl sleeping rough until a stranger had decided to join her, not taking her refusal kindly. She had sat in here, with paper separating her torn clothes from the fabric of the chair, smelling, while they waited for the doctor. It went against Sally Smythe's instinct to prevent a person from washing. Mrs Connor was quite a contrast. She sat in the anonymous room like a shy cousin invited to tea, and she was as clean as a whistle.

Soft-spoken, too, apparently grateful for her surroundings which she stated she liked very much, speaking with the voice of a well-trained guest. Raped and/or abused by husband, Sally Smythe read the doctor's urgent guess. Mrs Connor seemed in no hurry. She might simply be there for the enjoyment of the hotel accommodation they would have to arrange soon. Would be nice to make some headway first, Sally thought; nasty bruises on the wrists.

'Who attacked you, Brigid? Please call me Sally. Did your husband get a bit . . .' There was not even the slightest scent of sex. Brigid smiled her brilliant vacant smile.

'Oh no,' she said, 'not this time.'

There were some victims who were much more responsive to a man.

Ryan worked in the garden until after dark, as he had done every evening since his suspension. Against all the odds, it was not the emptiness of the days which threatened him, when his wife was at work and his children, ever adaptable to new conditions, either pursued their independent social lives on a prearranged course as if nothing had happened, or wheedled him for entertainment. Trouble at work, was all they knew, whatever else they had guessed; Dad considering changing jobs after a few weeks' rest. His children were a source of solace, distraction and intense anxiety by day. It was in the evenings, with his wife at home, that he felt awkward, claustrophobic and guilty.

The problem with his garden was no more than the time of year. It was too soon to begin on preparations for winter, too late to plant or prune. He would normally have sat back and enjoyed the late summer season: the flower-beds were weedless, although passing their best; his two fruit trees were free of blight and the lawn was healthy. There was nothing for it but to dig a pond.

Mary would have preferred him to concentrate on a number of things which required urgent attention indoors, but changed her mind. Anything which did not necessitate them remaining in the same room together for more than an hour at a time would do. If he was outside and she was in, they could behave normally. She would not be obliged to bite her own tongue in an effort to prevent herself from asking him, look, what exactly did happen on the night you went out with that girl? I know you haven't told me the truth. She would ask futile questions; each of them an accusation, a declaration of lack of faith which might be met with the mulish silence she dreaded, or the speaking of some truth she dreaded even more. There was a dull sense of *déjà vu* in all of this: there had been mutual infidelity in the past; enough evenings of silent recrimination, secrets and rows for neither of them to want a repetition.

She was brisk and calm. In bed, under cover of darkness, she had tried to make herself affectionate, but she could not pretend any real desire any more than he could respond. If he tossed and turned, it was better she did not know. The sleeping pills she had got from the doctor were remarkably efficacious, suppressing her boiling anger and letting her do what she needed to do: turn her back on him and sleep away the effort of being nice.

The pond had taken shape. Ryan, following instructions from an old *Reader's Digest* book, read first, dig your hole. The book did not mention what he was supposed to do with the resulting mountain of earth, except wheelbarrow it away to a site for a future rockery with the prospect of further time-consuming labour. Then, line your hole. Soon he could consider buying plants and fishes, then net to prevent marauders, then something to surround the pond. This task could go on for ever.

He was crouched on the edge of his hole, bone weary, rubbing soil from his hands. He stared at his nails, brown with the stuff, and rubbed the fresh callouses raised by digging. Gardening without the impediment of gloves, as he usually did, gave a man hands like sandpaper. His wife had been known to complain. He wondered whether Shelley Pelmore would remember encountering hands like that on her soft skin and, if she did not, would it be useful in his own defence? He could hear the question asked by a barrister with a voice to curdle blood: 'Surely, madam, you can remember if his hands were rough or smooth? Were they labourer's hands, madam, or those of a man at a computer terminal? Were they the hands of a man who digs a garden? You don't *know*?' In the last two years sitting in court to give moral support to the genuine rape victims who were his witnesses, Ryan had wanted to shoot the bewigged pompous farts who used questions like that to confuse.

Now, he would encourage it. He could take that girl and wring her little neck with his own calloused hands.

She was gorgeous, slim and lithe and gorgeous. Unquestionably affectionate, unlike his wife. So gorgeous, he could imagine burying her in a hole smaller than his pond.

The darkness of the August evening was not the real darkness of winter. His eyes had adjusted to it and he could imagine coming out here and seeing the glint of water, putting his feet in it on another night as warm as this, even though that was not what he was supposed to do with an ornamental pond. The strained voice of his wife floated over the lawn, shouting for him, trying not to sound impatient.

'Phone,' she said briefly, when he reached the harsh light of the back door, rubbing his eyes as he came inside. She watched, with resigned disapproval, as his dusty boots dragged dirt through the kitchen.

'Who?'

The phone had been so silent these last days, unless it was calls for the kids.

'Don't know. A woman, anyway. I asked her for her number for you to call back, but she wouldn't.'

Ryan rubbed his hands on his trousers and went into the hall.

'Help me,' said the voice. 'Help me, please.'

chapter eight

'Although juries must be told that "consent" in the context of the offence of rape is a word which must be given its ordinary meaning, it is sometimes necessary for a judge to go further . . . he should point out there is a difference between consent and submission . . . The jury should be reminded too of the wide spectrum of states of mind which consent could comprehend and that where a dividing line had to be drawn between real consent and mere submission . . .'

These were the words which excited him, would exonerate him if ever he needed it.

Both of the girls who had died had been afraid, although only initially. He would never have forced either of them, or any woman for that matter. The thought of doing anything so cruel shocked him. But even the most mature patient was timid, out of ignorance. There was nothing 'mere' about submission. One submitted to the dentist, the doctor, to life, even; submission was vital to survival. It was not a different state of mind to consent, but a close cousin. And in the end, one submitted to death; not consent, submission. What was the difference?

The law never mentioned redemption. The law did not believe in it.

The interior of the Rape House looked even more anonymous after cleaning. Plants, Sally Smythe thought; it needs plants.

'What did you do when he kissed you?' she asked the girl. There was silence.

'Nothing. I didn't do anything.'

'Well, he wasn't doing anything out of order at that point, was he? I mean, you didn't mind him kissing you?'

'No.' Her fingers continued to shred the paper handkerchief. 'I liked him, then.'

'They say you have to kiss a lot of frogs to meet a prince.'

'Pardon?'

Sally smiled to hide a sigh, reminding herself not to get clever. 'I mean, we all have to experiment, don't we?' How condescending she sounded.

The girl's answering smile was wan in the extreme. They were not going well and Sally felt as if she was wading through mud, not because of lies, but in pursuit of the words to frame the truth. Here was a plump girl, shivering slightly in the heat, preternaturally docile, although she had not been like that when the man she had liked took a deep-throat kiss as an open invitation to full-scale intercourse on the front seats of his van. She had fought like a cat, broken a window, all useful evidence, although it hadn't stopped him.

'Did he do anything else at first, apart from kiss you and you kiss him back?'

Another long hesitation.

'Put his hands . . . That's when I started to try and stop him.'

'Why? If you liked him?'

''Cos I wanted him to take me home. That's what he said. And it's all my fault, isn't it?'

She was crying steadily now, tears as plump as her hands. Sally moved the box of tissues nearer.

'Because I shouldn't have gone with him, should I? I shouldn't have fancied him at all.'

Sally gestured to her colleague to continue the good work and went into the kitchen. The slats of light which came through the Rape House blinds had begun to make her dizzy, but this girl had not wanted sunshine, she could only talk at all in the semi-dark.

The light in the kitchen was gloriously intense, reminding her of a tempting outside world and her own tired eyes. Brigid Connor had liked the kitchen, despite the view of a neglected backyard, or said she did, with her twittering politeness. She had even uttered thanks for a disgusting cup of soup; a charming lady, anxious to oblige, unlike the eighteen-year-old outside, who simply wanted to forget. Mrs Connor was so keen to please, so off-the-wall and, it had to be faced, so stupid, she would, and did, say anything as long as it received a smile, a nod of approval, or an invitation to continue in the same vapid vein. Didn't do so much talking at home, she volunteered; Aemon hated a chatterbox. She liked to take two baths a day, keep herself fragrant. She might have been in the bath when the man came to the door, but then again, she might not. He had no hair, that man. Your husband, Brigid? No, the man with the gorgeous eyes. At which point, Brigid would put her palms over her own eyes, as if the sight of his had blinded her, and then remove the hands after a minute as if she was playing a game of peekaboo with a baby. They should all have been in a play-pen together. Nervous exhaustion, Sally concluded; premature senility or a reversion to infancy. But, throughout it all, there was something horribly candid in her guileless face. There were throw-away lines, addressed to the kitchen window or her own tea mug. He did, you know; he sucked me wet and dry, he did; never touched me. Something had happened.

Sally filled the kettle, automatically. The medical examination, which Brigid had not resented, although informing the doctor there was nothing to see, revealed old bruises on buttocks, fresh bruises on wrists and ankles. They had not gone as far as arresting the husband; policy dictated otherwise. Surprisingly, Ryan had always concurred with this caution; don't charge in without being sure; work out which of them has got a screw loose first. In this case, a husband yelling about issuing a summons against the Police Commissioner, with no trace of a stranger in the husband's house. Her dressing-gown fibres apparent all over his suit, as they might be, but nobody had raped her.

Nor had the husband brought the chocolates and flowers which lay on the table. She was his wife, for heaven's sake, and a good life she had too. She was perfectly capable of buying those things for herself. Chocolates and flowers, flowers and hearts. Something had happened, but Brigid Connor had gone back to her old man, and that was really that.

No hair, no name, but flowers and chocolates. And ice. Phone Ryan. No, she couldn't phone Ryan. Not now.

Nasty little ritual, this, although Todd rather relished it, everyone else around shuffled a bit, changing weight from foot to foot as if it was cold instead of so relentlessly hot.

Todd adopted the informal approach, only safe in front of witnesses, including the man's miserable little brief. 'You know your rights, doncha? No need to say nothing, but silence ain't always golden.' Abandoning the strict wording also, handing him the sheet, which he received with a ghastly smile, like royalty receiving a perfectly repugnant gift and giving it to an aide. 'You attempted to rape Shelley Pelmore in the vicinity of King's Cross,' Todd intoned, leaving out the date for the sake of brevity. 'Got that? Anything to say?'

'Fuck off, you piece of crap,' Ryan said, before his solicitor could silence him. 'And where the hell's Bailey?'

''S all right,' said Todd, turning a benign countenance on the small man who was clutching Ryan's sleeve, judging from experience that unwise reactions often followed less-than-wise remarks. 'I shan't write that down. Hardly a response to the charge, is it?'

'Where's fucking Bailey, then?' Ryan demanded, louder. 'Where the fuck is he?' The cloth of his second-best shirt was bunched in the lawyer's fist.

'He's volunteered off the fucking case, is where, Mr Ryan. He wanted to go.'

Ryan reared back, pulling away. Controlled, sure, he had learnt control. He would not move; he knew he was powerless. He just wanted to look, for a minute, as if he was capable of butting his forehead down onto the bridge of Todd's nose. Todd did not wait. One swift jab to the solar plexus with the full force of vengeance behind it. Ryan doubled and moaned, thumped back against the wall.

Everyone was looking at the yellow paint above his head, pretending they were not listening to his breathing. It was in no-one's interest to record either the aggression or the reaction. Sad, really. The defendant was not entirely reasonable; like everything else, it was all his own fault.

Police officers, so Bailey had often told Helen, commit the same crimes as other people since they are prone to the same temptations, although their rate of offending was considerably less. And people like me are appointed to investigate on a rota basis. You do not, cannot, train a young man into total self-control; no training course was going to rid him of testosterone or the desire for the things in shop windows he could not afford. He has to have power in order to be useful; it follows he will abuse it. There were plenty of occasions when you wanted the man to have the strength of a vicious young brute, so that he could survive other, less-inhibited vicious young brutes who did not care if he lived or died. You did not wish to see a piece of animated cardboard policing a riot, but what the public did want was the kind of paragon not generally born of woman, with a lion heart easily moved to aggression or compassion, but never to anger or dishonesty. The public wanted muscle power, intelligence and perfect self-control. Well, they could not have it.

Across the desk was today's interviewee. He was older than most, ex-military, never learnt to control the cash requirements of the old wife and the new one, in deep trouble with money, making a false insurance claim. Not smart enough to get away with it. Following him would be the lad who bounced his torch back and forth across the head of a juvenile car thief. Bailey had more sympathy with him: that kind of crime had all the elements of rough justice. The sergeant with nowhere to go was claiming that he needed the money to pursue the course of true love, always an expensive commodity. I do not believe in the power of love, Bailey thought to himself. Dreadful things are done in the name of love, just as they are in the name of vengeance, and if anyone was ever again to say to him, I could not help it, when they talked about love, he was going to spit. Ryan haunted him. He went to take the phone call.

'Mr Bailey, sir?'

'Of course,' he snapped, regretting the recoil in Sally Smythe's voice.

'Sorry,' he went on, trusting her with a confidence to make up for the rudeness, 'but I'm interviewing a chap who is so riddled with self-pity I keep slipping through the holes and he's getting on my nerves. What can I do for you?'

All this was slightly overhearty, so she hesitated.

'You know what we were talking about when we met, about Ryan's little black book? The no-hopers?'

He did remember, all too clearly. That had been haunting him, too. So much so that he had mentioned it to Ryan's senior, and judging from the response of outraged laughter, wished he had not. She took silence as encouragement.

'Well, I think I've got another. Some of the same features. Ice.'

'I can't remember us discussing the presence or absence of that.'

'I can't remember us having much of a meaningful conversation at all,' she responded sharply, exasperation standing in good stead for confidence. 'But I should like to talk to someone and there isn't anyone else. No-one who'll listen.'

He weighed it up in his judicious way. Perhaps there was something to be said for leaving Ryan to the tender mercies of Todd and the rule of law.

'I can't be party to any plan to get Ryan off the hook,' he said portentously.

'That isn't the point,' she said, more exasperated than ever. But it was, as far as Bailey was concerned. There was no other point.

* * *

You don't care any more about the things you cannot change, Rose had taunted. Rose could taunt until the cows came home, and still remain an ally. That was the nature of friendship, or at least one of its many facets. If Helen had ever had recourse to much by way of family life since she had made the decision to ignore them in the manner they had ignored her for several years, she suspected she might have known more about how friendship equates to other states of being, such as sisterhood, brotherhood, parenthood. Her own background forced her to treasure her friends; she was glad, in many ways, to have been cast adrift. She hated the idea that the ones you loved had to be related by blood to give you the reason as well as all the obligations attached. Perhaps she was cold in her narrow little bones. I wouldn't kill for anything except my handbag, she'd said to Rose.

There were not many friends: she was too picky, and even in the realm of friends, love had this random touch. In lieu of the family I secretly crave, Helen had once told Bailey, I would like my friends to have the following qualifications: I would like them to be courageous, but not necessarily brave; stubborn, doing the best they can with whatever they have been given; full of self-doubt but sure of self-worth; honourable, if not always, at least by inclination; the sort who neither screams nor whinges for help until they really need it and makes suffering the stuff of jokes.

To thine own self be true, he had said. And in the meantime, Bailey had added, can they also be greedy, rapacious, dishonest, calculating? But of course. Nobody realizes, Helen had said, that you like people for what they are, which need not include conventional virtues, only the virtues you admire.

You said it, love. You like the people who are all the things you either are or want to be.

Am I cold?

No, just too analytical. I like you anyway.

She was sitting at her desk, crying with fury. There it was in the newspaper: the coroner's report, all on paper, no life to it at all. Girl found dead, two months before. Sweet twenty-seven. Pregnant, alone, a demise from heart attack. Nothing to show; not found for two days. How could it happen: death without cause in one so young? And how was it that she herself, so coy with friendship, so careful about the making of demands, considered not at all before she phoned Anna Stirland. Was it possible, she wanted to ask, to die of a broken heart?

No, no, Anna Stirland told herself, I rarely tell anyone what I do, especially now. Being a nurse covers so many questions, shuts them up nicely. Tell a man you're a midwife and he'll run for cover; tell a woman you work at a family planning clinic and she'll get you in a corner with anxious questions about her own thrombosis. Say you work in a hospital, they'll assume accident and emergency, like on the telly, maybe show you a blister or two. On balance it was best to keep quiet about being a nurse. They all want dramatic stories. They always avoid the question of pay and why you once thought you had some kind of vocation until the whole bureaucratic, form-filling idiocy of the NHS knocks it out of you.

All right; now I dispense pills, rubbers and other forms of birth control and assist in simple abortions. I wish I was still a midwife, really; but you could be a midwife for twenty years and still not be able to buy your own house. You can, if you work in a bank or sell cars. Abortion and the avoidance of pregnancy paid better and that was a fact, which was why a skilled and dedicated midwife worked for a private death clinic. She wondered if she might have been less vulnerable, less a potential victim, if she had been doing what she was good at; if she wasn't somehow defensive about what she did, since a person with such doubts about the nature of their work really did risk a kind of mental illness. Helen West had made her understand something, she said out loud as she walked round the park, namely that in her line of legal business there are no answers, no panaceas, no drugs which cure the problem. Anna had known that already, but she could not accept what he had done to her, even less what he might have done to others. Off his list, from the bowels of his computer and out of his notebooks, he would know exactly whom to choose for these little jokes. Because they, the patients, were like herself. They looked into his eyes and told him all their hopes and fears.

The park was the coolest place to be in the early evening. Not so much a park as a graveyard, sloping uphill away from the thunderous road into a canopy of old trees which left the grass, thin from constant shade, dappled with light. The gravestones were old, sticking up out of the ground round the church like gesturing fingers, the inscriptions long since worn away, making them little more than stumps of anonymous stone. There was no shame to sit up against them with a lunch-time sandwich. Few did; lying supine with a bottle of cider was more likely. It was not the kind of park which provided a landmark; not one of the perfect city parks which tourists in search of significant statuary would come to see. It was merely a green lung, always messy on the surface because of the leaves, slightly dusty because of the traffic; never entirely quiet. An old lags' park, with sinister overtones, a collection of bottles littering the grass each morning. Over the slope, beyond the sunken church, stood the coroners court, prettily Victorian, and next to it, on more anonymous concrete lines, the mortuary. There were many reasons why the park was not to everyone's taste.

Anna Stirland liked it, from time to time, when it suited and therefore soothed a certain morbid turn of mind, or, in summer, provided such coolness when the streets shone with ill-tempered heat, but she could not see it as a trysting place. Unless you had come to frolic with the dead.

She hefted her shoulder bag, full of food she might or might not cook, but bought as a commitment to ordinary life, and made for the gates, surprised as she always was to notice how the sound of traffic grew so much louder away from the trees. She passed a girl, marching in the opposite direction, walking with an air of pretended purpose, the way a shy woman might walk into a pub to meet someone, not quite sure what to do with herself if he was not there, except stare ahead and around, as if preoccupied. Her face was vaguely familiar, so that Anna was tempted to nod at her. She saw so many youthful faces in the course of her job, she was never quite sure when she recognized a woman or girl, if work had been the context. Simply a girl, strikingly thin, patently anxious. There were times when Anna did not regret the passing of the first apologetic years of youth.

Shelley Pelmore came to a halt within sight of the coroners court and paused. She felt less self-conscious now there was no-one to see her looking around. She stood with her hands on her hips, bag across her chest, long legs ending in heavy shoes, a contrast to her short skirt and loose cropped top, as fashion dictated. She flicked hair out of her eyes and stared at the stained-glass windows of the court. It would always be dark in there, she reckoned, on account of the trees; lights glowed inside, as if it was winter. The building held no fears, nor the concrete block adjacent; Shelley had no idea of the purpose of either and no curiosity. She would never voluntarily have gone for a walk, least of all in a park, but this slightly seedy area held some attraction. Sex alfresco had a great appeal, like doing something forbidden. Shelley Pelmore had never had to resort to sheds or the backs of cars; sex had never been clandestine. It had always been Derek, blessed by her bloody mother and, apart from the initial naughtiness, profoundly disappointing. There had never been anything faintly wicked about it. None of this palpitating tension, this sense of being out on a limb, this dreadful enticing fear. This desperation.

He never smelt of anything and he had the quiet footsteps of a cat. He could dance, too, this glamorous doctor. Shelley preferred to draw a veil over their first meeting, when she had talked her heart out, spitting out the particulars of her life for his edification, receiving back his sympathetic warmth. And then his hands on her, feeling gently, asking questions with his smooth fingertips, making her laugh, even as she lay with her legs wide apart and the cool instruments probing. An intimate examination was something she had first dreaded, and then dreamt about.

Maybe it was the relief at not being pregnant after all which made her bold. You ever go clubbing, Doc? Come on down and meet me and the girls. He was a little old for her, of course; it would not do to place him anywhere near her friend, the predatory manageress. She must keep him away from her. Shiny brown head under artificial lights, beautiful exciting eyes. But, oh yes, in the end he was too good not to share.

'Hallo.'

Behind her without a sound, arms on her shoulders. 'Where have you been?' she hissed.

'Missing you,' he said. 'All the time.' He was propelling her away from the court, towards the church where no-one went. She stopped abruptly, thinking it was time to make a stand, to tell him she couldn't go on like this. The world and its expectations were tearing her apart. She dreaded the morning, the afternoon, the evening and this time she really had to do something about the pregnancy, or she would be in prison for the whole of her life. Would he help her, please? Oh God, he owed her that. She turned on him, ready to be shrill, to embarrass him by screaming at him. But he stopped her. He held her head steady with one hand meshed in her hair, his mouth clamped on hers, the other hand briefly inside the loose top, squeezing a nipple, hard, then down beyond the waistband of the skirt, over the still-flat belly, inside her knickers, one long finger making her gasp. People would see; with eyes squeezed shut, she could imagine a crowd gathering, watching a man's hand snatch at her bush in broad daylight.

He pushed her gently into the deeper shadow of the church wall. She put both hands against it, feeling the cool stone scratch at her palms. He was behind her now, her buttocks supported against his thighs. Both hands fondled her breasts; then, bracing himself against her, he felt inside her thighs, parted the lips, slid his long fingers in and out, rhythmic and strong. Lovely, lovely cunt, he was murmuring, kissing her neck, feeling her legs slacken until she almost sat in his lap, the skirt round her waist, the G-string panties snapped, her breath ragged, her mouth forming, no, no, no, without making a sound, letting him do what he did. Legs straddled wide, coming round his fist in a writhing spasm and oh, God, no fucking with Derek was ever as safe or as dangerous as this.

She pressed her thighs together, trapping his hand for a moment, then relaxed with a shuddering sigh. It was at times like these, anger forgotten in a strange exhilaration, that she wanted to round on him, do something in return, fumble for the penis she had never felt and never seen, pleasure him somehow if only to even the score of need, or pleasure, or something. Other times, she would go home, practically howling for Derek and a straightforward unimaginative fuck to finish the business. Oh yes, he was safe. No risk of AIDS or babies with this man. Safe enough to share with friends.

There was low laughter from him, as if from a man satisfied. She could not understand him, nor did she want to. One of her friends, Becky, hadn't liked whatever he had done, the silly cow. Now he was talking to her, his body shielding her from view while his hands stroked her buttocks, held them apart, kneaded them. In a minute, she would want it again.

'I think it must be gravity,' he murmured. 'Blood rushing to the right place. Something to do with the fact that we might still be meant to go round on all fours.'

She leant back against him.

'Would gravity, or whatever, pull this baby out?'

'No.'

'You said you'd help. I helped you. I don't want it . . . I don't want it and Derek would never let me . . . When will you get it out of me?'

'Next week, at the clinic. No hurry.'

He smoothed the skirt over her behind. Her panties were on the floor; she picked them up and stuffed them in her handbag. It always amazed her the way they could walk and talk, like a couple discussing what to have for tea.

'Last time I came to the clinic, you weren't there.'

'Sorry.'

'And you weren't here yesterday.'

'Sorry again.'

'I can't go on like this.'

'I know.'

Fear paralysed her. Fear of not going on like this, with this occasional, insane, sick-feeling excitement.

'I don't quite mean that. Oh, I don't know what I mean.'

She was shaking, hanging on to his arm.

'Next time,' he said, 'I'll make it all all right. Promise. Now you've got to go home.'

Her face hardened. She was not ready yet for a pat on the head and being dismissed.

'Monday?' she said. 'Monday? Talk to me. Talk to me, or I'll talk.'

He held her gently, a soft kiss, like a continental greeting, to each cheek.

'No, you won't. Promise. Anyway, what would you say?'

chapter nine

'My man', said Helen West, always confused as to whether she should refer to Bailey as her partner, boyfriend, or anything as simple as a lover, 'is in a state of grief and confusion. He mutters in his sleep about treachery and chocolates. And what haunts him, poor soul? Another man. Do I have a problem?'

The nurse laughed. 'Oh dear. And where is it you're getting married. In church?'

'Nope. Register office.'

'Oh. The one in Highgate's very nice.'

'Is it? I only know the one in Finsbury, on account of being married in it once before. I thought he said Finsbury.'

There was something disconcerting about the way she found herself chatting in the surgery, as if she were anxiously ill, instead of guarding against an impending change of status by the superstitious precaution of a medical check-up. Getting the body scanned: heart, cigarette-stained lungs, hearing and sight, just so she would know, within the usual inexact parameters, the state of her health. Ready to present for duty, sound in mind and limb, as if matrimony were a mountaineering expedition. Chronic illness and the wedding was off. The medical practice at the end of the road was small and valiant. Helen could feel herself becoming apologetic as soon as she crossed the portals and heard the sound of coughing. Even this cursory examination made her feel foolish and more than a little exposed; there was a certain, in her case, garrulous, vulnerability in being half dressed, even in such a clinical atmosphere. A feeling of putting the body up for judgement, as if either doctor or nurse was going to add some scathing aesthetic verdict to the general diagnosis. (Thin here, floppy here, and OK, what does this corpse think it's doing getting married at its age?) The most embarrassing thing in the end was how idiotically talkative she became.

Bailey did not only talk in his sleep, these days; he talked when he was awake. Expounding Ryan's idiocies; what little Sally Smythe could tell him about Ryan's theories. Ryan and other forms of gaol bait wandered through his dreams. Her bridegroom.

The marriage had not been discussed. Most of the time, she liked it that way.

Anna Stirland laughed, a great big uproarious laugh which Helen remembered from their first meeting and had not heard since.

'Talk a lot? Patients? Oh, yes, all the time. To be encouraged, if only they weren't apologetic about it. Why else would I do it if I weren't so curious about other people's lives?'

A drink after work, a chat about anything, a little people-watching; turning out to be a good idea. 'Yeah,' Anna had said into her phone, not even cautiously enthusiastic. 'Yes, do me good. But one condition, mind.' A deep breath. 'Can we talk about anything other than my . . . attack? Honestly, it's weeks now, I'm much better, got my mind in gear.'

'What are you giving our Rose for a wedding present?'

'Wisdom?' said Helen.

'Not mine to give,' said Anna.

'Not mine, either. Impossible to wrap, anyway. A laundry basket, I thought, with a year's supply of all that boring cleaning crap: Jiff, bleach, dusters. Then I thought I'd add in extravagant underwear. Not his and hers, only hers.'

'I thought I'd make them window-boxes. Evergreens, late-blooming things. It'll be autumn when they come back,' Anna mused.

'Rose doesn't look after plants,' Helen remarked, remembering the cause of the last Rose and Michael quarrel.

'No more does anyone, given some boiled root azalea or a drooping palm for the living-room. She'll learn. You learnt with your garden.'

'Not really. I fiddle about, talk to it sometimes. Try and stop things throttling one another.'

'That's taking care. Michael will do it.'

'Was he a sweet child?' Helen asked.

'Oh yes, funny little squinty-eyed boy, went round with a bandage and specs, teased to death, then started to grow and grow. I met him out of school once; watched the other lads around him, baiting him, not even noticing how he'd grown. Michael picked one of them up, very gently, mind, lifted him into a rubbish skip and walked away. Never one to overdo revenge. I don't know Rose half as well. Didn't approve at first; love her to death now. I thought she was a gorgeous little slut; ever so glad I kept my mouth shut.'

'Gold dust,' Helen murmured. 'Hope the past doesn't come back to haunt her. Haunts me, and it isn't mine.'

'Should it?' Anna asked, curiously. 'Colourful, I knew, but . . .'

'Sexual abuse from a dad who probably murdered her mother – I shouldn't have said that.'

Anna nodded, as if receiving information on the weather forecast. 'What privileged and lucky lives we lead,' she said crisply. 'Will she make a good lawyer?'

'I hope not,' Helen said vehemently. 'I do hope not.' She paused. 'Kills your fire in the end, see? If you believe in it, it makes you cold. All this objectivity. As bad as the form filling. Never being able to do anything well.'

'Like nursing,' Anna said neutrally.

'Even being a midwife? All that new life?'

'Even that,' Anna said, blushing furiously. Somehow, the evening died and they were no longer easy with one another. Anna looked at her watch.

'You've lost weight,' Helen observed.

Anna smiled, shrugged.

'Decided not to sell my house, after all. I've worked hard enough for it. Besides, people want me to be better, so I thought I'd oblige them. Oh, it was all a silly episode,' said Anna, forgetting her own request not to mention it. 'Some throwback from his team sporting days, best forgotten.'

Ryan found the park again at about nine in the morning. No car, this time. The suburban train spat him out with the early commuters; he walked from that station to Euston. The air was as fresh as it could be in King's Cross; the park was sanitized by darkness and dew, the scrubby grass discernibly greener than in the afternoon. A man swept leaves, twigs and papers from the paths, moving with deliberate sloth, extending the task, enjoying it. The same old lag was sprawled on the same bench in a patch of sun. On a morning like this, the life of a drunken vagrant could seem almost romantic. Ryan trod by softly, noting, as before, the premature age of an old face with younger limbs.

The door to the coroners court stood open. Ryan leant against the outside wall next to it and stared up at the gasometers. If you built these now, he thought, great circular edifices of metal, the size of large buildings, composed of naked girders, some fool would call it modern art. They looked like a skeletal casing for a bomb; they invited a daredevil to climb up there and feel the breeze. They were monstrous, crouching like guardians, dominating the view, and yet he liked them; because they had always been there. Ryan straightened his tie. Wearing a suit after nothing but gardening clothes for the last few days felt like placing himself in a strait-jacket, but if he had not worn this uniform, which he did with an element of pleasure, he would deny himself the credibility he needed in the absence of a warrant card. No-one would demand to see it, or be aware just yet of its confiscation. He had never been a regular visitor to either the mortuary or the court or unexpected death, but the officers in the back room had seen his face once or twice before; so had the pathologist of the day. No-one would question his status.

Inside the foyer, there was a desultory collection of relatives, assembled sombrely to hear witnesses repeat the facts leading to the death of Aunt Mary or brother John, then listen to the coroner's verdict. Death by misadventure; one kind of accident to which the deceased may well have contributed himself, common for a drug overdose. Suicide, which needed proof beyond reasonable doubt; accidental, which meant what it said, and, most rarely of all, rarer than anyone supposed, unlawful killing. The bereavement of these relatives was already old news: they were not in the first stage of grief, merely anxious, looking a trifle lost, waiting for someone to explain procedure, concerned to do the right thing. Ryan was not the only one wearing a suit, with the difference that at least one of theirs bore signs of moth.

The courtroom itself resembled a church with pews for seats, plus the usual paraphernalia of judge's bench and witness stand. The sun glinted through the coloured windows, insufficient to illuminate an attractive restful gloom to the extent of making it possible to read small print. It was a place unconsciously designed to discourage hysteria; he found it difficult to imagine the staff even celebrating Christmas. Then he heard a shout of laughter from the office behind.

'DS Ryan. Dr Webb here yet? She promised me a word.' He introduced himself easily, nevertheless relieved to find his presence accepted. The pathologist occupied a desk, perched on it with the air of a regular visitor; she smiled sweetly.

'Oh, you again, Mr Ryan, with your awkward questions. What do you want this time?'

He felt as if he should be holding a hat in his hand, nervously turning the brim, like someone asking a favour from a duchess. Dr Webb was large, loud, extremely attractive and saw no reason why corpses, diseases and the inevitable fact of death should ever be discussed *sotto voce*, since she herself was congenitally incapable of whispering.

'A rehash of what we were discussing last time,' he said humbly. 'I seem to have lost my notes.'

She wagged her finger at him. 'Policemen should not be writing theses,' she said. 'And why should I mind repeating myself. Where were we?'

'I began', Ryan said, lowering his voice, 'by asking you if it was possible to kill a healthy young woman, leaving no traces, by the simple measure of inserting ice up her vagina. Could the shock of that cause a spontaneous heart attack?'

'And I', she said impatiently, 'said no. Not unless she had a weak heart. I told you it would not otherwise be a question of the temperature of the instrument . . . not unless it was so cold it burnt the skin. It would be more a question of the length. A long icicle, maybe? Where would he get such a thing? No. He might cause an undetectable death, even without injury, if his instrument probed too far, against resistance – death by shock – women died this way in backstreet abortions. The cervix does not like interference. People have strange ways of having fun. Not an icicle; maybe a syringe.' In defiance of the prohibitory sign and any intimations of mortality, she lit a cigarette.

'What I wanted to know', Ryan asked, 'is is there a technique a man could perfect?'

She considered and shook her handsome head.

'What technique? Technique for homicide, you mean? What a strange man he would be. Like an abortionist, he could perfect avoiding it, but not perfect the doing of it, I think. Your sexual murderer is more likely to be obvious. He does not have much control. He strangles, he bites, he stabs.' Hand and mouth, she gestured, biting, chopping.

There was a polite coughing from the far end of the room, where two of the coroner's officers sat with paperwork and phones, one looking at Ryan quizzically, trying to remember something, something he might have heard, perhaps. It reminded Ryan how much Dr Webb's voice carried; he remembered the waiting relatives, almost within earshot. Remembered also, his first protective chauvinistic impression, that a woman as beautiful as this should not speak so loud.

'Pleasant, outside,' he suggested. 'Shall we?'

She was, as always, obliging, and trailed her cigarette smoke into the warm outdoors. She sauntered into the park, stubbed out the fag end on a gravestone, sighed and looked at her watch.

'Pre-mortuary precaution,' she said, wiping her hands on her skirt. 'Takes away the smell. What next?'

'Another method of a man causing the death of a woman, in a sexual encounter, without leaving traces,' he began, pleased that he no longer needed to whisper. Her brow wrinkled.

'Ah yes. A similar thing. Death by blow-job. Shows there can be more things wrong with oral sex than just the view!' She roared with laughter. Ryan stood woodenly, looking at the grass, pressing down a ring-pull from a can into the earth. He noticed, with a sudden flush of horror, that he was wearing training shoes beneath his pressed suit trousers. He looked up again. No doubt the pathologist would cut off his feet for him if he asked her nicely.

'The vagina is full of delicate little blood-vessels. Vulnerable in pregnant ladies. The man doesn't do the normal: he actually blows into it. A bubble of air can enter one of the blood-vessels, travel round the system, get to the heart and poof! An embolism. You need ten cc. I told you. It's a bit like having an airlock in the central-heating system. She dies. No signs for me. Cardiac respiratory arrest.'

'I remember,' said Ryan, 'but could he be exact?'

'You ask for certainty, you can't have it; not in anything. More likely if you practice, but never certain. With a syringe full of air, more so. Oh, and only pregnant ladies, especially with vaginal verrucas.'

'How long would it take to die?'

'Oh, rapid. I must go. Is that enough?'

'Thank you. You've been very kind.'

'Good luck with your thesis. Don't come back soon.'

Another posse of relatives were huddled outside the entrance in order to smoke. They were a picture of controlled misery; Ryan guessed at the death of a child. He saw the officer who had coughed standing on the doorstep, looking over their heads, staring after him. No, he would not come back soon. Ryan turned and walked purposefully down the hill, wrenching off his tie, cursing his shoes. In this park he felt as if he was treading on skulls, one of them his own, and the shoes were simply a symptom of how far he had sunk and how much further he could go.

There was a man out there he had begun to hate long since. So nebulous a presence, the pursuit of him was similar to chasing a will-o'-the-wisp, a foggy London phantom, the discussion of whom would make him disappear into thin air. Unlike his own wife, who would stand by him until prison walls created the last barrier, and then, for the sake of the survivors, she would go.

The old young man slept, turned on his side to get the sun on his back. Ryan shoved his packet of cigarettes into a rancid armpit.

'Keep that bench warm for me,' he said.

'Look, Aunty Helen, when you and that old cadaver of yours get married, you will let me know, won't you? So I can come along and laugh? I don't know why the hell you're so neurotic about it.'

'I've told you as much as I can to explain it. And I'll tell you afterwards. But, frankly, can you see any point in asking you to grace the serious business of middle-aged nuptials with unseemly conduct? No, girl, get stuffed. This was always going to be a private arrangement, very short notice or I'd die of embarrassment, and don't ask why. Besides, Bailey can't ask Ryan—'

'I should think not!' Rose stormed. 'He's a fucking rapist!'

'—Overstatement and anyway, it seems to follow I can't ask my self-appointed, pain-in-the neck of a niece. There'll be a party, later, so you can offer felicitations and congratulations as appropriate, once the pair of us get used to the idea. If we ever do.'

'I don't understand you,' Rose stated.

Helen beamed at her.

'Good. If I were you, I'd avoid understanding. Tell me, is the man behaving well? Less of the nervous disorders?'

Rose considered.

'Most of the time, as good as can be expected, thank you, ma'am. Not always better, hardly exquisite in his manners, but not half bad, thanks. His lordship may still get the vapours when I let his botanical specimens die and when I spend joint money on going to an expensive clinic instead of allowing an ordinary doctor to get impertinent with me in the interests of birth control, but otherwise his health is excellent. How kind of you to enquire.'

'Is missy going to persist in this speech on account of watching a video of *Pride and Prejudice*, or can we get down to work?'

'Oh, did you see Anna?'

'Yes. Yesterday. She's going to make you window-boxes. You'd better look after them.'

'I'll use the bedroom one as a place to keep my cap. I'll plant it, instead of pinging it into the street, and grow little caplets . . .'

'Work, Rose.'

'OK, OK, but listen. You know I told you about the accident with the sodding cap? Well, it never came back, you know. I had to go to the clinic and get another one, didn't I? But the good thing was, it made Anna laugh. Laugh? I thought she'd split her sides . . .'

'Anna?' Helen queried.

'At the clinic. Where she works. Why else would I go to a place like that?'

'I thought she was a midwife.'

'Naa, not any more. More money in this.'

Only a little lie, Helen thought; only a small one. The sort of lie she always feared a witness would announce under oath; some little piece of secrecy or vanity which rendered everything else they said faintly suspicious, however true it was. She hefted the file off the floor and onto the desk.

'Work, Rose.'

'Fuck me. I forgot.'

'This one for trial. Read it, see if you agree. I've drafted the charge, you annotate the pages; six copies of each. Statements in order, so they tell the story in sequence. Code at the top for stuff which defence and prosecution might agree as purely scientific . . . away you go.'

Rose, astride the boxes in Helen's office, looked up, bullish and sulky.

'Look, I've read it. Cover to cover, honest. And I don't agree.'

Helen sat back. Examined her nails, thought of Bailey as Mr Darcy and thought, yes, there was quite a resemblance, not least in the fact that each had weaker friends.

'For God's sake, why?' she asked innocently.

Rose took a deep breath, as if about to sing solo and nervous with it. Helen's mind wandered; she reminded herself to ask some other time about this clinic Rose had mentioned.

'Because if you read her statement, it's perfect,' Rose blurted. 'Too perfect. The defendant's her ex-boyfriend, right? Can't stand the thought that she's left him for someone else, right? He gets lonely one night, comes round and knocks. She says she's afraid of his violence, which is why she got rid of him in the first place, but she lets him in. All lovely. How are you? Just come round to ask, and how are you too? Have a beer, she says. Sit and watch this video with me, she says. Nice to see you after six months, she says. Where's that coffee?'

'On your left.'

Rose grasped the handle of a half-full mug, used it to weight the hand making gestures.

'Then he jumps on her. *He* says, she likes it; been giving him the come on for the last hour, *he* says. Wearing a short skirt and not exactly putting a blanket over herself, he says. While she says, look, the whole thing came out of the blue. Why would she ever want to screw this sod when the kid's asleep and her new man's expected home any time? Well, I reckon this old boyfriend used to beat her like she said; he comes on strong like she said; she struggled a bit and then decided to keep the peace. What's once more for old time's sake, eh? Look, I think she's telling the absolute truth; she weighed up rape against a broken nose and settled for rape. And I know there's bruises on her arms, which he says were there before, because the new chap isn't so gentle either; not a scratch on him, though. But put that in front of a jury?'

Coffee dribbled onto the floor; Rose ignored it.

'They're going to say, why didn't she slam the door as soon as she saw him if he was so bad? Why didn't she yell

for help? By the time the defence has finished, no-one'll remember how that's actually a difficult thing to do. They
won't think like she would think: once more to stop him
hitting me, and I won't shout because of the kid in the next
room. She'd do it, and he'd be able to say either she consented, or he'd every reason to suppose she did.'

'She could have slammed the door.'

'You don't; she didn't, but no witnesses. Balance of proof.
Reasonable doubt. And you aren't going to get a six-year-
old to testify about mummy's distress, are you? Not even
you. As for the neighbours, they won't.'

Helen was out of her swivel chair, examining, through
their own dirty windows, the administrative staff of the
paint manufacturing company across the road. They had
revamped their mottled grey walls to make them greyer
still; the people merged with the décor in efficient silence.
All busy about some executive decision. Life-threatening
colour shades. She waved to no response.

'All right, Rose,' she said briskly. 'If that's what you
think, we'll bin it.'

'What?'

'The rape.'

Rose looked horrified. 'It might work,' she stuttered. 'I
didn't mean . . . It might . . . work.'

'A phrase not known in legal Latin. D'you want to argue
this point past Redwood's budget? You said it. If you can
see a reasonable doubt before you've even heard the argu-
ments, what the hell will a jury see?' Rose was silent. Then
she got up, opened the flap of a window, and made to heave
the file out. Helen stopped her.

'No good either. You want this woman's life all over the
street?'

'You made me say it,' Rose raged. 'You made me act

God! You made me say we should turn it down, even when we think it's true. Sometimes you're a bitch, Aunty H.'

'Wish I was,' Helen mourned. 'I really wish I was. But we can't run cases we know we're going to lose. Truth is luxury. And I don't like playing God, either.'

The apartment block was a strange building; once a school or institution, Bailey guessed, converted into flats of an unusual size with large modern windows, so that the façade stuck out like a sore thumb in a terrace of smaller, less-gaunt dwellings which had all succumbed to historically conscientious planning regulations while this building had escaped. It sat on the corner of two roads, defiantly marking the boundary between one kind of territory and another. Before it lay the metropolis, behind it the leafier squares of Barnsbury's genteel streets. You lived here for the view, perhaps for a feeling of power.

There were benefits to the flexible routine of a rota, Bailey knew. He had always managed to evade any kind of job which imposed too much of a regime, except that dictated by emergency. His creative evasions were becoming more difficult to achieve in an age where the formulae of accountability took more time than the work itself, but still, he managed. Provided he did excessive hours and obfuscated, he could still function in accordance with his own clock, leaving time for eccentric assignments like these: checking up on Ryan's theories, following up Sally Smythe's kindred fantasies about the no-hopers. Beginning with the most recent.

He had phoned in advance and met with truculence, smoothed by Bailey's natural diplomacy until Aemon Connor's rudeness diminished into a grudging growl. Sure, the policeman could come round and waste his time; waste his wife's time, too, for that matter, but not much of it. Ten minutes. There's little enough to say. She never did make a great deal of sense, he added.

There was a hotel-like carpet of more pretension than taste in the lobby and a tiny lift before Bailey reached the Connors' door. One myth, promulgated by the reports, was immediately exploded, namely that of a twenty-four-hour porter, sober or available at any given time.

Mr Connor was a man to whom anger was more than second nature; it was a state of being, only absorbed by frenetic activity, a constant position at the top of some heap, and the sense of achievement which came from physical exhaustion. Perhaps he was a cuddly bear when his children were around, but Bailey doubted it. Two teenage girls, he'd read, away for the summer, and, feeling the unnatural heat inside this high apartment, Bailey thought they were well out of it. There was no sign of the wife.

'In the bath,' Aemon said, briefly. He looked at Bailey's outstretched hand, wondering whether to ignore it, but since the man was smiling, he took it. Bailey wondered if a palm so calloused could actually feel the difference between a firm handshake and a loose one, but refrained from asking. Something about the quality of his own hand seemed to mollify.

'It was you I came to see, sir,' Bailey said. 'A chat, before bothering the little woman.'

'She talks rubbish,' Aemon muttered. 'Always did.'

'They often do, women, don't they, sir?' Bailey sighed in sympathy. 'Oh, I am sorry. Not the right thing to say, is it? I don't mean any disrespect.'

'You've got it in one, boy.'

A slight warming of the atmosphere was established by mutual head-shaking sadness, like a couple of men contemplating the keeping of a pair of iguanas acquired by accident and without adequate instruction. Bailey did not feel in the least guilty.

'And I thought the whole thing was closed,' Connor muttered. He had half a mind to offer the visitor a drink. Not such a bad sort of man, for a copper, and besides, he wanted one himself. Late afternoon, work going downhill, hot as all hell, with scarcely an evening made in heaven stretching away in front of him; a drink seemed a good idea. Just a large one.

'So it is closed,' Bailey said. 'But you see, sir, there's an aspect of the sorry business which might, just might, impinge on another inquiry, quite separate. Now, it seemed like your wife was fantasizing about a caller in the afternoon when you came home to find her in the bath . . .'

'I often do. She lives in there.'

'Yes, sure, but not usually for so long? That afternoon, when you had to send for the doctor. Look, we know, of course, there's nothing in this rape allegation against yourself; monstrous, of course, but I'm working on the possibility she did have a caller. One who frightened her maybe. Shocked her, made her hysterical.'

Aemon was listening.

'I can't think who she'd let in. Parish women. The priest, she loves the priest, for all he's a stern fellow to everyone but the undeserving poor.'

'Salesman?' Bailey suggested. 'Electrician? Plumber? Delivery man? Doctor?' he added as an afterthought.

Aemon shook his head. He was suddenly furiously defensive.

'A doctor? Why the hell would she let in a doctor? There's nothing wrong with her, is there?'

'Well,' said Bailey, looking at the clenched fists and wondering why the mention of a doctor tending his wife should touch so raw a nerve, 'perhaps nothing obvious. Perhaps she was feeling ill?'

Aemon snorted. 'Often says so, never is. Like a horse, she is.'

And, like an award-winning actress, faded, but never beyond a cue, the subject of their discussion wafted into the room. White towelling robe, an overpowering odour of roses, hair wrapped in a turban. Gloria Swanson, Bailey thought; Marlene Dietrich with a softer washed-out face and a bigger bosom. Never a Jamie Lee Curtis.

'Did you call a doctor the other day, Brigid?' Aemon asked, pleasantly, with only a hint of impatience. 'You know, the day when we all went on our pleasant little outing to the police station,' he added, bitterly.

She flinched, shook her head and smiled brilliantly.

'We've our own doctor,' Aemon explained. 'Sound fellow, sixty-four last birthday. Couldn't scare a cat.'

'Have you ever been to see any other doctor, Mrs Connor?' Bailey asked her. She shook her head vehemently and spoke quickly in a childish voice.

'Oh, no, I wouldn't do that.' Her face flushed scarlet. Her husband had poured her a large gin.

'Ice?' he barked.

'Oh, yes. A lot.'

The ice bucket was divinely old-fashioned, Bailey noticed; almost enough in itself to turn any ordinary drink into a cocktail. Aemon downed his drink in one without, in the end, offering anything to Bailey; it put him into a vastly improved frame of mind.

'Another doctor?' he chortled, stuck on the doctor theme. 'You'll be accusing her of going on the pill next. She'd never do that. Not when we still have time for a son.

Another doctor! Perish the thought! She won't even take her clothes off for me!"

Bailey, to his own shame, joined in with Aemon's laughter; let it travel over his face, make his body move while he tried at the same time to catch Mrs Connor's eye.

'I only ask', he explained, 'because we seem to have a man in this area masquerading as an innocent visitor. Possibly even a delivery man, sometimes, bringing in flowers and chocolates. He's bothered a couple of other women, that's all, got them upset.'

Aemon was thoughtful. 'You mean she needn't have been lying? She wasn't the only one being scared like that?'

'I wouldn't have thought lying was in her nature, Mr Connor.'

'Well, that's a relief. I hope you get the bastard.'

Aemon's eyes had strayed first to his watch and then to his wife.

Bailey saw her face, flushed and expressionless, as she passed an ornate mirror on her way to the window. A breeze moved the crystals of the chandelier making small clinking sounds. Mrs Connor leant against the window-frame looking downwards, intently, as if waiting for someone.

He saw scuffs on the glass, marks and streaks at odds with this daily-cleaned house.

She must have spent more time at the window today than she had in the bath.

God forbid he should be so happily married.

Ryan's blue folder. Two of them mentioning a doctor. Laughing it off.

chapter ten

'If, with intent to commit an offence . . . a person does an act which is more than merely preparatory to the commission of the offence, he is guilty of attempting to commit the offence.

'A person may be guilty of attempting to commit an offence (to which this section applies) even though the facts are such that the commission of the offence is impossible.'

Derek could remember their words, Mum and Dad and all the rest, but most of all he could remember the sharp intakes of breath he could hear when fellow men clapped eyes on Shelley.

She's a cow, Derek. Everyone's told you she's a cow. Pardon my French, said his sister. Let me tell *you* something, he would say, she's a lovely gel, just needs a decent bloke. She's done well, Shelley. Oh yeah, sure, she likes a good time, but she works hard.

He had recited this chapter and verse until it almost rhymed in his head, always singling out from the memory bank those times when Shell was really astoundingly pleased to see him. Times on which his devotion was more rewarded by her ten-minute enthusiasm than a starving pet with late-delivered food and everything forgiven. It was enough to nourish his dogged determination to keep by his side a bird as gorgeous and sometimes wanton as this. She could be a pain to live with, but they'd settled down, and oh, how his mates had envied him at first, whatever they said later. He could feel other men's envy like balm on the skin, massaging his fragile pride while they reappraised him.

'What you looking at, Shell?'

'Nothing,' she'd say, from her standpoint by the window, looking like a prisoner who would have knotted her bed-sheets together in order to abseil out quicker than she could walk to the big front door. It was not such an imposing front door, either, simply double glazed and ugly, steel-framed, paintwork with condensation stains, and a notice politely requesting that it should be closed quietly. Most of the other residents favoured security. Senior citizens, Derek said politely, content to accede to their requests for errands and the mending of kettles. Past their sell-by date, said Shelley, with contempt.

And he was slowly, very slowly, discovering that his lady love, his dearest, his chosen partner in life, was a girl to whom kindness was not second nature, a bit of a bitch, in fact. Derek had resisted any such conclusion, squirrelled it away into the realm of non-being, just as he hid from her his ongoing terror of her infidelity. He dampened his exclusive passion for this elegant sulky creature into round-the-clock good-natured solicitude which he couldn't stop even when he knew it got on her nerves. Nothing was comparable to the fear that she might leave. Not only leave, but go elsewhere.

'You're always looking out of that window, you,' he teased. 'Anyone would think you liked the view.'

She yawned in reply. 'Think I'll go round and see Kath,' she said.

'I thought you weren't speaking to Kath.'

'Well, I'll try. There's nothing good on the telly.'

Of course she was going round to Kath's while he went out for the evening shift. Like hell she was. She had all the nervous excitement and the faked yawns of a girl who was revelling in the idea of a cosy chat with a female pal and the pal's mother over a kitchen table. She was positively twitching at the prospect of drinking cocoa.

'I think you ought to stay in,' he suggested. 'Get an early night.'

'Well, I might do that,' she said, perkily.

His anger was always slow to build, easily hidden, only riled by lies. He knew what he was going to do and hated himself for doing it. He kissed her goodbye, went downstairs noisily and ignored the prohibition against slamming the door. Then he sat in the covered bus stop on the other side of the road and waited. Derek did not bother to crouch, disguise his presence, or wonder if she might see him. He knew she would fly out of the block without looking left or right, all memory of him eradicated with the application of her lipstick. He could imagine the possible destinations, too: The Wheatsheaf, The Crown, the wine bar by the canal. They were less glamorous than the second-rate West End clubs she really favoured, but still places where a girl could perch and get a drink or five for nothing and look around. The way she did on the rare occasions they were out together; she'd rather look at the wall than at him. But then in bed, later, it was another matter. Exquisite pains and pleasures from a sometime hoyden, sometime thumb-sucking youngster, sweetly demanding before the tyranny of sulks. Only a child.

There she went, like an arrow, long legs gorgeous in the late evening sun, and all at once the anger went in a sudden flush of longing for her, compounded by shame that he should sink so low as to follow her. No, he told himself; go for a walk, have a drink, calm down and then go home; have a showdown later. The conclusion that she was an incorrigible and convincing liar had been a long time coming. In fact, it might never have arrived with such finality in his slow but precise mind if he had not seen her, watched her with incredulous attention, when he had followed her the night before; seen her in the amusement arcade opposite the station, talking with gestures to that man, Ryan. The one who had been round their flat a long time ago. The one who was supposed to have raped her, reduced her to that humbled and whimpering state of need in which Derek had so delighted. He did not understand.

He had no head for drink, but he tried. He came from the same kind of stock as Shelley's mum and dad, less contemptuous of flesh, equally suspicious of drink, suspicious of a good time . . . Never take your eye off the ball, lad, or someone will have your job; ask about the pension plan when you apply at seventeen; life is for building a wall against the kind of poverty which killed your granny. Of course he had to sort this out with Shelley; you don't let go of anything you have. Not your bricks and mortar and not your woman. Especially if she was pregnant with your child, even if she thought that was her own secret. Ah, yes, he knew. And she didn't know that he had guessed about what she had done the last time. For all her cunning, she was lazy about the details, as careless with the receipt from that clinic as she was with the receipts for the clothes she hid, as if he had not built every hiding-place. The echoes of this contempt, as well as the drink, made him maudlin for himself and the lost child; more for himself, he had to admit. Even in the pub, he wept a little over his second pint and almost enjoyed the sensation. An older man came and sat next to him, one of the regulars Derek usually crossed the street to avoid, although at this juncture in the evening, when he should have been at work, when he should have been a man, not a wimp, he found he did not much mind.

'You all right, old son?' It was said in a sedulous whisper, with all the solicitous secrecy of the confessional. Derek noted with rare observation that the face, younger on close inspection, was lit with concern. Derek rallied slightly, bought the drinks the occasion demanded, confirmed that, yes, he was fine thank you and they chatted about the weather in the time-honoured fashion of strangers keeping company, until Derek could no longer stand the smell of summer sweat which was days, if not weeks old, nor tolerate the sight of dirt-stained hands with brown claw-like nails, trembling round a glass. One and a half hours killed; he left with pleasant farewells to find the world darkening beyond the doors. The traffic was lighter, the air pleasant on his forehead, and the scent of diesel fumes almost a relief.

Then he waited indoors, half watching a long film, sipping the brandy kept for special occasions. Sipping, dozing until hunger woke him as the credits rolled and he could not remember what it had all been about. Only that it was one in the morning and Shelley was not home. He blundered around, found Kath's number and phoned. Grumpy response. No, why should she be here? Let me sleep. Who were her friends, then? Real friends? Few enough. Giggly girls who did not last: none that he could count; none who lasted long. The thought chilled him. He was, really, all she had.

That was it; she was stuck somewhere and, oh Jesus Christ, that man Ryan trying to buy her off or something; she would always listen to a man and she was always worried about money. We've got all we need, Derek could hear himself saying, and her saying, all we need for what? He was cold and stiff and shrugging into a jacket, banging that damned outside door behind him before he was quite fully awake, panic rising like sap, full of renewed love. Silly cow! Why didn't she tell me? There was the echoing voice of a mate, saying, she don't tell you fuck all, that's for sure, not a woman like that. Ho ho ho. Fancy a dull boy like you thinking a bird like that would ever confide in your shell-like . . .

He was walking by now, shuffling at first and then, as became a man with a purpose, striding like someone with a preordained sense of direction, although one he made up as he went along. First The Wheatsheaf, eight minutes walk, faintly surprised to find it shut and barred. There was the feeling that they should open to his knock, purely on account of the fact that he was now wide awake, but he did not rap on the windows because he could see that even the manager had gone. He strode up Goods Way, silent in a misty heat, down past the ever-so-twee Essex-type yuppies bar above the fetid canal; slowing down now, realizing that his stride had no purpose and all but the juggernauts were well asleep. There was a train rumbling by in his dreams. The whole of this vibrating area had settled into a kind of brightly lit somnolence; nothing here much, and such as there was, on the way to somewhere else. The work overalls he had worn all evening made him hot. She would not be out at a time like this; she would be home by now.

Home. The shortest way was through the park, from the top end to the bottom, from the road below the gasometers, downhill to the road home. Gates locked, didn't matter, over the top next to a building with lights on inside; he didn't know why it existed and did not care, because he only remained in this district on his way out of it, like the long-distance lorries, with Shelley. Difficult to explain to his parents, less difficult for hers to understand his longing for a clean modern cul-de-sac. Not like this, a place which could not change, where he was ten a penny and the noise never stopped. The park had seemed larger when he was a child; once upon a time, he could have reached it without risking death by automobile. The dangers posed by humanity in here after dark were surely no worse than those encountered *en route*.

Quiet though; too quiet for Derek's urban soul, untuned even to relative silence. Silent and deserted, until he saw him: the man from the pub, bent over a gravestone, looking as if he was taking swimming lessons on a float; arms and legs waving in non-coordinated movements, thrashing at air rather than water. As Derek looked, he slipped down the side of the stone and lay belly up, humming at the still branches above his head. As Derek listened, the humming changed to words in a musical singsong.

Derek went across to him, drawn by the antics and the sound. As he got closer, he could hear the words, Oh dear, oh dear, repeated rhythmically. Oh dear, oh dear, oh *dear*, oh dear, oh dear, oh dear . . . For some reason, it made Derek smile, so reminiscent was it of a puzzled child, and so stupidly innocent the man's spread-eagled pose, waiting for a kick or a command to get up. Derek remembered the empathy at the beginning of the evening. Never mind that the sentiment had been drunken, it had still helped, for a minute. The man looked up at Derek, smiled sweetly. Derek's curiosity was diminished by the smell, it was worse here against the comparative freshness of the grass.

'Swimming lessons,' the man said and laughed. 'Every night, my swimming lessons.' Then he stopped abruptly, struggled into a sitting position. 'Oh dear,' he repeated warily, as if remembering something. 'Have you come to find her, then?'

'Find who, old man?'

'Her, of course.'

He pointed in the direction of the church porch. A sudden light breeze shuffled the leaves in the canopy of branches. The glow from the street lights prevented total darkness. Derek felt his heart contract. The man had begun to shuffle away from him, crab-like, sensing a change of mood. Derek walked uphill again, slowly but certainly.

Shelley lay in a pose which aped that of the vagrant, only more elegantly because she was incapable of adopting an ugly pose. Her legs were obscenely wide apart, one arm outflung, the other bent across her face, as if to shield it from the dim glow of the single light attached to the church wall. She could have been basking in the sun; she could, more like, have been lying in the way she lay at home in her own bed, after sex, guarding her discontented face from the prospect of the morning. Derek fancied he could smell sex as he squatted beside her peaceful form, catching the scent of perfume, betrayal, the rank odour of what she was: an alley cat. He moved the arm from across her face. Her eyes were open.

'Help me,' she seemed to whisper. 'Help me.'

He imagined these words, made them up later, the way he so often imagined Shelley pleading; but no help, not this time. Oh no, not this time. Never again was he going to believe in his little girl lost. There was nothing helpless about her; she was out in a filthy park, in the company of winos and that was what she had chosen. Her clothes were undisturbed; she was stretching, languorously, as though remembering the last man who had fucked her. Round her neck was a gauzy silk scarf; he felt it, recognizing none of the colours in this light, but knowing by the soft and buttery touch that it was expensive; not anything he would have given; not an item she was wearing when she had run from home as soon as his back was turned. The rage, held at bay by anxiety, returned in full force. He wanted to seize her head in both hands and bang it against the ground until it became indistinguishable from the grass; he wanted to fill her mouth with soil. Instead, he took the ends of the scarf which was twisted round her neck and pulled. Her head jerked; he pulled again. She made no attempt to resist, and, in that second, the rage died. A second or two, then he was loosening the scarf, slapping her gently on one cheek, then the other, saying, 'Come on, Shell, get a grip, come on girl.' Maybe she was drunk as well.

He got behind her, muttering encouragement, pushed her up so that she sat like a rag doll, supported by his weight.

'Put your head between your knees, Shell,' he urged.

There was no sound from her, not a single grunt of protest, not a breath. The trees had become silent again, accusing; making him realize she was dead.

He laid her back exactly as he had found her, even curving the arm back over her face. Although he had begun to tremble violently, there was precision in his movements and a certain fussiness in the way he wiped himself down. A trail of saliva ran from her mouth. Derek backed away, stumbled and finally tore his eyes from her face. The anger resurfaced, blinding. After all this time, you bitch, and you do this to me; well, I'm not going to prison for you, Shell, I'm not, I'm not, I'm not.

On the way out of the park, he looked for the tramp. The man was sound asleep, exhausted by swimming lessons, lying curled up by the same gravestone, snoring with his thumb in his mouth. Could she have been with him? No, the thought was clearly out of the equation; whoever it was had more power than that and she hated the smell of stale sweat. Somehow the thought of that filthy digit, stuck in the man's mouth with a tongue wrapped round it revolted Derek more than anything else.

When, in the sweet light of dawn, he reported his girlfriend missing, his complaint was met with indifference. Girls go missing all the time; what's a late night stop out between friends? Can't go into every case where a sweetheart fails to phone home. When he explained that Ms Pelmore was a witness in a case against DS Ryan, who had been bothering her recently, the interest increased considerably, but he was still told to wait and see. Some hours later, well into the afternoon and after Shelley Pelmore had been found, conveniently placed for the mortuary, and the glad tidings had been announced on local radio, Todd was also informed that he had lost a major witness. But it was still late at night before anyone called at Ryan's door. Out of the ten-year-old mouth of his favourite babe came the lisping truth, before Mrs Ryan flung herself between the child and the enemy. No, Daddy was not in. He'd been out all last night, too. Silly Daddy, he was supposed to be digging them a pond.

Sally Smythe went to the Rape House at eight in the morning, scarcely refreshed by a day off in which she had resolutely refused to clean her own house. She resented the fact that, apart from anything else, the duties of dusting and checking supplies seemed to fall to her in the Rape House, these days, or maybe she had simply assumed them in the absence of Ryan, whose domesticity, fussiness, even, was surprising, especially since he confessed to being the opposite at home.

It was one of the things she liked about him, the fact that he did not wait for anyone else to wield the hoover, plump the cushions or make the bloody tea.

The key slipped into the lock with suspicious ease, the front door yielding without any of the customary shoving. Although two of the team were expected shortly with a woman found in the public lavs at St Pancras, claiming indecent assault, to her knowledge, no-one had been here for two days. Which was why she was early to air the place; but the familiar smell of summer stuffiness was notable by its absence. Sally stood in the hall with the door closed behind her and listened to the silence. Her footsteps on the dun-coloured carpet of the stairs sounded unfamiliar.

There was a bed slightly disturbed and remade; the immersion-heated water was still warm from recent heating; the bathroom looked as if someone had been busy enough to wipe every surface, leaving a residue of cleanser. None of the cleaners they used on an intermittent basis was ever so thorough. The only sign of neglect was the used tea bags in the kitchen bin. Someone had been here. The place retained the residual warmth of a body. Sally thought of Goldilocks and the three bears. Whoever it was had rearranged the packets of cereal which, along with the packets of soup, was all the sustenance there was.

A couple of the lads from the nick taking refuge after a late night out? She knew there were several duplicates of an easily available, easily copied Yale key. The subject had been discussed when they first got the place and some bright young spark had dossed down here; a repeat performance was forbidden on pain of death. Victims deserved an

environment free of stale male germs and beer breath; the
Rape House was not a billet for someone who found himself incapable of driving. And, in any event, Sally did not
imagine that any hungover intruders would have been able
to cover their tracks so precisely. This trespasser had gone
in for overkill: the place was cleaner now than when he
found it.

Ryan, she guessed; and even as she tried to shove that
thought aside, it became so much a certainty, she almost expected to see a calling card propped by the fridge with
apologies for depleting the supply of long-life milk. Why
Ryan, she argued? Because the body concerned had oiled
the lock and conducted a sort of loving maintenance as he
went along; perhaps he had nothing better to do. He had always had a kind of affection for the place which Sally did
not share; kept talking about wanting flowers in the backyard.

But even so, this behaviour was a kind of critical disrespect. How dare he? He was either taking her for a fool to
assume she would not notice, or he was putting her at risk
by assuming she would say nothing. It was an abuse of affectionate loyalty, whichever way she looked at it, as well as
an abuse of the purpose of this house. Angrily, she threw up
the blinds.

The phone rang. 'Coming round soon, Sal, OK? No-one
in a good mood, though. There's a hue and cry out for our
Ryan, would you believe. Shelley Pelmore's dead, and he's
jumped bail.' Sally stood with her back exposed to the window, gazing intently at the details of the bland river scene
on the wall. She could have said something then; she could
have put down the phone and got Bailey or Todd or whoever. Instead, she thought of Ryan, running, thought of him
with profound sorrow and said, 'Well there's a turn-up for

the books. Oh, by the way, the front door's finally buggered, I had a devil of a job getting in, I'll get someone to change the lock this morning, OK?'

Bailey was changing his mind even before getting dressed. This jacket or this shirt? As if anything would make a difference to the weather. It was unlike him to be so indecisive, or rise sooner than he need, or to be so fussy about clothes. Helen never quite knew how it was that Bailey's suits and shirts marshalled themselves into neat ranks inside the hanging space he had built to include an ironing-board flicked up by hand so that a shirt could almost iron itself unaided. Her own wardrobe was a jungle; the choice of clothes made largely on the random basis of which were nearest and which were clean. Rose said clothes hung themselves free of creases automatically on a figure like Helen's and it was just as well. Helen was sitting up in his vast bed, watching him fuss around in the striped towelling robe she had bought him. She preferred its vibrant colours to his suits.

'Come here,' she said softly. 'Please.'

He did as he was told, half waiting to be asked, and sat heavily. A grey morning, she noticed. She put her arms round him, her chin on his shoulder.

'Begin at the beginning,' she said. 'I do like you an awful lot, you know. Even more when you talk to me.'

'What time is it?'

'You know very well what time it is. Early. Far too early for work.'

He was always like this, wanting to talk and wanting someone to force him to do it. Sometimes she had to take advantage of him in the early mornings.

'Ryan had a file,' Bailey said. 'If we'd searched his house, we might have found the duplicate, but we didn't, although Todd will sure as hell search his house now. The file's on the disk anyway. It was all no-hope fantasists who came in with weird stories about men they wouldn't, couldn't name, plus witnesses who couldn't help. I thought our Ryan might be keeping a book of screwball women who might not mind being screwed and could never give reliable information afterwards. There's a central register. You're only allowed so many spurious rape allegations before someone puts a question mark against your name. He was never fussy about type, Ryan; liked 'em all, in his way, but I didn't think he'd be so desperate. Although you never know. You never really know anyone.'

He slid in beside her and pulled the duvet up to his chest.

'But, if he was keeping the file for that, why keep the complaints of two women who died soon after he saw them? Unknown causes; heart attacks. Both pregnant. As indeed, it seems, was little Shelley Pelmore. Todd's flummoxed; and furious, which is why he phones me all day. Why I've got to help him nail the bastard.'

'Which bastard?'

'Ryan, the fool. For playing this so close to his chest. For fantasizing himself. Oh, I know he got his fingers burnt for even suggesting there might be a link between a few scared, confused, guilt-ridden women, where the method of attack described has no common denominator at all except for a total lack of forensic evidence on their persons. No semen, no fibres. He's either in their homes by some kind of invitation, in which case he brings flowers and chocolates, or, in the case of the younger three, showing a penchant for the great outdoors, or his car, also by invitation. No injury. A man they already know? Met in a club, says one kid; came to my house, says another. And the last recipient of chocolates and flowers says he has fine eyes. Well, according to fiction and anyone old enough for James Bond movies, creepy villains with great sexual potency and black cats always have mesmeric eyes. Personally, I think Sally Smythe has gone mad, too. And to think this was a man I trained.'

'Trained, not only in the systematic forms of investigation, but also the empirical,' Helen said.

'Not that empirical. You can bounce things off a wall, but only if you've got something to throw. Yes, I could kill him and I know he could have killed her; Shelley, I mean. He's capable of violence. More than one kind.'

He swung himself off the bed.

'Which is why I want to find him. I'm his best chance. The preliminaries show that Shelley, too, died of unknown causes. There was pressure on the neck, but it didn't kill her. Oddly enough, old Ryan had been asking a pathologist about how to cause death without trace, but that's neither here nor there. There's nothing forensic to connect him, nothing else either, if only he'll show his face and say where the hell he was, they'll have to drop the rape. The witness is dead; long live the witness! I hope he was out on a bender.'

He sounded gleeful; Helen hated him. Hated that flash of triumph in him which came from a death. A girl dead, and him smiling about it, thinking of nothing but a grand reunion.

'The witness dead. No evidence. Ryan being discharged. That's all you care about,' she said flatly.

'Not quite.' He dropped a kiss on her forehead. It felt like ice.

'Your mate, getting away with it. At the risk of a cliché, what about truth?'

'Oh, that?' he said, putting on a shirt without further indecision, scarcely pausing about the business of socks, underpants, trousers; always able to dress with speed. 'That can wait.'

'What about the fact that Ryan could be a rapist, a murderer?'

'That can wait, too,' he said, equally flat, his movements slowing down, less decisive. 'Truth often has to wait.'

'You detested that girl without knowing anything about her, and now you behave as if you'd dance on her grave.'

'That's an exaggeration.'

'What about compassion, then? Can you spell it these days?' she taunted, furious. This was her bridegroom, date fixed for the wedding, tomorrow, behaving like an alien with alien loyalties, underlining all her own doubts and fears. Bailey was all at once both defensive and apologetic.

'There's an order to things, that's all,' he began, then looked at her and decided not to continue, shrugged instead. They both knew she would not listen. Helen crept back inside herself and watched him go. The day was not only dull, but suddenly cold.

White was a cold colour. White flowers reminded Anna of snow and Christmas roses, and white daisies in a white living-room were just a shade clinical, even with the curtains closed. Anna was about the work of creation; playing around in there with the curtains open, of course, because it seemed sinful to close them just yet, but trying at the same time to imagine the place after dark. She could wait until nine, she supposed, when the light slipped away, but that was too complicated. Greenery with the daisies and a light behind them would soften the effect; so would the colour of the curtains and the rich throws she had arranged over her old chairs, and the high polish of the table . . .

It had to be envisaged by night, because it was by night

he would be there. She thought of how the evenings were becoming shorter and regretted the fact that she had painted the walls white at all. She could have made a cosy little snug of this room. Gone hunting for cheap second-hand curtains; velvet, perhaps, from that man in the market who had them sometimes. She could have had deep-green drapes. Suddenly she resented her own imagination and its shallow priorities. She had relinquished her vocation for the sake of this house and there were many days when she had thought she would sell her soul for the sake of going to a big department store and buying exactly what she wanted to beautify it, like Helen West had done, instead of the endless thrift required to achieve harmony. She chided herself for that ambition, too; having more money and choice would make no difference and would diminish the pride she had taken in her bargain hunting. Why would more money make any difference? The vast increase in her salary which had come from working in a private clinic had not made her happy either. As a substitute for a lover and a child, her obsession with this little house and large mortgage did not work. It was simply hiding a vacuum.

No, not daisies. Too cheerful and no scent. Something more fragrant was needed.

She had been smiling at him recently, exchanging the odd wry remark, and he had been reciprocating, convinced, of course, that all was forgiven and forgotten. If she sidled up to him and said, look, I'm cooking dinner tonight, why don't you come and share it? she was fairly sure he would say yes. He liked to be liked; he would want his reacceptance into the circle of her approval confirmed; he might not dare say no. Of course, a simpler form of revenge might be to poison his food, or indeed try to undermine his reputation, but she knew she was far too small fry to do that without her attempts being counterproductive. He would sail away and she would be sacked and branded as spiteful. No, this was the only way. It was not enough to injure him. He had to be humiliated and exposed and put on record. Anna's conscience was clear on that front; after all, the advice had come from a lawyer. The only way you'll get your own back, Helen West had said, laughingly, is to make him do it again.

Roses then, in that corner; deep-red blooms if she could get them. And she would not promise seafood, although he had told her he liked it, because the cooking of fish made such a smell.

Anna shook herself. She had become used to lying.

She remembered the ice, the worst aspect of all; ice touching neck of cervix and being welcomed as if to douse the heat. That was the humiliation which cried out for revenge, because that was what he did. He made the body lose control and take convulsive pleasure in itself, whatever the mind did.

And a nagging concern, which may have been jealousy, because the last name she had seen him extract from the records was gorgeous little Rose.

chapter eleven

'If the intercourse was with a woman of weak intellect, incapable of distinguishing right from wrong, and the jury found she was incapable of giving consent, or of exercising any judgement upon the matter, and that (though she made no resistance) the defendant had sexual intercourse with her by force and without her consent, that is a rape . . . however, it was afterwards held that the mere fact of intercourse with an idiot girl, who was a fully developed woman, who was capable of recognizing and describing the defendant, and who, notwithstanding her imbecile condition, might have strong instincts, was not sufficient evidence of rape to be left to a jury . . .'

'None of them have intellect! None of us has the kind of intellect which can prevail above need!'

He wrote on paper, the screen abandoned, knowing he should throw away this paper afterwards. His long slender fingers, unusual for an artist or surgeon, touched the vase by the desk and he did not know whether he was exhilarated or sad.

'Girls who are afraid of getting pregnant will nevertheless do a number of bizarre things in search of thrills,' he wrote. 'They are very willing to experiment, especially if they feel their experience leaves them behind their peers. So are those whose knowledge of sexual congress is nothing but a selfish coupling designed for the emission of seed and restoration of relative good humour of the male, usually an inarticulate young man who *has never studied anatomy or physiology and considers that his greatest suffering to date is an unalleviated erection in tight trousers. Such a boy does not know the good fortune involved in this kind of discomfort. He does not know what real pain is.'*

This was not part of the history he was writing, but he wrote it anyway.

'Despite disappointment,' he wrote, 'all young and youngish women are best approached in their secretory phase — immediately after ovulation — when they produce progesterone and, under the influence of this aggressive hormone, also a delicate watery mucus from the cervical glands. Progesterone production prevails for the first three months of pregnancy . . .'

He put down the pen, flushed with pity.

What chance has human nature against a cycle as relentless as this? Progesterone makes for imbeciles. The balance of the mind is disturbed; the body fair aching with desire, most easily pleasured. What price is free will to an empty womb which does not know it is empty for a purpose?

Sadness prevailed over exhilaration. It was the first time he had killed with such effortless proficiency, but there was no pride in it. Numbness and horror; more when he felt in his pockets and could not find the syringe, and then there was a moment of sheer panic.

There it was again: the wrong fear of the wrong kind of retribution, and then the old and crippling desire to be loved, coming back with a force so strong he took the empty vase and threw it.

He was weary of this game. Sick of it.

Even if there was another candidate waiting in the wings. Sweet little Rose Darvey, marrying a clod of a policeman with whom she already quarrelled, soon, no doubt, to reach a stage of bitter discontent; as slender as Shelley; as sexual. With a background devoid of love.

And also, Anna. Who forgave him, although there was nothing to forgive. She accepted what he was.
Maybe, after all this, there was redemption.

I used to believe in the redeeming power of love, Helen West told herself, but now I'm not so sure. Maybe it's only suitable for those capable of redemption.

First undertones of autumn. A smattering of leaves on the window-ledge, dessicated by the dry heat, carried a long distance, looking burnt and almost tropical. An ominous strength in the warm breeze.

Perhaps it had been a mistake to encourage Bailey to speak his mind if she was going to so dislike the result. Honesty was often death to harmony. He had been so disgustingly jubilant, a boy let off the hook of anxiety because his little friend was not going to get smacked. Going out of the house wearing a loud tie which suggested premature celebration, perhaps limbering up to the prospect of an interview which could be fixed. She could imagine how it would go. Where were you, the night before last, DS Ryan? Out finding a new way of making a witness have a heart attack by a little playful strangulation? What every boy does from time to time? No, sir; nothing of the kind. I was out and about in the business of my own defence against this heinous charge. Taking a break in order to get drunk with A, B and C, all of whom will stand alibi to squash any suggestion that I might rape or terrorize some poor little wench who once trusted me. Happens all the time, sir. Honestly, all I did was breach the conditions of my bail. Slap my wrist.

Helen could not concentrate. She looked at today's set of papers. A case with the usual qualified hope of whatever it was they called success, as if imprisonment was success.

The best level of success in a rape case was the victim being believed; and then believed to the extent that there was no room for the jury to be distracted by sympathy for the accused. She was sick of this kind of Russian roulette. One sought a confirmation in the mind of the victim that she had not deserved this violation, without the whole process of law making the nightmare worse. *'Any penetration is sufficient . . .'* At the moment, Helen felt that a kiss from Bailey would feel like a bruise. Intimacy with a stranger she was supposed to marry tomorrow, who did not care about truth, only about his brutal little friend.

In the present case, as Redwood would say, the evidence was sound. With injuries like that, there was no question of consent and that was all which need concern her. Mary and John, whoever they were; their careers; their future life, were not hers to record. She judged the lives of others on the episodes she read; on evidence of misspent passion; love, turning first to disapproval, then to hate. She only evaluated them on a reasonable prospect of conviction.

Helen loved Bailey with reservations. Bailey loved Ryan to the extinction of conscience. Yes, she preferred to know people only on paper. And she knew this angry litany of accusations against Bailey was unfair. He was not the only one tainted with hypocrisy. She was fuelling her own cowardice by blaming him for something. Anything would have done to excuse the fact that when she thought of marriage her feet were cold.

'I do not judge the living, I simply dissect the dead,' Dr Webb told them. 'But I liked your Mr Ryan. He said he was writing a thesis. Such a need for certainty.'

'The hell he was writing a thesis.'

Todd's ruddy complexion was pale with irritation. There

was a sheen to his skin which might have been sweat or the rain, a half-hearted drizzle which dampened the hair and clung to clothes. They stood outside the mortuary, Bailey smoking, apparently nonchalant, impervious to the damp which the brown grass of the park drank greedily. If he looked at the grass long enough, he was sure he would see it change colour.

'Amazing,' said Todd. 'Absolutely bloody amazing that he should be asking you about how to kill women without trace and then one of them's found dead, on your doorstep, of a bloody heart attack.'

'Complete cardiac and respiratory failure. That was the cause. There is nothing to indicate that this death had anything to do with Mr Ryan's research. It's unusual, sure, for a healthy woman to die with such spontaneity, but not unknown. Strange things happen in pregnancy.'

'But he tried to throttle her,' Todd snapped. 'Someone tried, but not very hard. And, as far as I can tell at this stage, she was already dead. Too late for the skin to bruise; she was already turning white and blue; she hadn't tried to defend herself. No, she just lay down in the park and went to sleep. No level on drink or drugs yet, maybe she took some pills. If there was a combination, well, who knows? Death by misadventure. I don't know about fibres and other stuff; nothing I could see.'

'He had to do it,' Todd fumed, talking to himself. Dr Webb stood back from him, Bailey noticed, looking at him as if he was a specimen on a slab, her posture revealing a mild dislike, but then Todd had this way of standing too close. An habitual invader of private space, as if he wanted everyone to share his flowery aftershave, worn as a precaution against mortuary smells.

'He knew all about it,' Todd said stubbornly.

'All about what? About an air embolism being fatal?' She was becoming irritated, felt that both men had her standing out here in order to make her accuse on evidence not yet gathered, purely to give them some sense of direction where there was none. They weren't even the officers investigating the death which she had not even called homicide.

'Look, an air embolism is fatal, but I do not know if one existed. And what do you think he would have to do to create it? Put a straw up her nose? A long blow-job?'

Todd sniggered. Nerves and embarrassment.

'Getting a quantity of air into a woman isn't easy. It has to get into her bloodstream. An injection would be best. Giving an injection isn't easy, either. How would your nice Mr Ryan know how to do that without leaving a needle mark?'

Bailey was silent; Todd sulky.

'But the fact he asked you . . .' he began, wagging his finger, hectoring, so that she stepped back even further.

'Means what? He first asked me about his thesis four months ago. Someone he knew, someone who'd complained of an attack, died mysteriously. Set him off thinking, he said, but he was slow to learn. Needed everything repeating.' Like you, she might have added, but refrained.

'Where is he?' Todd muttered darkly. 'Where the hell *is* he?'

Bailey thought of the Rape House and held his tongue. The rain fell harder as he looked downhill towards the traffic. He saw a man huddled by a gravestone, pulling his sweater up round his ears.

Ryan could live like that; Ryan could live in a phone booth. Ryan could be the perfect chameleon, changing colour with the landscape.

I never knew you, Bailey thought to himself. I never really knew you at all. He turned to Dr Webb, smiling his cadaverous smile.

'To kill a woman without trace, Doctor, would take some skill, wouldn't it?'

She looked at him with scarcely more approval than she had granted to Todd. They were both imbeciles, one slightly better than the other.

'Yes.'

'Medical skill?'

What did he think she meant? The skill of an engineer?

'Maybe a plumber,' she said. 'A medical plumber.'

That was what they all were, Anna Stirland thought as she tidied the third surgery, aligning the instruments in order, wiping the padded examination table with antiseptic and then putting a new sheet of paper over the top. Sensitive technicians in human tubing. The idea was to make them feel that internal examination was no more than having in the plumber to take a quick look at the drains, and all this was going to be as relaxing as half an hour on a sunbed, although rather more expensive. No prescriptions without examination, no surgery without express permission, sympathy unlimited, but absolutely nothing doing at all without money up front. The voice of the receptionist, asking how miss or madam would like to pay, writing down a credit card number like one transcribing a precious secret, was only as dulcet as her own, asking, Are you sure this is what you want to do? It's only a little scrape, dear. Oh, hallo, Miss Smith. Are you back again? How odd it was that even women in extremes of anxiety were prone to fall in love with the doctor and ignore the nurse. How odd it was that such a variety of people came here, even those whose general practitioners offered free access to advice and treatment they could otherwise ill afford. Ah, but there was something about payment which was supposed to guarantee quality and safety, discretion and soft, soft hands. Of course, one would have to pay for a clinic which offered such individual attention and such comprehensive appreciation of the whole female psyche. From the waist down.

Of course they did good, she argued with herself; they helped women avoid the ruination of their own lives. And they gave one doctor a playground.

Anna often fancied she could hear the echo of a baby crying in the murmuring quiet of this place.

She scrunched the used paper from the couch and put it into a sealed bin. A nice little girl, the one who had left, happy with her cap and happy with her life, and, like most of them, squeaky clean for her visit. If only they would not wear perfume, as if embarrassed by any possibility of their own smell. Clean underwear for the doctor, as if this was a brand-new date, and no thought about how he might be allergic to their artificial scent while being immune to what was natural. No, that little girl with her steady relationship and determined control over her own future would not be one the good doctor would choose.

It would be someone like Brigid Connor, Anna surmised. Someone who came in full of fear, who would have worn a paper bag over her head if she could, because the mere fact of begging a doctor to find something wrong with her, and then pleading for the means to avoid a late and dreaded pregnancy, was so obviously wicked that she had shaken with the fear of it. That was the type of person.

Anna told herself she only wanted to know what he was

doing. Why it was he accessed certain personal details from the confidential records again and again, preferring the ones he had treated with conspicuous tenderness. Why he could continue to express such interest in the insecure, sometimes the downright ugly, and then treat her as he had.

Passing down a long corridor, footsteps silent on the carpeted floor, she paused to nip a bud from a plant. She took a deep breath, knocked and assembled a brilliant smile. 'Tonight OK, then?' was all she would ask. And he would say, 'Yes, fine.'

Her house would be bursting with flowers. The window-boxes she was creating for Rose were beginning to flourish in the backyard.

Rose stood by the office door, pulling faces at Helen's back. She had said hallo twice to no response. Miss West gazed through the window and there was a suspicious smell of cigarette smoke. 'Tut, tut, tut,' Rose said loudly; Redwood would never forgive that. Major disaster, perhaps; general cock-ups in the administration of justice; poor timekeeping; innocent souls languishing in prison; cases lost by negligence; anything which would not easily be found out, but an infringement of the clear-desk and no-smoking policies was certainly a hanging offence.

'Wake up, Helen, there's a good girl. Oh, what are they doing now?' The occupants of the office over the road never failed to cause amusement. It was like watching a video without the sound; trying to decode the body language from a distance of twenty metres and through two panes of glass. Once they had all seen a fight and since then Rose and Helen watched all the time. Nothing quite as exciting had happened since, forcing Rose to invent a situation of seething rivalry between two men in suits lorded over by a lady of large size, indeterminate years and sultry authority.

'She's putting on weight again,' Rose said, pointing. 'Shame, after she was doing so well on that diet. All those apples. She'll have to stop pigging out at lunchtime. Hamburger and chips, I've seen. What's the matter? Speak to me. I've brought you a memo.'

'Great. Do you suppose someone has given her a memo about her weight and that's why she hasn't spoken to anyone all afternoon? That one at the other end, for instance? The one who could be Redwood's cousin?'

Rose peered. 'Oh, yeah, for sure. He looks the type. They could do with a few plants over there. It always looks like an open-plan greenhouse recently visited by locusts. Oh, and I bought you some flowers to go with the memo, in case Redwood forgot; you know what he's like.'

A small and delicate bunch of freesias landed, without ceremony, on the crowded desk.

'Thanks,' said Helen, touched and, only as an afterthought, suspicious. 'What have I done to deserve this?'

'Nothing,' Rose said carelessly, running fingers through the spikes of her hair. 'Only I heard on the Michael grapevine about everyone being out looking for that bastard Ryan. They all had it in this morning's briefings. I didn't think it was the kind of news which would be making for a happy atmosphere at home, that's all.'

'No,' said Helen. 'It won't.'

She yawned and stretched. The scent of the flowers drifted upon her and she had a sudden and inexplicable urge to cry. Any act of kindness could have that effect, but she rallied since there was no point in public tearfulness if she could not explain it and she knew she did not want to make the attempt.

'So what does the memo say?'

Rose shrugged and offered a chewy peppermint, her panacea for all office ills.

'Reorganization. Again. Me to go to outer Mongolia and you to go to Special Casework. Extradition, forgery, counterfeiting, a lot of it about. No more rape.'

'That'll be the day,' Helen said. 'Which part of outer Mongolia?'

'Camberwell Green. He told me he thinks you're bad for me.'

This time, the urge to cry was becoming real.

'Maybe he just thinks rape isn't good for either of us.'

'C'mon, Helen. It isn't good for anyone.'

The afternoon was thunderously dark, the rain gentle and relentless.

Rain filled the pond which Ryan had dug in his garden and lined with polythene before leaving it incomplete. Mary Ryan, along with the youngest child, who was wearing bright-red wellington boots, both threw clods of earth into the hole which had been designed for exotic fish and now resembled nothing more than an overlarge puddle. The child whooped with delight; Daddy might as well have made him a scarecrow or a makeshift coconut shy, or simply have given him something to smash or throw things at. And where was Daddy now? And why had the house been turned upside down? All a game, darling; Daddy's lost his cheque book and these friends of his are trying to find it. And Mummy isn't saying anything about the note which Daddy left, which she destroyed not because it told her to do so but because it made her incoherent with anger. 'Got to go,' it said. 'Things to do, or we'll never get this sorted . . . can't explain more, yet.' As if he had ever explained anything at all. No, please believe me, I love you etc., not that sentimental words or promises loomed large in their relationship, but there were points like this when she might have clung to any endearment or plea for help. So she had stood by, mutinous, unco-operative and monosyllabic while the house was searched, only vaguely grateful for the fact that her status as a detective's wife, even one charged with rape and suspected of worse, meant that they were tidier and more considerate than they might have been. She remembered his tales, told with glee when he was a younger man, of how easy it was to trash a house when some guilty thief had flown. The only other saving grace was the absence of Bailey from the grim-faced number. She would have hit him with a hammer.

'Time to go indoors, love. We're soaked through.'

The child was too old to be playing such childish games. Retrograde behaviour, like her own in stuffing her face with chocolate and making herself feel sick. Maybe Ryan had dug the hole for the pond as a place to bury himself. She wished he had.

Then she looked at his flowers, the shrubs, the blooms, the riot of colour which had been his creation. In the damp air of the early evening, she tried to convince herself that he was incapable of savagery, but she could not. The only things Ryan loved were plants and children: growing things. Women were never in the same league.

Women could be stupid, but only as stupid as men. Stupidity was the place of last resort and Helen knew she had reached it when she found herself calling herself a silly bitch and then correcting the description to say – on the top deck of the bus, watching as the rain ceased and a sky appeared, purple as a fresh bruise – that although she merited the description of silly, giddy, irrational from time to time, it wasn't a constant state of being and, try as she might, she was not what she herself would call a bitch. A female dog was never, as far as she knew, accredited with anything more malicious than a habit of fighting with a competitor when under the influence of hormones, and then fighting twice as hard to protect her young. It wasn't such a bad thing to be a bitch. Silly bitch was nothing more than a description for a kind of giddiness, a lack of steadiness in the head, an imbalance of vanity against reality, the optimism of prettiness against the ugliness of age and so on. It was Bailey who loved the Oxford English dictionary, with its definitions of so many words which had become, essentially, so bloody meaningless. Like 'bloody', for instance. A word removed to the fringe of language, by misuse.

Helen got indoors, with the sky still purple, and set about the task of clearing up the kitchen debris, working to some mental calendar which told her rubbish was collected tomorrow. The desire to weep for no particular reason other than a universal sense of failure was still prevalent.

After a cursory rummage round, the sink was clear and the rubbish sack in the bin underneath was far too full. She rammed it down with force, trying to be deliberate. The second finger on her right hand shoved itself against the rim of the chicken soup can of the day before yesterday, standing proud with its nasty serrated rim. What a lot of blood, she thought bleakly; what an awful lot for such a pedestrian accident, and what a very distinctive, unmistakeable colour fresh blood has. She was running her finger under the tap at the time, wondering if traces of chicken soup could be infectious, condemning herself for choosing the kind of sustenance so bland to the taste and yet with a container so malicious. She was thinking, too, about whether the disablement of this little digit could stop her holding a cigarette for ever. The desire to cry was ever stronger.

She moved her finger from the kitchen sink, swathed it in layers of kitchen towel and still it bled. On the floor, in the sink, wherever she tried to keep it out of harm's way, it bled. She managed to avoid drops on the carpet, but any admonition to her finger did nothing more than make it spout blood even faster. She held it above her head, like a trophy, wrapped in kitchen towel and still it bled. The Elastoplast was somewhere, she forgot where, inaccessible. Finally, she went into the garden. Blood was surely good for the soil.

The rain had stopped, but the sky had turned from purple to a bleak grey.

Signs of neglect out here, Helen remarked to herself, crossing her hands across her chest. Anna Stirland said you had a care of your plants if you could stop them throttling one another. Which, revived by rain, they were about the business of doing; she imagined she could see them moving, the whole thing a jungle, praying for attention, made aggressive by nourishment.

Gloves, then; let the finger bleed inside the sleeve of her stiff gardening gloves, hanging by the door, awaiting a mood like this, when care and control of the garden seemed more important than anything, if only as a substitute for control over her own life. Nothing hurt when she worked in the garden; she would surprise herself later with the discovery of unconsciously acquired scratches on arms, legs and torso, regarding them proudly as symbols of the fact that, though she might not be an expert, something in this small wilderness had received the benefit of her energy.

There was a school playground on the other side of the high wall which bounded the back of Helen's garden and made it so private. She liked the presence of the children she never saw, although on days at home she heard the raucous playground screams, always amazed at the sheer exuberance of their noise and the deafening nature of the quiet which followed. Remembering now, as it grew dark and silent around her, how long it had taken to feel safe in this garden. She pulled at the convolvulus which made the ivy look shaggy, tore at it as if it was a real enemy and, as the pile of weedy rubbish grew on the grass, she felt the beginnings of satisfaction. The dark grew gently deeper, summer dusk turning inky black, so that soon the only light spilt from the kitchen window and it was silly to go on. Helen paused, thirsty, and turned to go indoors.

It was then she saw a figure crossing the patch of light, disappearing into the shadows. Her elderly cat had died in the spring and its presence haunted her still, but she knew it was not the cat, or any ghost. She was suddenly engulfed with a fear which was at once strange and yet appallingly familiar. There was more than one kind of ghost in this garden. Bailey would not joke like this; he knew her fears and respected them, but all the same she called his name, her voice quavering uncertainly.

'Bailey? That you?'

Silence. The tree which shrouded the corner seemed to sigh, shuffling a full head of leaves and loosening the very last of the rain. The scrape of a shoe on stone.

It was a small garden by country standards, large in urban terms, but now it felt enormous, the distance be-

tween herself and the back door the length of a long mine-
field. She stumbled in her headlong run to the rectangle of
light which represented safety, her glove skidding against
the rough surface of the wall, her hair flicking into her eyes,
all of her sick with fear. Falling into his arms.

There were lights from the upstairs windows of the
houses on either side, their promise a mockery. Her scream
ascended unheeded as she had known it would; she was in
the midst of a crowded street and it made no difference.
The creature who twisted her body round so that he held
her neck and clamped a dirty hand over her mouth might
as well have been holding her over a cliff on a shoreline devoid of humanity for all the help she could summon.

'Shut up,' he snarled. 'Shut *up*.'

She nodded her head, let her body go limp. The hand
moved from her mouth to her throat, his other arm pinion-
ing her round the waist, pressing her against his groin.

'Lovely Miss West,' his voice murmured. 'And you never
knew I cared.'

She could feel his penis stir against the soft flesh of her
buttocks; his palm strayed to brush across her breast and a
deep shudder passed through her. Then she began to tremble.

'Obviously mutual,' the voice continued. 'Always knew
you fancied me rotten. Shall we go inside, love? Get ourselves comfy, eh?'

It was Todd who kept stating his wonderment about how
Ryan could disappear, repeating himself stupidly without
thinking about what he was saying. Bailey had no such confusion and he was bored of listening to the ramblings of
frustration. Despite his years as an officer, Todd had never
somehow taken to the streets; he had formed no affiliations

there and still could not understand how a man like Ryan, who had so often failed to make his own way home in the evening, could remain at large now. Bailey thought the quickest way to flush him out would be to stop his credit cards; let him play cat and mouse if he would; he himself was tired of the game and angry with Ryan for prolonging it.

'I feel sorry for the boyfriend,' Todd said, nursing his pint like someone slightly afraid of it, sitting there in the uncomfortable company of Bailey, guilty for being in a pub at all, but knowing he would feel guiltier if he simply gave up. He was like a dog gnawing at a bone, turning it over with one paw and chewing the other end. If he had been Ryan, he would have given up on the subject long before now and gone on to his summer holidays.

'He seemed a decent bloke,' Todd went on.

'He probably is,' Bailey agreed, recalling a lad with a large ever-mobile Adam's apple and eyes full of tears, whose stress he had thought owed as much to fear as to grief. Eyes darting everywhere whenever they forgot to maintain a self-consciously sincere contact with those of his interlocutors. Lying about something, Bailey thought; the boy was suspiciously relieved to have it stressed that his dearly beloved had not died of strangulation, and even more suspiciously confused and angry to learn there had been no signs of sexual attack. Then he had cried. Bailey had disliked him even more than the manageress in the shop where Shelley Pelmore worked: a bitch from hell, who, even in the midst of genuine shock and tears, remembered to flirt. Bailey had failed to tell Todd that after this pint he was going back to see her.

'Did I hear tell you were getting married?' Todd was

asking, trying too late in the day to be conversational. 'A triumph of hope over experience, is it?'

Only Ryan was allowed to tease and Bailey could feel himself about to snap, until he realized it had slipped his mind. Slipped? The thought of marriage had sunk like a stone. When was it? Next week? Tomorrow? Christ, tomorrow. Perhaps, after all, he was already married; to Ryan. Go home, Todd, he urged silently. Go home and let me get on.

'What? Oh. Yes.' Tomorrow. Jesus wept. 'Excuse me a minute, will you? I've just got to go and phone her. She does like to know when I'm going to be late.' Todd nodded, with an understanding smirk which made Bailey cringe.

Bailey dialled, drumming his fingers on the shelf inside the booth. Perhaps there was something to be said for mobile phones; they would be mandatory soon for him, just like a radio for every beat copper, and then they could all stand around on street corners in common with half of the population, yelling at one another like lunatics. She answered after interminable ringing. Bailey imagined her out in the garden, or ironing a garment. Doing something frivolous and feminine, the way he secretly liked to imagine her, such as lying in a scented bath, with her tan-coloured skin turning pink.

'Look,' he said, before she could even say hallo. 'You haven't forgotten, have you?'

There was a long pause, laboured breathing.

'Forgotten what?'

'Wedding,' he said tersely. 'I'm sorry, I was so . . . brisk this morning.'

'Have you found Ryan?' she asked.

'No.'

'What a pity. I expect he's closer to home than anyone imagines.'

Her voice was high; then she seemed to explode in a fit of coughing, ending as if she had been thumped on the back. There had been no coughing this morning, not that he recalled.

'I don't want to talk about Ryan. I've had it up to here with Ryan . . .'

'. . . But he's very close to you, I'm sure he is . . .'

Her voice was now so strained, it sounded almost as if she was trying to swallow. Choking on something, possibly laughter.

'Listen, love, are you ready for this? Ryan doesn't matter as much as us. Eleven-thirty in the morning. Don't be late, will you?'

Again, he allowed himself that fond imagination of Helen peacefully at home, sorting out her special-occasion wardrobe. He loved her clothes and the way she wore them. Then he heard the sound of clinking glass; a voice, which could only have been Helen's, turned sideways to the phone, saying shush. Then a male voice, very close, whispering, and the sound of smothered laughter. A cork being pulled from a bottle.

He could feel a sensation like a mild electric shock, then a feeling of despair. Shame on her, Helen drinking for Dutch courage. Finding someone else for reassurance? That was it, then. Hadn't he always known there was a risk, a big risk that she would run away from commitment to him in the end, that marriage terrified her, and that his middle-class, professionally qualified, passionate but cool-as-ice Helen would decide she could do better than him and find someone her own class would approve?

'Bailey?' She seemed lost for words. It was only ever guilt which made her speechless.

'Look,' he said wearily. 'It's up to you, isn't it? I could call round later, only . . .'

'Not *later*,' she spat, then fell silent. Bailey could not think of a single thing to say. On the other end of the line, he could hear someone whistling in the background. Someone thoroughly relaxed in her house. Slowly, he replaced the receiver, unable to listen.

'You look so glamorous in those gloves,' Detective Sergeant Ryan remarked. 'So why doesn't a smart woman like you change into gardening clothes before she stoops to do the garden? I always do, myself.' Helen looked down at herself. The gloved hands were folded in her lap; they had made it awkward to hold the phone. She sat in the least comfortable of the kitchen chairs by the window, noticing, at his prompting, the dirt on her workday skirt and blouse, thinking, yes, perhaps she would be an all-round better person if she remembered to change her clothes before making an onslaught on the garden, and surely Bailey would know there was something wrong. Don't come *later*, come sooner. Feel concern for my cough. Wonder why I mention Ryan.

Ryan took the phone off the hook.

'Just in case he phones back, eh? Then he can think you're cosily engaged.'

'Why did you make him think someone was here?' she asked.

'I didn't make him think anything,' he said. 'I just told you to get rid of him before I hurt you and also because, if he comes round here, I'll kill him. Only he won't. If he thinks there's someone else here, he'll simply go into a state of shock. Not a jealous fellow, Bailey, just in a state of constant dread. He doesn't deserve you, you know,' he added, mimicking her voice. 'Oh no, never did.'

He took a swig from a tumbler of whisky; she looked at him with a mixture of amazement and contempt, shivering at the memory of his body pressed against hers. She noted the growth of beard, the training shoes, and felt strangely resigned now that she had spoken to Bailey, scarcely caring at that particular moment about the carving knife which glinted on top of the fridge, well out of her reach, but easily within Ryan's. She pulled at the gloves; the one on her right hand was firmly stuck; she tugged at it, grimacing, releasing it from her fingers, letting both gloves drop on the floor. Her hands felt light and cool; she pushed her hair away from her face, a small attempt to make herself tidier than she was, a minute effort in the difficult exercise of self-control. Ryan's eyes suddenly widened; she shrank from him in alarm. This was the moment, then; this was when the rapist would go berserk.

'Christ, Helen, I didn't do that, did I? Oh God, did I do that?'

She had put her hand to her face, the first gesture of self-protection, noticed that it was covered in dried blood and fresh blood oozed from the injured finger.

'For God's sake,' he said, dragging her towards the sink by the wrist. 'Put it under the cold tap, you silly bitch.'

Always some act of kindness which did it.

Made her cry.

chapter twelve

Perhaps I could love someone. Perhaps they could love me. Perhaps what has happened to me is all a figment of my imagination.

Perhaps I did love her. Little Shelley, who wanted the thrills, the decadence, the dirt. Or perhaps my current sombre mood is a reaction to murder.

But she consented, even to that. It was not submission; it was consent.

Women have such a capacity for forgiveness. Perhaps it is not too late for me. The love of a good woman.

I must not do this . . . now I have perfected it, my own power terrifies me, and it will corrupt. My hands itch to hold the implement, insert it between soft lips . . . nothing but the air we breathe . . .

Her life would have been wretched anyway. She would have made it wretched because she was far too afraid to change it.

Maybe it's not too late for me.

I could always try again. I could try and see if love redeems me. Redeems my flesh, and blood.

* * *

The blood ran away under the tap. She gazed at it, mesmerized, watching the pale pink of the water.

'Should probably have a stitch,' Ryan said. 'But a plaster would do. In the bathroom, are they?'

The bathroom was down the hall; the exit door next to the kitchen. She nodded, but he caught the enthusiasm of the nod and shook his head sadly.

'I'm not going to fall for that one, am I? You don't know where the hell they are. Women without children never do. Have kids, you get used to the sight of blood. Here, don't be a cry-baby.'

'I'm not a baby. I'm not.'

He grunted, doing a passable job with more papertowel and an elastic band from a dish which held assorted letters, paperclips, vouchers and bills. Then he seemed calmer. Shoved her back into her chair and sat opposite.

'Now you can get drunk if you like. Here.'

He had found a bottle of the heavy red wine she had been keeping for winter. In other circumstances she would have loved the sound of the cork. She thought of the damage a violent man could do with a corkscrew, such as gouging out an eye, making scoremarks in skin. The wine was a warm claret; the first sip sat like a sour sponge on her dry tongue in the damp heat of the early night and yet tasted like nectar. There was more rain on the way; she could feel it gathering; the kitchen was stuffy. As if reading her thoughts, he stood and pulled down the window, letting in the air. She imagined the front of her flat from the road, unlit and empty; a basement where no-one was home. She had reached a state of subdued hysteria, preternaturally calm; the tears had dried to salt on her cheeks and she sipped the next mouthful as if she was someone standing on the edge of a party, trying to make her wine last and look busy at the same time.

'To what do I owe this pleasure?' she said. 'I mean a drink among friends is all very well, but I can't remember inviting you.'

'Must have slipped your mind,' Ryan said. 'Can't think how. Mind, I've been a touch difficult to find over the last thirty-six hours. Found a bed last night,' he leered. 'She chucked me out so I thought I'd better find another.'

Waiting in the back garden; getting into her house over the back wall from the playground, she thought; Ryan would know about that. She was hot and sweaty, conscious of her grubby clothes.

'We travelling rapists, see? We can't be picky, can we?'

She nodded and sipped a little more wine.

'Do you remember the first time I came in here? No, you don't. It was when that mad youth attacked you. I happened to be passing.'

'I've never forgotten,' she said slowly. 'I let you in. I leant on that entry-phone buzzer until I passed out.'

'And never liked me since,' he said.

'True.'

'I often wonder if you knew that he was deep dark in love with you, even then. Bailey, I mean. Perhaps you didn't.'

'No, I didn't. I only knew about my own reaction to him.'

'And I was taking a long route towards finding out that maybe my wife was the best woman in the world. Comparative studies, I think they call it.'

'You've a funny way of showing your feelings. She must be worried sick now.'

'What do you want me to do? Phone home? Hallo, wife, it's good to talk . . . be back after a rape or three . . . See ya . . . Look at me, Miss fucking West. Look at me.'

He seized her shoulders in a grip which would bruise. Calmly, she looked. She had faced men accused of rape, possibly murder, always with a barrage of fences between them. The dock, the courtroom barriers, her own protected space. This was a hard-edged face on a muscular man, handsome in an obvious and sexy way she had never found appealing, like the good looks of a football star. Capable of kindness to children and animals. She made herself think that he had the brown eyes of a cow. In response to the scrutiny he had invited, Ryan blushed. He touched the paper-clad finger and started to speak.

'No, I don't like you much. Nothing personal; I don't like lawyers much. And I don't like what you do to him. But I thought I'd bust in here, rather than down at Bailey's gaff, because you might believe me. Also, it's the last place he'd look and I don't want him finding me, yet. I don't like you, but you listen. Bailey does, sometimes. Responds to signals, know what I mean? But he's always got something else on his mind. Jumps from one thing to another. Got a mind like a series of traps; comes of doing too many things at once. I know what he'd say. You're off the hook, laddie, if you play it right. What more do you want: justice? Got a cigarette?' For an answer, he rifled her handbag, lit one for both of them.

'But you,' he said. 'You listen. You'll take a leap for the fucking truth. Obsessive about it, you are. Or something like it.'

'I prefer evidence,' she said.

'So do I, doll, so do fucking I.' And then, to her horror, he began to weep, a controlled weeping which meant that he kept his hand near the knife on the top of the fridge while his eyes filled with fat tears, rolling down his chiselled cheeks and making him look like a clown. Weeping made him dangerous but also ridiculous; she did not like to see him weep, although she could not feel an ounce of pity.

'I don't want to look like this for my wife, see? I don't want her looking at me and saying I'm crazy. Mad or bad, what's the difference? Only that little Shelley Pelmore; she told me a thing or two. Wife wouldn't believe. Nor would I, except . . .'

'I need some more,' Helen said, extending her glass. He sloshed wine.

'Start from the beginning,' she invited. Let him ramble while she stalled for time.

He took a deep shuddering breath, spoke almost dreamily. 'It all begins with girls. Women, girls bored with sex or romance. Either with difficult histories, abuse perhaps, or simply unrealistic expectations of the whole thing. Girls who dread pregnancy; disappointed girls; girls afraid of it. Girls who want sensation, not through drugs. Screwed-up girls. Girls like Shelley Pelmore: bored with life, dying for a kick. Or another kind of girl, who can't wait to get rid of innocence . . . hungry for a man . . .'

'Which all girls are, of course, is that it?' Helen asked, attempting to jeer. He looked at her, half amused.

'In my experience, most of them. Don't interrupt. Girls, women with unfulfilled sexual needs or bad sexual histories, fantasize about it. I've heard a lot of fantasies about men doing amazing things with bottles, with implements, with ice, making them beg . . . Only then I heard a series of fantasies, like that, but all featuring a bald man with wonderful eyes . . .'

Helen stared at him.

'He seduced, he humiliated, he played jokes, he corrupted. He corrupts. That's what he does: he corrupts. And in two cases, two of these confused women died soon after they'd made their confused complaints about a man who visited them at home. We'd listened to them and turned them out. No forensic, they wouldn't give us a name, but they were humiliated. Two died of natural causes – pregnant kids. Then there was Shelley Pelmore's friend, picked out of the gutter; unhurt, apart from what she'd done to herself; half dead with shock. Something happened to her; some sexual trauma, I don't know what.'

He stared into the dark garden.

'Know what I think? I think the greatest humiliation for a woman is sex they've somehow invited, willingly. They let themselves in for it, innocently, and while they know it's wrong, the body responds. And when the body has responded, then the shame becomes excruciating.' He coughed. Even to his mind, this was extra fanciful and he couldn't explain what he meant.

'And then there was wee Shelley herself, who wouldn't say anything for the record, but somehow wanted to boast about something or someone. She says I met her twice; in fact I met her more than that. She told me about the bald-headed man; she actually confirmed his existence; before that, I only had this odd unconvincing dossier on him. Shelley adored him, but she was afraid of him, teased me with bits of information about this demon lover who was, she said, "too good not to share". Shelley loved a kind of perversion; she'd persuaded a couple of her friends to try . . . she thought he'd made Becky come round the neck of a bottle. Wouldn't you like to know who he is? she'd say to me, and I'd say, yes I would, and what did he do to you last time? Once I'd got her a bit drunk, she'd tell me. He made me come against a park bench, she'd say. Used his dildo; used an icicle. They were conspirators of a kind, Shelley and him; she was proud of it, but she was afraid of him, too. She set me up for the rape to stop me looking for him. They planned it. I fell into the trap, oh, so neatly.'

He smiled, ashamed of himself. 'It was easy, you see. All this drink and dirty talk. I fancied her; I let her tease me; I wanted the information; I prolonged the quest for it, even though it was him I was after; I half enjoyed it. And I really did leave her in the pub. I forgot the jacket; I think she hid it behind a chair. And she could see I had fingernails full of soil from the garden. As if I'd been grubbing round in the park.' Helen did not entirely follow, then remembered.

'You must have hated her for that. If that's what she did.'

'Hated her? Oh yes. Oh yes. "Hated her" would be the understatement of the year.'

She wanted to ask, Enough to kill her? And if so, how? But it was his mention of the icicle which somehow seemed more important. Ryan was in a world of his own, continuing without prompting. He seemed to have forgotten the knife.

'I hated her a bit less after she'd called me at home. She was frightened and wanted to see me. I met her once, but she shilly-shallied about, wouldn't really talk. Then a second time, much the same, in the amusement arcade. Then I lost my temper, wanted to strangle her. She went off in a huff. I followed. That park, by the mortuary . . .'

'Where she was found?'

'Yup.'

'And?'

'I left her,' he said bitterly. 'I was hungry and angry and

I left her. I didn't think she'd be meeting him, but then I thought, shit, I bet she is. By the time I'd doubled back she was dead. And I thought, I'd better not go home.'

He paused. 'Such a pretty girl.'

He might think the place was home, decorated for Christmas, there were so many flowers. Anna thought perhaps she had overdone it. Once, twice or three times he had said how much he appreciated flowers; she had brought them to his desk. Snowdrops last winter, daffodils in March, never thinking then that there was something unconventional in a woman courting a man with flowers, as if she was being the male for both of them. She removed the lilies from the living-room; like the daisies they were too white and too much of a contrast to the roses. She wanted the room to have the atmosphere of a study rather than a boudoir; she was excited and he was late, and it was the excitement that bothered her most. Keep a clear head, she told herself; just one glass of this stuff. The champagne, not quite real; an Australian lookalike, which is what she thought he would expect from her, rather than the far more expensive real thing, sent flutters of trepidation through her abdomen. She felt she was full of air.

Bruises, bodily fluids: evidence. She had a dim idea of how to create the bruises by replicating kitchen accidents she had suffered in the past. If she left the back-cupboard door open and belted it with her hip, that gave a hefty bruise, as she already knew. There was the cabinet in the bathroom; she had once hit her head against the open door when straightening up from brushing her teeth and now always kept it closed. The bruise, complete with a graze in the middle of her forehead, had looked quite dramatic and had given rise to teasing from colleagues. That one would

have to be self-inflicted later; she couldn't meet him with a
face like a balloon; she was trying to seduce the man, for
God's sake. She caught sight of her face in the bathroom
mirror. Well, she murmured to herself, that won't do it. A
face to launch a million ships? This one wouldn't get a
rowing boat out onto the Thames, and why was she so in-
sanely cheerful? When the doorbell rang, she was composed, rehearsing words. Oh do come in, how nice to see
you and how good of you to call . . . the last words made her
put her hand across her mouth and stifle a crazy laugh. She
couldn't say such a thing, she really couldn't. She should go
downstairs to her door and open it with decorum, hoping
she didn't look overdressed or even faintly vampish with
the extra make up, but no perfume. The house was full of
it, from the flowers.

He rang again, and when, with suitable stateliness, she
let him in, she remembered to be casual.

'Sorry that took so long,' she said, smiling. 'I was out the
back, come and see.' He bowed from the waist, giving her a
glimpse of the top of his smooth head. There was nothing
better to get a man indoors and unwary than a kind of distracted friendliness. Nothing sinister about his examination
of Rose's evergreen window-boxes and a discussion of why,
after a downpour, the flowering shrubs grew crooked.
Good smells wafted from the kitchen. She chatted like a
starling; she knew she was amusing. Hope these clothes are
right, she thought. A pretty loose-weave top over an uphol-
stered bosom, multi-coloured skirt almost to the ankles,
neat leather pumps. Not particularly sexy in themselves; the
pretty clothes of a plump, budget-conscious, working
woman, better chosen than most and, only incidentally,
easy to remove. He had brought flowers and chocolates.
Such clichéd gifts annoyed her; wine would be better; they

hardened her resolve, but there was one troubling feature. In some utterly bizarre way, she really was pleased to see him.

'What a lovely room this is,' he said when they took the second glass of the cold fizz into the living-room. 'How clever you are.'

It was as if he had never been here before. He moved from object to object, glass in hand, commenting on the watercolour seascape which had been such a delightful bargain, the bright-coloured porcelain of no known make which she had so artfully assembled on the shelves to make it appear striking and valuable, the pastel-patterned throws which made her chairs look inviting. 'I haven't the knack to do this,' he was saying; 'I can't create comfort, I wish I could. I have a living unit rather than a home, and oh, what's this?' holding, gently, the favourite of her few, carefully chosen ornaments. A small clay bird, nestling by the vase of abundant miniature roses.

He was turning back the clock; he was the soul of natural charm, behaving in exactly the right slightly shy, curious way; alert to her answers; concentrating his interest in everything which was hers; smiling appreciatively. It was exactly the way she would have wished him to act on his first visit. A courtier, humble but proud; the way a man should be if he was seriously interested in her. Oh praise, the wilful nature of it; she wilted and simpered beneath it. Her sofa was the perfect casting couch, the ironing-board was as absent as his memory of it, the burn marks on her arms as vague as they always would be, and her capacity for revenge was somehow dulled, and his mellowness was all too soon. And she was, because of the unusual amount of sipping which had gone on in the afternoon while she experimented with bruises, slightly drunk. More on hope and revenge and tension than wine, but still not entirely in control.

She laughed with him; she poured more wine; she shook her head roguishly, making the thick shoulder-length hair which was her finest feature move in tune with her own animation. Pressing the bruise on her thigh to remind herself of her purpose, she wondered, in spite of everything, whether clocks could be turned back. She ached with a sense of what might have been.

It was all going so much like clockwork, there was not even an audible tick. They ate by candlelight in the kitchen, the back door open and the smell of flowers competing with aubergine, oil, spices. He had the right kind of admiration for the food, too: not exaggerated; asking how she did this or that, eating well, talking about work in between. Why he did this and not something else, mutual commiseration about the state of medicine. She found herself longing to tell him how much she wanted a child, the hideous and direct contrast between herself and most of the patients at the clinic, but that one would wait. She had thought, in the planning stage, that this might be a sexual ploy he could not resist. Now it seemed ridiculous. The food, eaten sparingly in her case, sobered her a little.

'Tell me,' she said, casually, as she moved dishes from the table and brought the perfect fruit and cheese, 'why is it you take so much more notice of some patients than others? So much longer with them? And then look them up on the computer after they've gone?'

His glance was suddenly intense, then he laughed.

'Do I?' he said. 'Do I? If I do, I take more notice of the unhappy ones who need me.'

She sat down again, her face flushed.

He leant across the table and took her hand, turning it

over. Even in the candlelight, the V-shaped mark of the burn from the iron was visible on the underside of her wrist.

'How did you do that?' he asked gently. Anna let her hand rest where it was.

'You did it,' she said. Because it was too late for pretence. 'You did it.' Her voice had become shrill. He shook his head, in disbelief.

'Oh Anna, darling, I didn't realize.' Those fine brown eyes were full of sympathy.

Bailey detested the shop manageress with an intensity he had no difficulty disguising. Even conceding that his present mood would make him dislike any human specimen of the female sex, he wondered, as he sometimes did, how he was able to dissemble so easily. Natural talent, he told himself without any smugness; perhaps one shared by this glamorous harridan. Or perhaps she really did enjoy his company; she showed every sign of it. A bar-stool percher of the old school, difficult to age unless one looked very closely to see the crow's-feet round the ever-smiling eyes with their long lashes, or observed the lines on her forehead which were artfully concealed by the blond fringe. It was hair which resembled spun gold, looked careless and youthful in style, although he suspected it would feel like steel wool, solid with fixative. Bailey thought of the scar on Helen's forehead and her understated, sometimes untidy, elegance. Of course, she had always been too good for him.

The manageress had already established he was a bachelor. He had parted with several bogus particulars of his own life in order to advance the conversation and he suspected that what she had told him in return (a dreadful divorce, life so hard for a woman on her own) might have been equally contrived. They approached the subject of Shelley Pelmore obliquely, by the route of mutual flattery and three drinks each, Bailey pretending throughout that his interest in Shelley was strictly professional, while his interest in the manageress was anything but. There were times when he despised himself more than others.

'Such a divine-looking girl,' she gushed. 'I mean, really lovely. A credit to us, but wasted in a shop, really. Should have spread her wings a bit. But I suppose, in the end, it's best to knuckle down if life's given you a nice man, isn't it? So rare to find. That's what I told her, anyway.'

'But you went out together?'

'Oh yes, lovely fun. Just a bit of clubbing, you know.'

'He was tolerant then, her boyfriend?'

'And why not? She never *did* anything. Far as I know. Mind, there were a couple of blokes came in the shop, liked her. A lot. Oh yes.'

'Anyone in particular?'

Music came from the far end of the bar where the place merged into a club. She looked towards Bailey, who hated dancing and was grateful Helen had no time for it either, and had an unbidden thought that dancing with this woman would be like dancing with an easel: all sharp angles and a picture of a face in a frame.

'An Arab who was rather persistent. She made him buy so much, clever girl! Actually, a couple of those – both fat. Shelley would never go for a fat man. Oh, and then there was this beautiful chap; bald as a coot, but ever so attractive. I've got a feeling she used to see him outside, but I never was sure.'

'What did he do? I mean, for a living?'

'Oh, it's not my business to ask what anyone *does* . . . not the men, anyway. They aren't usually buying lingerie for their wives, you know. But come to think of it, it said Doctor something on his credit-card slip.' She gave the distinct impression that the title of doctor gave a man a touch more kudos than that of police officer. Bailey could not blame her for that; most people thought the same. Most people were unwilling to talk to police officers; they would talk their heads off to a doctor. Suddenly he felt extremely uneasy and, for the first time, smiling into the woman's eyes, he also felt the first stirring of pity for Shelley Pelmore.

The mixture of one pint and three indescribable cocktails, as well as the frozen glance of the manageress after she had conceded that, yes, it was possible to reclaim a credit-card slip and of course she would do it tomorrow, only to find that whatever she promised, he was leaving her to her lonely perch, all combined to make him feel queasy.

The darkness was not complete; the rain began again and he was hungry and lonely. He drove, illegally he suspected, from the West End to Helen's street and parked outside. What price pride, boy? What does it matter if she has a drink or two on the eve of her wedding and decides, in the company of some old friend, that the best thing to do is regard it as a joke? Maybe it was his fault for taking Ryan more seriously than anything else this last week or three, behaving like a bear with a sore head. No wonder she needed a little last-minute frivolity. She wasn't the only one, he thought with a flash of irritation; what made her think he was so confident about it?

Bailey knew as he approached the door that there was someone inside. Empty flats echo with their own vacancy; this one did not. The front windows, visible from the street, were severely curtained, showing not a chink of light; that in itself was unnatural. The phone, when he had tried *en route*, was permanently engaged, for which he read, off the hook, and now repeated ringing at the doorbell brought no response.

All right, so he had his own key, but they had their own set of rules and, godammit, he wasn't going to beat the door down to see her if she so clearly did not want to see him. If she wanted to hide, let her. He was hurt to the quick. Silly bitch; a phrase without meaning, but echoing in his head all the same as he got back in his car to drive home. Halfway there, he stopped, bowed his head against the wheel, weary beyond belief, and this time more than slightly nauseous. He felt overwhelmed by the kind of grief which had first afflicted him when he had been woken with the news about Ryan; a sense of panic about how empty life was going to be. Then, aware of the prospect of a passing patrol car, although he was confident by now, on completely unscientific grounds, that his own emotion had digested the booze at double speed, he continued. Speeding up dangerously on the final stretch as a last coherent thought occurred to him.

Maybe Ryan was waiting at home.

'Let me go,' she was roaring, beating at his face with her fists, scratching, pulling away, tugging towards the door, going on and on long after the car engine died away and she knew he had gone. Ryan held her back with almost contemptuous ease, even though she stamped and yelled like a fractious child. Restraint of hysterical human beings, children included, was second nature to him; he knew how to subdue, exactly how to spread his fingers across her face so that she could not bite, then let her punch and kick and tug until she was exhausted. A brief slap brought all resistance to an end; the sound of it in her kitchen, unnaturally loud above the humming of the old fridge, like the announcement of the finale.

'Silly,' he said, half apologetic, half impatient as he pushed her back into the same chair. 'Shh, be good, now. It didn't really hurt, you know it didn't.'

No more than the cut on her finger had hurt. There was only the humiliation. The sting on her face was less painful than the utter futility of resisting at all; the reminder of the ultimately debilitating truth that in a straight fight with a man, a woman is no match and that is the cause of a primeval fear and anger. Helen did not want to kill Ryan; she would dream at other times of watching him being slowly and relentlessly overpowered until he begged for mercy for this simple illustration of his own power and what he had made her do: lie to Bailey, deny him access, make him believe her a treacherous fool. A silly bitch. At the back of her mind was the real terror of what he would think of her and the awful realization that she cared for Bailey's good opinion more than that of anyone in the world. And then another realization filtered through her shameful agitation. It was that although she wished Ryan every kind of pain as she looked at him, speechless with fury, she was no longer afraid of him, and it followed, somewhere along the line, that she believed what he had told her.

He poured the last of the wine as if he was a solicitous host, continuing an interesting conversation merely interrupted by a telephone call.

'Bailey would dismiss all this as a load of nonsense,' he said conversationally. 'Turn me in for my own good. He doesn't mind speculation, as long as it's his own speculation. No point telling Bailey anything without evidence.'

She spread her hands on the table, willing them to stop shaking. Blood seeped through the paper towel, and she wondered vaguely what Ryan would do when he needed to go to the lavatory.

'The only thing I don't see', he continued, 'is where my fantasizing ladies meet their bald-headed man. Except for Shelley and her friend, there's no common denominator, not the same backgrounds, clubs, dentists . . .'

'A clinic,' said Helen. 'A women's clinic.'

'A clinic?' he repeated stupidly.

'A place where women go', she said, 'and tell a doctor all about their lives. The way we do.'

Tell me about your life, Doctor. Tell me what has made you such a gentle persuasive monster, so sure I would never complain, and would, after a time, want you back; want you until I ached in my bones. Something in the way you joked and made life deathly serious, but less than serious. Something about the hands, the eyes, who knows? Tell me I am drunk and my mind is not engaged in this, although this is what I wanted, isn't it? Revenge? I wanted to tempt this man into my body and then cry rape, because, even if I were not ultimately believed, I should have made him feel as powerless as he made me. Humiliated by my body's desire.

I must let him do this the way he wants.

He called me darling. He said, my darling, I am sorrier than I can say to have treated you so despicably, you of all people, the one I liked best, respected most, but I had to push you away as brutally as I could. You do see that, don't you? No, I don't, I don't . . . Listen to me, my love, he said; you are the only one who forgives. Let me make love to you. Please. Beautiful.

I am not beautiful, but I am here, obedient and waiting,

nerves stretched like wire. Lying, at his invitation, on my
own bed; he has resisted the casting couch. I must, repeat
must, let him do this in his own way. I must pretend. I must
be his slave in order to find out *why*, or how. Not criticize
him for his failure to remove all his clothes; he has a broad
chest, hairless, which is odd for a man of such dark skin, or
is it, how would I know? How many men have I ever
known? Only a few. Pretend enjoyment; he has promised
that this, and his explanations afterwards, will make
amends. Why does he wear those awful synthetic-fibre
trousers? And he a man of such taste. Unbuttoned at the
waist, though; when I reached to touch his nipples, he shivered. Pretend? I am not pretending.

Kiss, kiss, kiss. Tongue going down my throat, neither
too wet nor too dry, tasting of the wine. Stay still, he com-
mands; let me do this, let me admire you, please.
Whichever way he wants, let him; I could not stop him if I
wished and I do not wish. Breasts fondled like rosebuds,
one held while he feels how wet I am, his knuckle kneading . . . I feel as embarrassed as if I were producing sap . . .
I want him, want him; he must smell desire by now. Sweet
words, too: darling, darling, gorgeous darling, a word
which can be such a mockery and is not, here and now. I
touch his head and close my eyes against my own naked-
ness. Let him do it his way, that was always the plan, but I
want him inside me, I do, I do, I do. Licking me like a cat
with a rough tongue; I once heard a tale of a woman who
made her dog do that, with a bigger, rougher tongue; it got
to like the taste. Mutual release is what I want, but he told
me to close my eyes and keep them closed and I do what he
says. There is no light in here. The room is at the front with
the curtains drawn and a bit of the street light coming
through. I've always been ashamed of those curtains: cheap

and nasty, and Christ – why call upon him at a time like this – Christ, I can't stop . . . go on, go on, go on. He's as cold as ice. Cold, cold, cold. Enormous.

I can't keep my eyes closed and open them to find myself in the arms of a man who kisses and caresses while I convulse around the neck of an empty cheap champagne bottle.

I wonder if he rinsed it first.

When he removes it, there is the loud and hollow sound of a cork being drawn. Wroop. Louder than the normal sound; a vintage cork, pulled with an echo and a sensation in me like a plaster pulled from a raw and weeping wound.

Breathe deep, you silly bitch. You asked for this; he knew all along and you, you . . . consented. Now he takes off his trousers, like a man settling down for sleep, having done his duty, ready to confide, and I have never felt such hatred in my life.

I reach out to grab what is exposed. A firm fist with the greatest possible intention to cause maximum injury.

In my imagination, it could all come away in my hand. I handle an ugly, flaccid, unarousable piece of rubbery flesh which never ever responded to me. A brief fight for repossession, with one of my eyes drawn to the green bottle he has carefully placed on the window-ledge; him trying to speak, me trying to scream. Unable, but I frightened him. I could see the fear as I lie paralysed and he tries to slink away.

But you did consent, he says. I did what you wanted and I am what I am made, and I do, love, you.

Silly bitch. The phone was sounding in his ear. Bailey drew himself up onto his elbow, bile hot in his throat. He heard her voice and knew what time it was, the way he did; late for a man whose only recourse was sleep or food, and there was no food. On the edges of London, major capital of the world, and he a sophisticated man in it, there was no food and his stomach heaved. The height of his eyrie, the multi-colours of the duvet, all mixed on a palette with this dreadful sadness. A book lay unread on his pillow and he could scarcely hear.

Be there, she said, and I'll be there. Will you?

But the phone was silent. All he had received and all he could remember was the answerphone message from earlier in the day. Silly bitch, too late to say sorry and far too late to care. Then his skinny legs on the floor on the way to the bathroom. So who the hell was that? Colours blurred; voices, too, and his last surviving image was that bitch in the club, her with the spun-gold hair and a face with a scar on the forehead.

And a dim memory, too, of the phallic-looking syringe in his pocket, which the park vagrant had given him out of his own.

chapter thirteen

'As to the admissibility, in cases of rape and kindred offences, of the fact that a complaint was made by the victim shortly after the alleged offence and the details thereof, not as being evidence of the acts complained of, but as evidence of the consistency of the victim's account and as tending to negative consent . . . such complaint cannot be regarded as corroboration and it is a misdirection to refer to it as such.'

Wait for the morning, Helen said. The morning will shed the light of reason on all this. Neither my Rose nor Anna will answer their phones; why should they at this hour? Ryan could not quite leave it alone. Got to find him, he kept saying, long after two a.m.; got to find him.

What exactly has he done, Ryan?

He corrupts. Like I said, he corrupts. Makes women mad. Kills them; kills their spirit.

What evidence, Ryan? What offence?

Don't know. Got to get inside that clinic. If they've got records of all those women . . .

You can start a war. But you can't bust in there, can you? Even when we find out where it is?

I can't. You can.

Which was why at seven in the morning, showered, dressed and half crazy with fatigue, Helen was walking to Anna Stirland's house on the day she had arranged to be away from the office in order to get married at eleven-thirty. Perhaps that could be retrieved, but this was a priority. She was too tired to think in advance of what she was going to say, feeling an irrational anger against a nurse who lied, and, despite Helen's single effort to phone, failed to answer at antisocial hours, although, on reflection, an answered call might have achieved nothing. It was better to face her, feeling aggressive with anxiety, and say, look, Anna, I don't want all of the truth, only a little scrap of it. Such as, where do you work and what is his name? She would have been happier involving Rose; Rose would be good at this, but involving Rose meant more complication and, besides, Rose did not deserve it.

Crossing the road, even so early, was dicing with death. In the middle of an intersection where lorries stormed from left and right and she was the only pedestrian in sight, Helen felt anonymous and irrelevant, marooned amongst hurtling metal. A train rumbled over the bridge beneath which she stood; there was too much unsyncopated vibrating noise to allow for thought as she ran for the other side. The road surface was damp with drying rain; the freshness of the day swallowed in alien smells, and she wanted, at every third step, to turn back, go to Bailey, who, Ryan had said, would not listen either. So she also believed, reluctantly, because it was, after all, Ryan who knew him best. I may miss my own wedding, she thought, but Bailey would want me to do this.

Anna's door was as freshly painted as she remembered, the street quiet, with the traffic a distant backdrop, like the bass sound behind a tune. She knocked and rang and waited, repeated the process and waited again. Come now, she chided Anna in her mind; life is not so unsafe that you cannot open the door at this time of day to what might be a postman with a gift.

There was the rattling of a bolt and the door opened a crack. Enough to show something less than a vision of loveliness. A poached face, pale, puffy, otherwise expressionless and slow to function. Then it trembled into a half smile with lips moving uncertainly, halfway between a grimace and a frown.

'Oh no,' was what she mumbled. 'Go away.' And then, beginning to push the door closed, repeating it more urgently. 'Go away; this is all your fault.' Helen shoved herself forward and found that, despite Anna's bulk, the resistance was weak.

'I need to know where you work and what the bald-headed doctor's name is,' she shouted, standing in the hall and watching Anna pull her dressing-gown round herself. Anna began to laugh, an ugly sound which she seemed unable to control until the words forced their way through the chortles of someone sniggering at a dirty joke.

'What?' she asked. 'What! You, too? Well, well. I would never have guessed.'

'What do you mean?'

'Another one. Fallen into the trap of Dr Littleton's charms . . .'

'I don't know what you're talking about.'

Hangover, Helen was thinking. Big-time hangover here. She had that disorientated look. This was not a woman who was fit for work today, but Helen could not be concerned with Anna at the moment. She could not even feel vaguely sorry for depriving Anna of an hour or two's sleep which might have made a difference between feeling like death and a state where life was possible.

The kitchen was surprisingly clean for someone who had so clearly been on a binge. Bright, tidy, odour free, not a sign of a bottle or a glass. It took an obsessive character to manage to eradicate any sign of conspicuous consumption. Perhaps Anna was a little that way inclined.

'What time is it?'

'Not long before eight.'

'Oh, shit.'

She sat at the kitchen table and let her head fall onto her crossed arms. Helen prodded her impatiently.

'Who's Dr Littleton and which clinic?'

Silence.

'C'mon, Anna. The bald doctor. I need to know.'

'Wha' for?'

Helen thought wildly of something which would inspire an answer; something which would make the woman talk. The words were out of her own mouth before she had digested them, a natural cunning driven by a rush of adrenalin.

'Because Rose has been to see him and I don't like it. I need to know who he is, where he is.'

Anna stirred, raised her head and gave a long sigh.

'Joseph Littleton. The Wilson and Welcome Clinic, Camden Street. Near the park.' The words seemed to exhaust and amuse her. Then she yawned. 'Do me a favour, will you? Tell them I'm not coming in to work today. Maybe never,' she murmured to herself. 'I'm sick of it.' She turned a half smile to Helen. 'That's why I drink, see?'

Helen had paused, conscious of some kind of lie, but unable to define it. She was aware of the sweetish taste of red wine still sour in her own throat as she left the house and walked away. She turned left at the end of the road, following her instinct while wondering all the time what to do. Should she go straight into the lion's den, with none of the legal power of a police officer to demand information which they would not give? Pretend to be a patient, asking for the only doctor she could name, and be told to come back next week? Or sit down somewhere and work on her slim talents for subterfuge, and all for what? What, after all, had the man done? Where was the offence, and where would be the proof?

The world was, by now, thoroughly awake, the traffic heavier, the noise greater and the adrenalin less. She wanted direction and she wanted Bailey. Instead, she walked to the unpretentious front door of the Wilson and Welcome Clinic, to read a sign which said it opened at ten-thirty. On the other side of the road was a café of supreme grubbiness, where Helen sat and waited, after she had struggled with the question of whether to phone Bailey. Ryan had pleaded with her not to do so; would she be able to phone Bailey, make the peace, make some explanation which would convince him without mentioning Ryan? She doubted it, but knew she had to try. Summon up more subterfuge. So she stood in a phone box which stank of last night's booze and listened, three times, to the polite message which said he was not there.

I am going to miss my own wedding. But I am doing what Bailey would want me to do, aren't I? And my feet are cold.

When Bailey phoned Todd in the early morning to say that he was too ill to come to work, it was scarcely an exaggeration, but he still felt a *frisson* of guilt. He did not mention he had booked the day as leave; it would have meant nothing. But then if neither Todd nor any of the others had been wise enough to question the vagrant in the park, they hardly deserved him either. Especially since they were operating at cross purposes. His only hope as he knocked on the door of the South Moulton Street shop, admiring the window display of silk, and thinking how a certain colour of chocolate brown would suit Helen, was that the manageress would be less brittle in the morning than the evening, or at least she would look her age. He received the credit-card slip from heavily ringed fingers; the thing presented like a lottery prize, with a brilliant celebrity smile. Maybe it was the effect of himself, looking so much less attractive and so much more sinister in daylight.

It was no trouble, with the use of a little official muscle, to worm out of the credit-card company the address of a suspected felon, who, it transpired, rarely used the facility and always paid his bills. Bailey found himself going back to King's Cross; floating out of the station, carried by the crowds who celebrated rush hour with absent faces and copious luggage. It would be nice to take the train. Up to Scotland or some deserted part of the Yorkshire moors; anywhere cooler and greener than here. He passed the red brick of the monolithic British Library, saw the cars gridlocked as he detached himself down a side-street and found the place.

It was a dusty old mansion block, with a scroll above the door, spelling out in stone that it had been built in 1914; time not favouring the place, but unable to diminish a certain dignity to the solid door, despite the lack of paint and the grime of the first-floor windows. Still, a block for renters rather than owners. A placard on the left wall announced that for 'Passports Inc', press the entry buzzer and follow directions to the third floor, while for 'Graficko', he should act similarly and go to the second. Small businesses, hoping to grow big; scarcely a sign of a resident, despite the plethora of other bells, and nothing showing the name of Littleton. Nevertheless, when he buzzed the business bells and the door opened without any challenge, the foyer smelt of old cooking, overlaid, somewhere, with a fresher scent of bacon. Bailey knew he should have eaten *en route*. Helen never understood his hypoglycaemia.

Eleven-thirty, the register office. Ah well, she was not at home or at work; he had tried in call boxes, checked his own messages; best not to think about it. Easy come, easy go, you can't deal with neurosis. But down in the heart of him, a terrible misery made him hate the man he had come to find for his oblique part in all of this, or more aptly, for his part in Ryan's imagination and the need for Ryan's exoneration. Foolish of him ever to think that Ryan's rehabilitation would be achieved by the death of that girl, Shelley. Her death had only put everything else into a melting pot. Bailey had accustomed himself to believing that the sometimes volatile Ryan could be capable of rape, but he knew he could not murder in cold blood. Hot blood, yes, he thought, as he climbed the stairs and looked through the gloom of dark corridors, wishing his spectacles helped to read in dim light the small printed cards in brass fittings on the mahogany-coloured doors. Not a calculated killing, planned over days; Ryan would never carry it through. Which left the bald man, this creature of a dozen fantasies, suddenly more substantial. There he was on the label at the fifth out of six floors; Bailey resented him, even for that.

The door was opened by a Filipino girl, whose pear shape, adorned with pink overalls and the hose of a vacuum cleaner gripped in her hand as she led it behind her, startled him. Likewise her disingenuous response, which was so unworldly wise as she smiled and explained about cleaning the place on this day of the week, and no, he was out, at work, she supposed, like he usually was, and of course his cousin could come in.

She had a face like a nice round cheese, eyes like raisins. He was expecting me, Bailey said; he told me midday at the latest, but I'm early. All that announced with the answering smile which could terrify a guilty conscience, but not this innocent. And if you don't mind, he added, I shall wait.

Of course. He's a good man, your cousin; good to me. But only, it seemed to Bailey, marginally good to himself. An adequate flat, because of the generous proportions of the living-room, but still a chunk, carved from grander accommodation, with an air about it of the temporary and something suggesting the perpetual student, or the genuine academic to whom surroundings are transitory and a taste for comfort a distraction not yet acquired. The mean furnishings granted by a landlord, with little added; indulgence discovered in the kitchen cupboards when the Filipino girl obligingly left him alone and went on to her next job, closing the door behind her so softly she could have been in a convent.

The man liked food; he had all the taste of a delicate gourmet who lived alone. Packets of smoked salmon and trout, speciality soups, olives, lemons and a variety of flavoured oils and green leaves in the fridge along with free-range eggs and a vacuum-packed loaf labelled as containing sun-dried tomatoes. Nothing here a really hungry man in need of a high-cholesterol bacon sandwich in white sliced toast could really crave, but Bailey noted the bread for future reference and did a mental inventory of the herbs for interest only. With a cup of coffee made in the man's cafetière and flavoured with the man's skimmed milk, he

strolled into the bedroom which doubled as study. He was
Dr Littleton's cousin, after all.

It smelt of flowers in here. The whole of the small high-
ceilinged room was dominated by the desk rather than the
small single bed which was simply cramped against the far
wall; the bed a white-coloured couch with a much-washed
cover; bare walls. There were no posters or pictures to indicate interests; the room of a celibate, with a random selec-
tion of unmatched clothes on a rail. Bailey touched a dozen
polyester shirts, trousers of a synthetic linen-look mix and
wondered. The only thing he liked about this man was the
quality of his coffee and the fact he was good to his cleaning
girl.

Perhaps there would be a clue to everything in the sheaf
of notes spread all over the desk, the only untidy feature of
the whole place and a complement to the piles of books on
the floor. A confession, neatly word-processed and double-
spaced. In a long life, Bailey had never come across such a
thing, but this area, for sure, was where the good doctor
kept a life.

The window was double-glazed, making this room
alone semi-quiet if not entirely so. Bailey could see why the
place was unsaleable for development, what with that subdued roar in the near distance, the slight vibration of the
underground which would rattle nerves on the ground
floor and still echoed slightly at the sixth. He waited, listened to nothing, waited. He found a medical card for the
doctor; fluttered his hands over piles of paper, and then
began to read. He was sitting on a good chair, built to hold
male weight; supportive without being cosy and, even so,
the subdued traffic hum was oddly seductive; the room felt
warm, but protected from another hot day. His own eyelids
heavy as lead.

Time passed. When he opened his eyes, there was the doctor's life, told in code. And his own rumbling belly.

Two rings, then dial off, then ring again, that was her code for Ryan from the phone box outside the clinic, and when Helen reached him all he could say was, get in there, girl, like someone encouraging a greyhound. Well, at least she didn't have to phone work. The day off today had been organized well in advance, although she did not expect to spend it this way. Pretend you need an abortion or something, Ryan said. Helen stroked her own stomach, a trifle swollen from half a loaf of bread and three milky coffees from a thick white mug in a café where no-one took much notice, provided she did not stay there long enough to interfere with the small breakfast crowd and the serious trade at noon.

There was no-one of the doctor's description going out or coming in, but she could well have missed him. Her predominant feeling was one of intense foolishness. Trying to appear unconcerned, wishing she knew as much about pretence as she did about keeping secrets. All I want is sight of the man, she told herself.

Proof he exists.

The reception was small, comfortable without luxury, a sensible-looking place with a counter reached through swing doors and flanked by four armchairs. The glass-panelled swing doors muffled the noise of shouting. Leaning across the counter was a woman with a large bosom and red hair, clutching the blouse of the receptionist in one fist and shaking the other, yelling, 'I want that doctor; I want Dr Littleton . . . where is he?' with the receptionist, trying to repeat, 'He isn't here, he isn't here,' her face flushed with panic as she tried to avert her head from the woman. It was difficult to detect what was being said, although the import was clear, the voice rising in insistence, the fist ready to connect, the receptionist looking round wildly for help, but it was not the kind of establishment which ran to a security guard and the door both in and out minimized sound. In an instinctive copying of Ryan's methods, Helen ran forward, grabbed the raised fist and twisted the woman's arm behind her back, her other arm round the neck, pulling her back, holding her still. The hold on the blouse was relinquished, the woman suddenly still.

'There, there,' Helen said in her ear. 'Now what was all that about?' What she did not know was how long she should hold her captive, so she let her go, slowly, patting her shoulder, making calming noises, the way she used to talk to her cat. 'Dr Littleton is not here,' she said calmly. 'That's a pity, isn't it? I was hoping to see him, too, but we can't, can we? Why don't you go home and phone him tomorrow?'

The aggression seeped away. The woman seemed accustomed to obedience; she produced a brilliant tremulous smile, straightened her hair and her cotton jacket and made unsteadily for the door. She wore a dress with a sweetheart neckline, appropriate for a little girl rather than a woman; she smelled of baby lotion, her arms shiny with it. Helen opened the door for her with a flourish. The receptionist sank into her own seat, gratefully.

'Get many like that, do you?'

'No . . . I didn't know what she was going to do . . .'

'Don't worry about it; hope she doesn't come back. Look, could you help? I'm Dr Littleton's cousin; I've been away for a while and wanted to make contact. Could you give me his home address? Oh, and I've got to give you a message from Anna Stirland. She won't be in today, touch of flu, but you know what she's like, probably fine tomorrow.'

It was easy. Stepping out into the road, Helen looked right and left for the redheaded woman, grateful for her intervention which had made the difference between co-operation and the lack of it. She found that she was shaking, caught between a desire to laugh and another to run, with an underlying shame at how easy it was for a person who so prized truth, to be a liar.

She looked at her watch. Was there any point calling Bailey again? To say what? A lovely mess, this was. A gut-churning mess which was set to damage life beyond repair and there was nothing she could do to redeem it, except be braver and more reckless than she felt. A silly bitch.

Bailey made toast out of the bread with the sun-dried tomatoes, detested it and chewed it solidly, without benefit of butter, since there was none of that. At least the bread had been vacuum-packed, otherwise he might not have chosen it, reluctant as he was to touch what the doctor had touched with his own fair hands. The doctor's bathroom was as clean as his kitchen; it was not a lack of hygiene that made his skin crawl.

'Juniper extract, overdose fatal,' he read. 'Hellebore and aloes . . . iron dust, ivy . . .' all used to effect an abortion. 'Internal douching, strong brandy, water as hot as possible, brine vinegar . . .' Abortifacients, first swallowed and then inserted via syringe as time passed and more was known. Abortionists using a Higginson's syringe, or an enema with soapy water, stirring up the contents of the uterus with a long sound . . . Syringing was the commonest form of death because it was the commonest practice . . . it risked the inclusion of air . . . death by air embolism could produce a fatal airlock in the lungs and brain within minutes of the procedure. Fat embolisms may be produced by soapy particles used in solution. But most, death from air, entering the bloodstream via vulnerable dilated blood-vessels . . .'

And in the doctor's bathroom cabinet, two packeted syringes. Sixty millilitres, bladder wash, womb irrigation, for the use of, like the one he had left in the park. Nice souvenirs the man kept.

He was an historian of his trade, that was all; nothing more sinister than that. There were library cards and certificates and, in the drawers of the desk, the history of a long and failed legal case. The doctor seemed to divide his interest between obstetrics and law. Not a humorous person, Bailey surmised; there was nothing in his book collection which suggested the least desire for entertainment. Bailey started in on the legal documents, wearily but intensely interested, sitting on the edge of the chair, his body tense, so that when the doorbell went, he sprang to his feet clumsily, cramp in his calves, scattering paper far and wide, then moved in ungainly fashion towards the door. He had a right to be here, he told himself: he was the doctor's cousin, and beside the doctor, a picture of health.

Rose was feeling in a mood of more than usual insolence. Even though she thought it was nonsense, there was something about the impending state of being a married woman which had a stimulating effect, as if it meant joining the real world, giving up the conversation of a girl and entering a club of those who could justifiably moan about men from a position of established authority. The wife. As in a nagging wife, scolding wife, she-who-must-be-obeyed wife;

mustn't let it go to her head, it was only the party which mattered, but all the same, another life began here and she had no regrets about the one she was ending. What day of the week was it, now? Days of the week did not matter in this office or a courtroom; there was no routine which made the same thing happen on successive Mondays, not even a canteen with the same weekly menu. The only reason she was thinking about the days of the week was counting down. One afternoon and two working days to go, and then she and Michael would be off to Majorca, via the wedding, of course. Such a lot to do. Sneaking out of the room she shared with five others, down the corridor where she joked with the workmen who were replacing the lights, into Helen's office where she could use the phone in peace in order to check the progress of the damned cake. Being a busy bride-to-be and making them laugh in the shared room was all very well, but there was a limit to how much they could take. Rose knew colleagues did not always like you for being so volubly happy; there were times in her own working past when she had teased a wedding candidate, mercilessly, with the crudest jokes she could find and she wasn't sorry for it.

Standing in Helen's room, wanting to tell Helen about the dress, watching the staff across the road in the early afternoon, she leafed through Helen's diary. Now why had Aunty H wanted a day off? The page-a-day diary had a line through today's date with the initials B-RO. Didn't mean much, possibly an interesting assignation with a washing-machine man. Rose saw the supervisor of the paint people opposite sitting near the window, chewing in what Rose imagined was a furtive manner; she felt sorry for those who could not eat as they pleased and stay thin, as she could, and, in the same breath, thought of Anna. Give her a call, too. Leave her a message in case she forgot to organize the flowers.

She was surprised to get an answer. Wasn't anyone but herself and those in the immediate vicinity at work today? Was the rest of London at home in this muggy warmth? Anna's voice was cool but apologetic, saying wasn't it unutterably silly and downright embarrassing to have got measles at her age? Confining her to home quarters, forbidding her the joys of weddings or flowers; sorry, sorry, sorry.

The woman over the road continued to chew and Rose tapped her fingers on the desk, impatiently, mouthing commiserations, chatting a bit, being as nice as she knew how and all the time thinking, well, never mind the flowers, then, who needed them? Knowing that Anna's measles were more important than her floral decorations in a few days' time, but nevertheless annoyed, because it meant something else to do. She didn't much care about bloody flowers, but other people did.

Get well soon, then. See you after Majorca. Byeee.

What did RO stand for?

Register Office? The old cow.

The two cousins of Dr Littleton met on his doorstep without much more than an initial shock of recognition. The progress of Helen's day was making her immune to surprise and her heart had been beating so fast with fear at what she might encounter, this kind of surprise was a relief.

'Hallo.'

'Do come in,' he said politely. 'Who referred you? Was it treatment you wanted, or merely a consultation?'

His smile was false; she felt suddenly and profoundly ashamed.

'I'm glad you're here, though I don't know how or why,' he continued, waving her in blithely as if he owned the place. 'I've been needing some help. Doctor Titillation here has an interesting desk. Needs some deciphering.'

He sat on one side of it, she on the other, like a pupil at an interview with the headmaster.

'I can only presume that you know something about the resident of this not-very-nice apartment,' Bailey went on in headmasterly tones. 'The theory being that he used his job at a clinic to pick out disturbed or unhappy women, either pregnant or not; gained their trust; offered or foisted upon them some kind of alternative treatment and then raped them.'

'A kind of rape.'

'A kindred offence, then. Which all were either too ashamed or too confused to report accurately. There is another category who actively enjoyed his powerful attention, but, in the case of Shelley Pelmore and two before, there was a real risk of them blowing the whistle. So, using a method he had perfected from study . . . or practice of old abortion techniques, he persuaded them into co-operation with the use of a syringe which created an air embolism, which killed them. It may not have been deliberate. It may have been accidental. They may have asked him to do it. Are you with me, so far?'

'It couldn't be accidental.'

'Yes, it could. It could be in the course of an abortion. And, anyway, there's no-one alive to say otherwise. If you consent to sexual experiment, or to cheap makeshift abortion, are you consenting to death? And although the good doctor is prolific in his notes, including love-letters so ambiguous they may as well be in Greek, his jottings do not include confessions. Although he gloats a little about his lack of hair and his choice of fibre-free clothes, there's nothing else to indicate either a criminal mind, or a conscience.'

'Where does this leave Ryan?'

He looked at her quizzically, saving questions for later. A hard stare which left her uncomfortable.

'Ah, the good doctor could be very useful there. He's very kindly kept the particulars of several victims, if you can call them that, including Shelley. By which I mean he's copied personal details from the records of the place where he works and brought them home. Incriminating, in a benign kind of way, since names on his list coincide with a series of women who went to the police with vague complaints which, at best specified his appearance, at worst nothing. The doctor's list is longer, of course. Includes Lady Hormsby something, lives near you. Ever met her?'

'I may know ladies. None with titles.'

'He stocks good coffee, this man,' Bailey said. 'Which is kind of him, since he had no idea he would be offering hospitality to strangers.'

'I'm no stranger. I'm his cousin; to get this far.'

'So am I.'

'But I'm the only cousin on the distaff side whom he longs to see,' Helen said, desperate to make Bailey smile in this oppressive room. 'He and I have corresponded for years. We were childhood friends. We played doctors and nurses. Very clever boy he was. Only the slightest tendency to rape. Had an ambition to be a plumber. He knows me well.'

'How lucky for him. I don't,' Bailey said.

He left the doctor's desk and paced the room.

'How odd, how little one knows. I was contracted to marry a woman who looks vaguely similar to you, an hour ago. I hithered there on the dot and thithered hence, in case

she arrived, but it was all in my imagination that she had
ever meant what she said. So I came back to act the doctor.
Do you think I look the part?'

Helen felt that if she touched him, her fingertips would
freeze from cold. Bailey's skin was pale; he looked old.

'You look like Doctor Death.'

'It's only the names he collects', Bailey said, 'that make
him deeply suspect of naughty play. A new phrase I've invented. Like your legal phrase, it won't work. Although it
will work, to prove Ryan had a bona fide investigation, an
honourable intention in his silence, and there is another
candidate for the attack on Shelley and her untimely death.
We can blame everything on this doctor. Except . . .'

Then he laughed, but she could not laugh with him. He
paced the room again, still laughing.

'This man', he said, 'needs beating up on a street corner.
Like we were allowed to, once. A kick in the balls. If his
balls, or his prick, would suffer.'

He seemed to find all this funny, extremely funny. He
removed a large handkerchief from his pocket to absorb the
tears of laughter. Fountains of water appeared on his gaunt
cheek-bones, showing up the contours of his face. He
looked cunning: a fox with a shiny nose; she found it repel-
lant.

'Where was I? Oh, yes. Only Ryan could pursue a rapist
who can't rape. Can't rape anyone, this customer. Impotent.
Ugly. Chemotherapy burns. He sued them over his cancer
treatment gone wrong, but it got him nowhere. Poor bastard.'

Helen sat stunned.

'No wonder he likes his food,' Bailey added irrelevantly.
'And another thing. If the good doctor comes home, I have
no right to be here. No search warrant, no nothing, since

there is not a scintilla of evidence that the man committed any crime, only evidence that a series of women fantasized about him, unpleasantly. That might be enough to restore official faith in Ryan, provided the doc does not get a lawyer and, quite rightly, stop us referring to illegally accessed private papers. In fact, it would be highly convenient all round if the poor blighter left the country and never came home. Where is Ryan, do you know?'

She felt as if she was giving him a blow beneath the ribs.

'At my house. Doing the garden.'

He faced the window, unable to look at her. Picked up the strange-looking vase which was the only ornament, studied it and put it down carefully.

'The poor emasculated doctor has no-one to trust,' he said. 'I think I know the feeling.'

chapter fourteen

*'The charges of rape and attempted rape are punishable
with imprisonment . . . other than in the most exceptional
circumstances, an immediate custodial sentence should
be imposed following a conviction for rape in order to
mark the gravity of the offence, to emphasise the public
disapproval, to serve as a warning to others and to protect
women. The length of the sentence should depend on all
the circumstances.'*

There were no newspaper headlines about rape or even the
sexual peccadillos of cabinet ministers. Parliament was not
in session; the late-summer news was dominated by a new
royal scandal and the abduction of two British children by
their Spanish father. The last week in August had brought
more rain and the trickling home of the holiday crowds.
West End shops swelled with mothers and teenagers, quar-
relling about the most appropriate clothes to wear for the
new term at school. Members of Aslef, the union for railway workers, went on strike and, for two blessed days, the
larger stations were as hushed as museums.

A doctor who had gone missing failed to return home. It
was thought by his employers that he might have made a
sudden and inconsiderate decision to holiday abroad with a
cousin.

A man in north London referred his wife to a psychiatrist for her habit of wandering the streets on the rare occa-

sions she consented to get out of the bath; a hitherto unknown form of agoraphobia was diagnosed.

Miss Rose Darvey prepared, with glee, to change her
name. 'I never liked it in the first place,' she said.

Detective Sergeant Ryan was admonished by his superi-
ors. His reinstatement was close to a foregone conclusion,
pending the convening of the right kind of committee.
Someone was obstructing it.

A famous English cricketer announced he was gay.

Ryan and Bailey sat in the latter's large clean flat, watching
the sunset. It had been a long lunch.

'I suppose I'm meant to feel sorry for the bloke,' Ryan
was saying. 'And I suppose, in some ways, I do. Fancy,
overdose of chemotherapy, you said? Ouch. It's more difficult to be terrified of a chap with such an affliction and a
prick as useful as a chipolata. Why the hell didn't he win
his negligence case?'

'Because he'd interfered in his own treatment. Thought
he knew best. Misdirected a technician. Arrogant.'

'So some of this was his own fault? Naa, you can't say
that. Getting cancer wasn't his fault. I mean, it isn't as if you
ask, is it? Make a prayer, like, go on, God, disfigure me,
why don't you?'

'He was brave, apparently. Stoic, philosophical, courageous in the face of pain, all that. And is admired as a doctor for his holistic, sympathetic approach.'

'Oh yeah? Loves his patients, you mean?'

'And still, poor sod,' said Bailey softly, 'wanted to be a
lover. Don't we all?'

'Steady on, guv,' said Ryan, not wanting to get maudlin,
or not yet, anyway, and then getting angry. 'I mean, steady

on. What do you want me to do? Be sorry for this fucking ghost with no balls? What did he do, then? What did he do? He had trust, sacred trust, the sort you and I get in a month of fucking Sundays, handed to him on a plate. And he used it. For what? Some kind of fucking revenge. A power trip. Made girls hate themselves, made them mad for him, made them trust him and then killed them; or made mad fools of them while he fucking experimented.' He was speechless with rage. 'I mean, what kind of fucking wanker does that? Gets a job like that?'

'Your use of the word fucking in this context is hardly apposite,' Bailey interrupted, primly. 'And he might not have had much choice about his job.' 'The fucking hell he would! He's a doctor,' Ryan shouted. 'He ain't judged by his balls! And a fucking doctor, like any other man, should know that disease and disappointment is what you get from being alive. You've got no licence to spread it. And just because you've taken some fucking Hippocratic oath that's going to keep you all right with the pension plan, you don't have the right to abuse. Jesus, Bailey, you've gone soft in the head. Stop finding fucking excuses. There was pleasure in what he did; love wasn't involved. He was experimenting with lives; he was full of self-pity, the worst. Can't you see evil any more? Even when it puts its tongue into your mouth? Sod the excuses. He's still a monster, because he knew what he was doing. There aren't any excuses. I just wish one of his women had found a way to retaliate.'

His anger faded into a dull ache. He settled himself back into the depths of the enormous sofa, squinted round this minimalist but colourful room and thought, benignly, how he had always considered it a bit cold, although it wasn't really, and quite comfortable, even with all that space. At least he didn't have to walk across the car-park-sized floor for the next sustenance, which stood at his elbow. Personally, he preferred the clutter and noise of his own home, like everyone did, despite the superior quality of the whisky and, really, if he had to choose between the two, he liked Helen's place better than this. Now there, even with his many reservations, was one hell of a woman. She had spent hours on the phone with his wife, squaring it all up, so that he could go home and explain it again, knowing he was halfway there. He felt suddenly ashamed at his own good fortune and his own role as the one who persisted in getting away with it. And Bailey's reluctance to condemn enraged him. He would never dare ask if Bailey had ever actually believed the rape charge against himself. If he had actually done it, Bailey should have shot him. That would have been justice, instead of all this analysis and trying to understand. Ryan still wanted something.

'It wasn't all in my mind, was it? He does exist, doesn't he? Can I tell a liar from a lover? I dunno.'

There was this fact about Glenmorangie: it kept on tasting good. Not as good as the first sip, but still good.

'No, he wasn't entirely a creature of fiction. Maybe fifty per cent the fevered imagination of those reporting on him, but more than a grain of truth.'

'The man's a bastard gone to ground, wherever he is. Where the hell has he gone?' Ryan grunted, resolving privately, as he had publicly, that he personally was never going to search. They would turn over what they knew to the medical establishment, let them hound him out. If Littleton could not practice, he had no base for manipulation. It irked him that that was all they could do.

'Where's he gone? People asked the same question about

you a couple of days ago,' Bailey said. 'What makes you think you're the only one with licence to disappear? The doc's got plenty of money. Goes where he likes, and when. Earned money, own money, a mixture of both; mystery man. You're a shit, Ryan. Why didn't you trust me?'

Ryan remembered to pause and think about his answer. Bailey had spent years teaching him that.

'Didn't. Couldn't. You had a job to do and you know me too well. You knew I could have gone off the rails; you know how close I've been . . . Besides, I wanted to hit you for not being able to spring me out of there. I wanted to hit you. Kick you. In the balls. But you were always out of reach; like Helen always seems.'

'Helen isn't out of reach,' Bailey said, 'merely absent.'

'Are you accusing me of fucking it up; the wedding, I mean? Well, stone me; if you have to get married in secret, you ain't got a lot going for you, have you? I didn't believe you'd ever do it; nor did she. Funny what she said in the middle of the night.'

Then he found Bailey standing over him. Pulling him up by the sleeves, shaking him like a rat, the sound of cloth tearing. Controlled violence of some intensity, designed to intimidate. It had been a good shirt, once.

'Oh, for God's sake, leave it alone, will you? Would I ever touch your woman, you stupid idiot? Even less, would she touch me? Hates my guts; don't fancy me either. Nor me the other way round, if I'm being frank. Leave off, Bailey. There, that's better.'

Bailey returned to the opposite chair, calm as a sleepy spider. Jealousy had not really featured in his action; merely a vague suspicion that Ryan's sabotage of his own marriage plans had been, in some sense, deliberate.

'She talks in her sleep, that's all, and she talks loud. Carries through to that sofa in the living-room where she parked me for the night. All sorts of stuff. Like she thinks she don't live up to a man like you. Well, thinking the way you think – namby-pamby, forgiving everybody – she may be right.'

Ryan became restless, the way he did with emotion in anything other than a professional context. He could handle weeping women, provided they were strangers. Emotional men were another matter, and besides he was not being entirely truthful. He'd always thought Helen was a very tasty piece, likeable or not.

'So what's the state of play now?' he demanded. Bailey misunderstood, deliberately.

'Oh, stalemate. There's not enough of anything to justify getting out a warrant for the doctor's arrest. The verdict on Shelley Pelmore will come back as death by misadventure. The pathologist suspects embolism, but can't put a hand on her own cardiac machinery and say for sure; could have been a freak result of the couple of drinks and couple of paracetamol she had on board . . . If the doctor came back, we could question him, that's all. And if he said nothing, that would be that. And we could go back to the women in your little black book, but since they gave unreliable accounts first time round, they'd never be credible. And then there's this Anna Stirland, who's off sick and told me on the phone she's not saying anything. Amen. Can't force her. All we know is that he couldn't be a rapist. Not with his equipment.'

It was repetition of old ground. Ryan was sick of it.

'Do you have to pay a cancellation fee if you don't turn up at the register office?' he asked, politely.

'Only what you've paid already. They're used to it, apparently. Some don't turn up. Others turn up every few years.' Bailey was not going to be drawn further.

'I hope they don't reinstate me before I finish the pond,' Ryan said.

Helen was not to be drawn either.

'All right. If you didn't get married, now that Ryan's off the hook, you'll do it, won't you?' Rose was asking.

'Stand still. The label's sticking out at the back. There.'

'. . . Only don't do it without me. Promise?'

'Promise. Cross my heart and hope to die. You look . . . well, wonderful.'

' 'S all right, innit?'

Rose stood before the full-length mirror, stuck out one hip and crossed her eyes. Her hair was soft and full, a compromise between spikes and curls. Small nuggets of silver sparkled in her ears. The dress was a short-sleeved shift of soft crimson. Designer label, courtesy of Oxfam. Who would know, Rose had asked, and if they did, who would care that it cost five quid? Must have been a person who got too fat for it and gave it away in a fit of pique. My good fortune; meant for me. I'll do the same. Watch me, lover, watch me.

Standing back, Helen compared the effect to a young Audrey Hepburn *en route* to breakfast at Tiffany's. This was no sacrificial lamb; this was breathtaking.

'I sort of wish this was in church,' Helen said. 'So the vicar would faint.'

'Stuff 'em all. S'long as Michael likes it. Here we go.'

Michael at his mother's, chewing his knuckles; Helen and Rose in the upstairs bedroom, watching for the car, making the last unnecessary adjustments to perfection. It wasn't so much the dress, Helen thought later, as Rose's total appearance that brought gasps of admiration on the town hall steps; it was the poise, the complete assurance, which brought tears to her eyes and a pang of non-malicious envy to her heart. Oh, to be like that, to have such belief that you would make everything work and that what was broken you would fix.

If she had ever had that kind of confidence, she no longer had it, but she rejoiced to see such utter certainty in another. There was such a thing as true uncomplicated love. There was, but it simply needed belief in itself to flourish. A childhood deprived of it, perhaps, so that it was easy to recognize and vital to preserve in a tight fist. That was what Rose had: a rigid grasp on reality. Her kind of true love was not so fanciful after all.

There was a brief exchange of vows; the hall was full to bursting, extra chairs provided. On Rose's express instructions, issued on pain of death, each woman was dressed to excess. I want you costumed over the top, she had ordered. There were hats with feathers a foot long, puffy taffeta skirts, ear-rings the size of tin lids, plenty of sheer thigh, and a total inability on the part of the crowd to keep quiet. Chatter only fell to nothing during the making of promises, when a snuffling into handkerchiefs replaced it. Standing next to her, one of the few men who looked at ease in a suit; Bailey dug into his pocket and handed Helen his hanky. The extra-wide brim of her overlarge deep-blue sombrero, worn low over her forehead, hid the act of blowing her nose.

'I don't want anyone sitting down,' Rose had said of her own reception.

'It creases the frocks. I want 'em all moving around, eating and drinking and showing off and talking to one another.'

Which they did in the hotel room with buffet and garden attached, where food was less important than drink and the sixty of them, chattering, made a fine volume of noise amid too much of a squash for anyone to notice the dearth of floral decoration. Bailey unbent from his great height, enjoying himself, Helen hoped, since she was herself, out of relief as much as anything else, because it was turning into exactly the kind of thrash Rose had planned. They would probably leave before the lights came on in the garden and the music, Rose's secret weapon to subvert the tendency to speeches, began to invite dancing.

'What kind of dancing?' Bailey asked suspiciously.

'Any old kind of shuffle. We've got three generations here.'

'So I can waltz, can I?'

'We can watch, first.'

He took her hand. They sat in a corner of the garden; he observing, with evident pleasure, the ranks of Michael's aunts and uncles towing each other about with concentrated movements, some serious, some laughing throughout.

'I don't know if it's possible to have a wedding without relatives,' Bailey shouted above the din.

'No fun at all,' Helen agreed.

'I think I've only got two left,' he added. 'I don't know what I've done with them all.'

'Me neither.'

'Look, Helen,' he was bellowing. 'We can't go on like this, we really can't. It's no good, it's become a neurosis.'

She could feel herself freeze. She did not want a conversation about the issues between them; not here, not now.